"So you're planning on staying, then?"

Despite the casual nature of her question, Vadim heard the serious intent behind it.

"I thought I'd made that quite clear."

"Are you afraid I'll go nuts if you don't?"

He smiled down at his coffee. "No, I'm afraid I'll go nuts. I don't think I would function very well if I couldn't be with you."

Ella slammed her mug down on the countertop. "Morosov, don't *say* things like that. You're supposed to be running away from me, not offering yourself up for more punishment."

"It's just the way it is."

"I don't like it." She bit into her bagel and crumbs flew everywhere. He resisted the urge to fetch a dustpan and brush and gather them up. Maybe it would be better to wait until she'd finished....

"I can't change my nature, Ella."

"As to that." She swiveled on her seat so that she could face him. "What exactly are you? I know you're a swan shifter and some kind of Fae royalty. Is there anything else you'd like to tell me?"

"Don't you think that's enough to be getting along with?" He darn well hoped so. He had no intention of telling her the rest unless he was in mortal peril. "I'm sure you have questions."

She'd kicked off her slippers. Her toenails were bright pink with orange sparkles. He wanted to kiss them....

He was in deep shit.

**Also available from Kate Pearce
and Carina Press**

SOUL SUCKER

KATE
PEARCE

Death Bringer

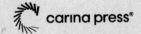

carina press®

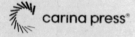

ISBN-13: 978-0-373-00234-4

DEATH BRINGER

Recycling programs
for this product may
not exist in your area.

www.CarinaPress.com

Printed in U.S.A.

Dear Reader,

Death Bringer is the second book in my Soul Justice series, and starts right where *Soul Sucker* left off with our uncomfortably mated-for-life couple, empath Ella Walsh and Vadim Morosov, the shape-shifting Fae. Not only are they going to have to work out how to stay together, but also how to survive when a killer wants to drag Vadim back to his least-favorite place in the magical universe: Otherworld.

It's really more Vadim's book, as we finally get a chance to explore how he came to leave his homeland and the dark secrets of his ageless past. But Ella isn't the sort of woman to sit by while her world goes crazy, and she's determined that if anyone is going to kill Vadim, it's going to be her.

It's always fun writing about a city you love, like San Francisco, and even more fun to weave the real places into the fantasy world you've created for the book. I've now moved to Hawaii, so it will be interesting to see if I can set some of my new books there!

I hope you enjoy *Death Bringer,* and please feel free to contact me and let me know. I love to hear from my readers.

Best wishes,

Kate Pearce

www.KatePearce.com

Death Bringer

PROLOGUE

San Francisco

BRAD DAILEY WOKE to sunlight streaming through open blinds and wondered where the hell he was. The last thing he remembered was a bar in the city, being dumped by his chick and ending up talking to the bartender and the only other guy left in the place. Nice guys who'd drunk with him until he couldn't remember the girl's name, let alone why he'd liked her in the first place.

Her loss.

He swallowed, and his tongue stuck to the roof of his mouth like spit to an envelope. What the fuck had he ended up drinking? He was going to have the hangover from hell, and he was due in class at ten. He grabbed his cell phone and squinted at the numbers. It was already nine thirty. Even if he busted a gut, he'd never get there in time.

But he had to go. Dr. Blinz was a bastard. He'd be chucked out of the class if he didn't show up again, and his parents would kill him. With superhuman effort, he rolled out of bed and staggered toward the bathroom. First, he needed to pee real bad. That accomplished, he turned on the faucets and faced his reflection in the mirror.

And screamed.

ONE

"WHAT DO YOU mean, I can't spend the night?"

Ignoring the interested glances of the other passengers on the packed Blue & Gold ferry to Tiburon, Ella glared right back at Vadim.

"You can't."

"Why not?"

"Because you haven't asked nicely, and I don't like being taken for granted. We might be stuck together for life, but it doesn't mean you own me or anything." She walked away from him and looked back at the city. The incoming fog crawling in under the Golden Gate Bridge was slowly swallowing up the gray, square lines and glinting glass buildings.

"Then why didn't you say something when I got on this damn boat with you?"

He was right behind her again. His voice was quiet, but fury emanated from every pore. He wore a long dark coat and blue cashmere scarf that screamed Italian designer. Tendrils of his black hair danced coyly in the breeze, caressing his awesome cheekbones. He might look like a model in the middle of a photo shoot, but he was much more than a pretty face.

She shrugged. "I don't know where you're living. I assumed you must have moved over here."

"I haven't moved anywhere. When the hell did I have time to do that? Alexei left for Russia this evening. I paid off his extortionate bill, but kept my room on."

"Well, that's lucky. You can stay on the ferry and go right back again."

"You know damn well that this is the last one to-night."

She swiveled to face him, her arms crossed over her chest. "Then you know what you can do, don't you?"

"What's that, Ms. Walsh?" He moved so close that she could see into his dark blue eyes. So much bluer than the murky waters of the bay, and so much more dangerous too... His gaze flashed black, and her pulse jumped in her throat.

"You can use magic, Morosov, and fly away home."

"Yes, I can." He slowly let out his breath. "What I don't understand is what the hell is wrong with you. You've been treating me like dirt all day."

"What's new?" He didn't lighten up, and she looked away from his intense gaze. "I just need an evening to myself, that's all."

Silence greeted her remark. She concentrated on maintaining her mental shields, even though if he really wanted to get through them, he could do it with ease.

"You nearly died yesterday."

"So?"

"We've spent the last twenty-four hours being de-briefed by the SBLE authorities, and now I want to sleep for a hundred years. With you."

"It's not just your decision, is it?" She hunched a shoulder at him. "Oh, for God's sake, Morosov, don't get all primitive and possessive. I really can't handle it at the moment."

"You can't handle it, period. That's why you don't want me here. You're scared."

"And you aren't?"

"At least I'm trying to deal with it."

"Well, good for you."

The ferry slowed and shuddered against the pull of the tide as, engines churning, it turned clumsily toward the dock. Seagulls flew off the sea wall to encircle the craft, looking for rich pickings from the tourists.

Ella pushed past Vadim and walked over to the stairs that led to the lower deck. She stomped down them and joined the line of passengers ready to exit the boat the moment it docked. She felt rather than saw him fall in behind her.

"Go *away*, Morosov."

"I'm just getting off the ferry."

"And then what will you do? Sit on the beach all night?"

"If I have to."

The older woman in the line in front of Ella turned around. "Is he annoying you, dear? Do you want me to call the cops?" Her gaze drifted up to Vadim's. "Wow, he's really cute. Are you sure you don't want him, because I'd take him off your hands in a second."

"Be my guest." Ella smiled at the woman. "He's almost house-trained."

"Ms. Walsh."

There was a definite note of warning in Vadim's tone, but when had that ever stopped her? She turned her attention to the deckhand who was opening the gate and shuffled forward with the rest of the weary commuters. The salty air hit her like a shot of tequila, and she breathed it in. After twenty-four hours stuck

at the Supernatural Branch of Law Enforcement, she'd
wanted to scream. Only the thought that her testimony
would put on record who had been killing empaths had
made her stay and endure the endless, repetitive questions from a bunch of morons who should know better.

"Agreed."

Vadim's voice echoed in her head. Damn, she must
be tired if she couldn't keep him out at this stage of
the evening. She stumbled on the uneven deck, and
he attempted to catch her elbow. She jerked away and
almost fell again.

"Ella, let me help you. You're weaving around like
a drunk."

"I'm fine. Go away."

He took hold of her arm and spun her around to face
him. "I'm not going anywhere. I'm taking you home,
where we will go to sleep. If you want to continue this
discussion in the morning, when we're both refreshed,
I'll be more than willing to do so." He paused. "Are
you *mimicking* me?"

"I can't help it. You get so polite and Russian when
you're pissed with me."

He let go of her and looked down at the ground. "I
can't do this right now. Can we just go home?"

Without giving him a direct answer, she set off along
the coastal path and up the hill, toward her basement
apartment. Things really were bad if they didn't have
the energy to fight with each other. He followed her
silently, his breathing even, his presence a comfort she
refused to acknowledge.

She still couldn't deal with the fact that she was
a) alive and b) mated to an enigma. She'd confidently
expected to go nuts in a week, when she turned twenty-

seven. It happened to empaths. She'd assumed it would happen to her and had lived her whole life accordingly. But in a strange twist of fate, she'd ended up with Mr. "I'm not quite human" *GQ*.

She snorted. Strike that. He wasn't human at all. He was Fae fucking royalty.

"What's wrong?"

She'd stopped walking and was breathing hard through her nose.

"Nothing!"

Perhaps it was a good idea to let him spend the night. When she'd rested, she'd make sure to interrogate him thoroughly about his family in Otherworld before she let him eat or have sex with her ever again.

Not that she needed to have sex with him like she needed her next breath.

"Do you want a push up the hill?"

"I'm fine, thank you." She kept walking, her gaze fixed on the looming Victorian house with its white railings, steep steps and gabled roofline.

"I'll get the door."

He disappeared ahead of her. Could she do that now? Use magic to get stuff done? She hadn't actually asked Vadim how much of his power she could control and manipulate, now that they were bonded. She'd tried not to ask him anything at all.

By the time she reached the front door, he'd turned on the lights, started a fire in the grate and put the coffee on. Her mail was stacked on the countertop, and he was already in the bathroom sloshing water around. Not that she minded. He would always leave the place cleaner than when he'd entered it. It was one of his more endearing, yet annoying, habits.

Wearily, she stripped off her coat and hat and threw them toward the back of the couch. All she wanted was a shower and her bed and two days to sleep.

A blast of fragrant steam billowed out of the bathroom, and Vadim came out. He picked up her coat and put it over his arm.

"The shower's on. You go ahead. Do you want me to bring you some coffee or anything to eat?"

Ella just stared at him until he took her by the hand and gently pushed her into the bathroom. By the time she opened her mouth to reply, he'd closed the door behind him, leaving her alone. She took off her clothes and got into the shower, sighing as the hot water streamed over her. It took all her remaining energy to lift her arms long enough to shampoo her hair.

When she finally rinsed out the conditioner and could see again, a mug of herbal tea stood on the ledge next to her. Had Vadim come in while she was showering, or was he no longer hiding the extent of his abilities? She guessed the latter. After sipping the tea, she stepped out onto the fluffy mat and found two warm towels and her favorite pink bunny pajamas awaiting her.

Damn, the man was good.

She dressed and didn't bother to dry her hair, just wrapped it up in the towel and went back into the kitchen. He was standing at the kitchen counter, drinking coffee and watching something in the toaster. He'd taken off his coat, jacket and tie and rolled up his shirtsleeves.

"Are you sure you don't want something to eat?"

"No, thanks. I think I'll head straight to bed."

He looked up. "Good night, Ella."

"'Night, Morosov."

When she closed her bedroom door, she realized he'd put the bedside lamp on and turned on her heated blankie. With a sigh, she threw herself into bed and wrapped the warmed quilt around her. *Bliss.*

Twenty minutes later she opened one eye and listened intently to the silence around her. Where was Vadim? She couldn't sleep without knowing what he was doing.

She got out of bed and opened the door a crack. The scent of toasted bread floated over her, but the kitchen was in darkness and so was the bathroom. Had he really gone? A feeling not unlike terror clutched at her heart. She opened the door wider and stepped into the hallway.

"Morosov?"

A slight sound made her peer into the gloom. Was that a hint of white on the couch?

"*Ouch!*" She recoiled as her knee collided with the chair arm.

"Ella, are you all right?"

She fumbled her way to the seat, still holding her knee, and sat down. "You're sleeping on the couch?"

"Where else would I sleep?" His voice was low and husky. "It's better than the beach."

She touched his leg. "I thought you'd gone."

"Do you want me to?"

"No."

His fingers curled around hers, and he brought her hand to his mouth and kissed it. "Then go back to bed."

"Okay." He let go of her and she slowly stood up. "See you in the morning, then."

"I'll be here."

"Good to know." She went back to bed and slid between the sheets. With an exhausted sigh, she closed her eyes.

"You don't need to come and find me. You'll know if I've really gone."

"How?"

"You won't sense me in your head."

"That would be a blessing."

She waited but he didn't reply, and she gradually relaxed again. She might not have come to terms with him, or anything in her life yet, but she was glad he was there.

In her head.

In her heart?

With a groan, she rolled over and went to sleep.

"Coffee?"

Vadim held up the half-empty pot as Ella came out of the bathroom. She stared at him as if he were speaking Russian and briefly closed her eyes. Her blond hair was standing on end as if she'd stuck her finger in an electrical outlet. He wouldn't put it past her. Concealing a smile, he found one of the mugs he'd just rewashed, filled it with coffee and put it on the countertop next to her.

"Do you want me to toast you a bagel?"

She clambered up onto the kitchen stool and nodded, both hands wrapped around her mug of coffee as she inhaled the rising steam. He sliced the bagel, put it in the toaster and went to the refrigerator to get the cream cheese.

"I went out for a run earlier, so I got some supplies."

She sipped at her coffee, and her shoulders slowly

came down from around her ears. It had been a stress-ful couple of days. "Thanks."

"You're welcome." He turned away and studied the newspaper until the bagel was toasted. "Did you sleep well?"

"I think so. I don't remember dreaming or any-thing."

"That's good." He'd have enough nightmares for both of them. He was surprised he hadn't woken her. "I'm not planning on going into the office today. How about you?"

"Hold it. Stop with the casual small talk." She pointed her knife at him. "Why aren't you on that plane going back to Russia with Alexei?"

"Because the SBLE decided I should stay here."

"Why?"

He shrugged. "I have no idea."

"They don't know about…us, do they?"

"I should imagine they'll work it out fairly quickly when you don't start going insane on your birthday."

"Oh, damn. I'd forgotten about that. Maybe I could pretend to go nuts?"

"And lose the job you love so much?" Ignoring her impression of sticking her fingers down her throat, he stuck another bagel in the toaster. "And remember, they won't necessarily know *whom* you're mated to, just that you are mated."

"But won't everyone wonder why you're still here?"

"The last I heard, everyone was hoping I'd stay be-cause I'm the only partner you've ever worked with that you respect."

She stuck out her tongue at him. He handed her an-other bagel.

"So you're planning on staying, then?"

Despite the casual nature of her question, he heard the serious intent behind it.

"I thought I'd made that quite clear."

"Are you afraid I'll go nuts if you don't?"

He smiled down at his coffee. "No, I'm afraid I'll go nuts. I don't think I would function very well if I couldn't be with you."

She slammed her mug down on the countertop. "Morosov, don't *say* things like that. You're supposed to be running away from me, not offering yourself up for more punishment."

"It's just the way it is."

"I don't like it." She bit into her bagel and crumbs flew everywhere. He resisted the urge to fetch a dustpan and brush and gather them up. Maybe it would be better to wait until she finished…

"I can't change my nature, Ella."

"As to that." She swiveled on her seat so that she could face him. "What exactly are you? I know you're a swan shifter and some kind of Fae royalty. Is there anything else you'd like to tell me?"

"Don't you think that's enough to be getting along with?" He darn well hoped so. He had no intention of telling her the rest unless he was in mortal peril. "I'm sure you have questions."

She held out her coffee mug. "Fill this up first, and then we'll talk."

He studied her bunny pajamas and tatty white robe. "Don't you want to get dressed first?"

"Why? We're not going anywhere, are we?" She slid off the stool and headed for the couch.

Vadim waited until her back was turned and swiftly

cleaned up the crumbs, put her plate in the sink and wiped off the surfaces. Picking up his own cup of coffee, he joined her on the couch. She'd kicked off her slippers. Her toenails were bright pink with orange sparkles. He wanted to kiss them…

He was in deep shit.

"So tell me about the shape-shifting first."

He forced his gaze back up to her face. "One of my…grandfathers is the current swan king. I get the ability from him."

"It's not much use is it? What can a swan actually do? Peck someone to death?"

"They can do much more than that."

"Yeah?" She tucked her feet up under her. "I hear they're really good at ballet and telling fairy tales, as well."

He took a long, slow breath and let it out through his nose. "Are you just going to mock, or are you actually interested in learning about the abilities you've acquired?"

"You have no sense of humor, Morosov."

"I believe you have enough for both of us." He stopped talking and just stared at her.

She sighed. "I suppose you can fly, right? That's quite useful. Can I do that?" By mating with him, she'd acquired his Otherworld powers, and he'd stabilized her empath abilities. In fact, she'd come out of the deal really well. Maybe she should be more grateful.

"If you practice."

"Do I have to shape-shift?" She leaned forward. "*Can* I shape-shift?"

"I'm not sure. With my other powers, I can just

grow wings and fly. I should imagine you'd be able to do that too."

"That's kind of cool." She picked up the cushion next to her. "And if you shed, I'll never have to worry about stuffing my cushions again."

He sipped his coffee. "How long are you going to keep this up?"

"The jokes?"

He inclined his head a frigid inch.

"For as long as I can think of them."

"Fine. Do you have any other questions for me?"

"I sure do, buster, don't think I'm that easy. Why didn't you mention that your grandmother is the queen of the Fae?"

"She's one of the queens. There are several warring factions in Otherworld."

"I know that, but I asked around the office yesterday, and she's considered the most powerful one at the moment."

"I didn't mention it, because it never came up."

"Bullshit. You didn't mention it, because you hate being associated with anything from Otherworld."

"Maybe that, as well." He was willing to concede the point if it kept her from inquiring further. "And as I told you before, the more I talk about my Otherworld connections, the more likely they are to become aware of me."

"Because you've been trying to hide out here and pass as human."

"Obviously not very successfully."

"You were doing pretty well, until I dragged you back there."

"Trust me, I'd love to blame you, but Rossa already

knew I was here and was keeping an eye on me. It was just a matter of time before my grandmother found a way to try and force me back there."

"Why does she want you back?"

"Because I performed certain tasks for her and the Fae."

"Magical ones?"

"Usually."

"But what good is a shape-shifting swan?"

"You'd be surprised." She'd be horrified, but he definitely wasn't going to get into that. He stood up and held out his mug. "I'm getting more coffee. Do you want some?"

"No thanks." She handed him her empty mug. "Stick it in the sink. I'll use it later."

With an inward shudder, he put her mug in the dishwasher and refilled his own. "You're still a bit low on food. Do you want to go to the supermarket?"

She stretched her arms over her head and yawned until her jaw cracked. "I suppose I should."

His cell phone went off, and a second later he heard hers ring too. She wandered into the bedroom to get it as he answered his.

"Mr. Feehan."

"Vadim. We have a situation here. Can you liaise with Ella and meet her at San Francisco General? There's a man there I want you both to see."

"I'll do that, Mr. Feehan. We'll see you there as soon as we can."

He looked up to see Ella in the doorway of her bedroom, phone clamped to her ear. "It's Feehan. He left a message. He wants us to meet him at the hospital." She pouted. "So much for our day off."

Vadim shut his cell phone and put it back in his pocket. "How soon can you be ready to go?"

"Give me five minutes." She checked her cell. "There's a ferry leaving at ten, if we hurry. Where did you put my coat?"

"In the closet with mine."

She turned a slow circle. "Which closet?"

"The one by the front door, where you are supposed to hang things."

"Really?" She wandered over to it and opened it. "I always wondered what it was for."

She tossed him his coat and suit jacket and retrieved her own. "I'll just be a minute."

In less than ten, they were walking down the hill toward the ferry, which had just docked. A stream of tourists poured from the gangplank, their eager faces scanning the small town and exclaiming at the views back across the bay. Getting through them made Vadim feel like a lone salmon fighting to swim upstream against the current.

They made it just in time and headed for the top deck. He would never tire of the view or the experience of approaching a great city by water. It was the first place he'd ever considered putting down roots. He glanced down at Ella in her blue and orange knitted hat, denim jacket and pink ripped jeans. But maybe it wasn't the place. Maybe it was her. His grandmother might have meddled in his life simply to force him back to Otherworld, but she'd started a whole chain of events he didn't even dare contemplate. He had no doubt that less benign forces would soon be on his tail, demanding his return. But now he had a mate to fight for and a reason to live.

He slowly shook his head. He was not going back willingly. They'd have to come and get him, and even in this realm, his powers still trumped most of theirs. With one snap of his fingers he could annihilate the entire city that lay before him. He smiled as they approached the pier. Let them come. He'd be more than ready.

TWO

"Hey, Jose. This is a colleague of mine, Vadim Morosov. Jose's the charge nurse on this floor." Ella waited as they exchanged pleasantries. "Is our boss here yet?"

"Mr. Feehan?" Jose pointed at the closed door of the hospital administrator's office. "He's in there."

"Cool. We'll go and join him. Thanks, Jose."

He winked at her and she winked back before knocking on the door, Vadim right behind her. The hospital was its usual busy self, the hallways as crowded as the subway one minute and just as empty the next. She sensed Vadim strengthen his shields and did the same. You never knew what crazy magical shit lingered in a place like this.

Feehan opened the door and ushered them in.

"You found each other, then?"

"We did. What's up, boss?"

"I'm not quite sure." Mr. Feehan glanced at the petite blond female sitting behind the desk. "Ms. Phelps, this is Ella Walsh and her partner, Vadim Morosov. When necessary, Ms. Phelps acts as a liaison between the hospital staff and the university. Perhaps you should tell them exactly what happened."

"I'll certainly try." Ms. Phelps gave them a distracted smile. "Brad Dailey, one of our second-year medical students, didn't show up for class this morning. As it was a scheduled test day, his professor contacted student-support services to follow up on him. This student has missed quite a lot of school this year, and Dr. Blinz wasn't happy about it. He wanted to make sure Brad received an official warning."

"So what happened?"

"One of the junior administrators called his apartment. Eventually Brad picked up and started screaming incoherently into the phone. The administrator alerted the emergency services, and they went to check on him. When the police forced their way into his apartment, they found Brad in the bathroom trying to rip his face off." She shuddered. "At first the paramedics assumed he'd taken some kind of drug that hadn't agreed with him, but after he was sedated and brought here, the doctors realized that wasn't the case."

"So what do you think is going on?" Ella asked.

"As I was just telling Mr. Feehan, I have no idea. The poor boy can barely form a sentence. The staff has run every test they can think of, and nothing abnormal is showing up. In these cases, we normally contact you." She looked helplessly at Vadim. "I do so hope you can help him."

"We'll certainly do our best, Ms. Phelps," Vadim said. "Is Mr. Dailey capable of speaking to us yet?"

"I believe so. He's been restrained for his own safety, but the medication should be wearing off by now. Not that you'll get much sense out of him. He's just babbling."

"What's he saying?" Ella turned off her cell phone and stuck it back in her pocket.

"Something about that not being him in the mirror. A classic hallucinogenic drug response, but he's not testing positive for anything at all."

"Maybe there's something new on the street. Do you remember the frozen addicts?" Feehan glanced at Ella. "No? You're probably all too young, but in 1982 in Santa Clara County, right down the street from here, some addicts took a new substance called MPTP that brought on the symptoms of Parkinson's and literally paralyzed them overnight."

Ms. Phelps nodded. "That's a possibility we are aware of, but until we can confirm anything, we'd still like you to take a look at him."

"Morosov and I would be glad to help, wouldn't we?" Ella raised her eyebrows at Vadim, who was still smiling at Ms. Phelps. "Can you show us to Mr. Dailey's room?"

"Sure." She rose to her feet. "I'll make certain you aren't disturbed."

When Ella came out of the office, Jose handed over her white coat. "Here you go, babe. Are you free for dinner tonight?"

"Sorry, no." She patted his arm. "But thanks for asking."

"Ella's busy," Vadim added and placed his hand in the small of her back to usher her along. He didn't say anything else, but she sensed both his sudden alertness and a hint of his magical power wafting around.

"Keep it down, Morosov. You're like a skunk marking his territory."

"That guy wouldn't pick up magic if it bit him in the face."

"Don't you mean pecked?"

"You're hilarious."

"I know, and by the way, don't call me Ella at work, okay?"

"As if I would dare." His smile showed a lot of teeth.

Ms. Phelps stopped at the last door in the hallway. "Mr. Dailey is in here. I'll ask the nurse to step out of the room, but she'll be outside if you need her. If you require more urgent medical assistance, just press the red panic button."

"Will do." Ella went in first, nodding at the nurse as she passed her in the doorway. Brad Dailey was strapped to a gurney on the far side of the room. His face was bandaged like a mummy's, and his terrified gaze darted around the space, fixing avidly on Ella as she approached.

She sat on the side of the bed and took his shaking hand in hers. A hint of residual Otherworld magic trickled through her senses. "Hey. I'm Ella Walsh, and this is Morosov. Can you try and tell us what's wrong?"

His chest heaved and he started to struggle against his restraints, his hands turning into claws. Vadim came up beside her.

"It's all right, Mr. Dailey. We just want to help you. Take a deep breath and tell us what's wrong."

Ella shivered as she felt Vadim push some kind of calming magic through her and into Brad. Whatever it was, it seemed to be having the right effect, as he slowly relaxed against the gurney and his breathing evened out.

"It wasn't my face in the mirror. What the fuck happened? Who the fuck am I?"

"When you say it wasn't your face, do you mean you saw someone else's reflection in there with you?"

"No, it was just supposed to be me."

Ella glanced at Vadim, who was listening intently. "And it wasn't your face."

"No. That's why I tried to pull it off."

"You thought it was, maybe, a mask of some kind, a practical joke?" Vadim asked. "Did you get drunk last night?"

Brad nodded eagerly. "Yeah, yeah, that's what I thought, that some of the guys had gotten into my room and stuck stuff on me to scare me, like, you know?"

"Medical students love their pranks."

"But it wouldn't come off." Brad's voice rose. "It was me, but it isn't me!"

"Since you damaged your face so badly, it's hard to tell what you looked like before this happened. Do you have any recent pictures of yourself?"

"Sure, on Facebook and my cell."

"Would you object if we looked at them?"

"You can look as much as you like, but you won't ever see me with brown eyes and black hair. I'm fucking blond like you."

Ella checked out the thick black hair sticking out from the top of his head. It didn't look dyed, either.

"Okay, so if we accept that you woke up this morning with someone else's face, how do you think that happened?"

He went silent, his gaze fracturing, his whole body caught up in some internal struggle Ella could only guess at.

"I don't know. I don't fucking know." Tears slid down his face. "What's going to happen to me now? Who am I? What am I going to do? My girlfriend dumped me last night for being too immature, I sat and had a few drinks with some guy and that was it."

"Did the guy come home with you?"

"Don't think so. Although I'm not sure how I made it home."

"Perhaps he helped you?"

"And took my face?"

"Maybe. Do you remember what this man looked like?"

"Not like me."

"Like you now, or before?"

"Neither. He was like kind of older than me." He glanced at Vadim. "About your age, but sort of average looking. You know, unremarkable?"

"Can you tell me the name of the bar you went to and your girlfriend's name?"

"It was the Blue Flamingo in Little Italy, and my ex's name is Penny Jordan. She's a student nurse here at the hospital."

Vadim was busy recording the information, so she focused on Brad. Part of her wanted to reach into his mind and extract the terrible memories, but she couldn't do that yet. They needed more information from both him and his associates before they could make any firm decisions as to how to deal with his horrific recollections.

"Listen, Brad, will you concentrate on getting better while we go and gather more information for this case? It's possible that something or someone did steal your face. We'll do our best to get it back for you."

"You believe me?"

"Somebody has to." She held his gaze. "We work for the SBLE, and our specialty is solving cases like yours."

"You're like the *X-Files*."

"Kind of, but keep that to yourself." She squeezed

his hand. "All we need you to do is hang in there. Something is very wrong, and we're going to do our best to fix it, okay?"

He took an unsteady breath. "Okay."

She stood up and Vadim walked to the door and held it open. Ella gave Brad a brisk nod. "We'll be back. Stay strong."

He nodded and they went out past the nurse. Ella kept going until they reached the sanctuary of the administrator's office. Feehan and Ms. Phelps weren't in there. She shut the door and turned to face Vadim, who was already firing up Brad's cell phone and investigating his wallet.

"That poor kid." Ella shook her head.

"He's hardly a kid. According to his driver's license, he's twenty-three."

"Don't split hairs. Would you like to wake up and not recognize your own face?"

"Some days, yes."

"Morosov…"

His smile was brief. "I agree that this is a difficult situation. Did you get a sense of Otherworld from him?"

"Yes, but that was pretty much a given, wasn't it?"

"I don't know. There have been some pretty inventive human serial killers."

Ella perched on the corner of the desk. "You think the guy in the bar drugged Brad's drink and brought him home, intending to carve up his face and kill him?"

"It's possible."

"Apart from the fact that we both felt Otherworld magic around him." She chewed slowly on her gum and blew a big pink bubble. "It's got to be Otherworld."

"Why, because you can't imagine a human doing such a terrible thing?"

"Of course I can. I've seen those movies with Anthony Hopkins."

"Who plays a fictional character."

"I *know* that." She glared at him. "Why don't you want it to be Otherworld?"

He put down Brad's phone and met her gaze. "Because there aren't many beings like that even in Otherworld, and those are usually incredibly powerful and well connected."

"Damn." She blew another bubble. "So we're going to have a hard time finding this guy and executing him."

"Oh, I think he'll come back."

"Why?"

He shrugged. "I just do. I'm going to suggest to Mr. Feehan that we restrict access to Brad's room and that he's monitored 24/7."

"And *I'm* going to get hold of Liz and see whether she has any data about similar crimes."

"That's certainly a good place to start. Do you want to go ahead and leave me to talk to Feehan and Ms. Phelps?"

"No, I'll wait. They'll probably be back in a moment, and we need a ride from the boss, remember?"

Vadim subsided into one of the chairs. "I'd forgotten." He passed Ella Brad's cell phone. "He definitely doesn't have black hair."

While she waited, she flicked through Brad's photos and then checked out his social-media pages. "Gawd, I hope his parents haven't seen these pictures. If I was paying for my kid to attend medical school, I certainly wouldn't appreciate seeing him grinning, drinking, and fondling women in every bar in the city."

"I'm sure your parents felt the same way."

"They never saw a thing." She tossed him the phone. "That was one good thing about the empath college being in Otherworld."

The door opened and Feehan came back in with Ms. Phelps.

"What did you think of the patient?"

"Well something's not right, is it?" Ella slid off the side of the desk. "We're going to talk to his ex-girlfriend and visit the last bar he was in."

Feehan hesitated. "Ms. Phelps has a request."

"What's that?" Ella turned to face the administrator, who'd taken up her original position behind her desk.

"Brad Dailey's grandfather is a retired senator for the state of Michigan."

"So?"

"His father has political aspirations too. The family has requested that the information about Brad is kept between the hospital, the Dailey family and the SBLE."

Ella cast a sidelong look at Vadim. "Like we'd gossip to the media about a case."

"I'm sure you wouldn't, Ms. Walsh, but we'd just like to make certain we're all on the same page. Brad's parents are flying in later today to see him."

"Do you think that's advisable?" Feehan followed Vadim to the door. "If he's obviously unstable, that might complicate things."

"We'll make sure he's sedated." Ms. Phelps stood too. "I hope to hear from you as soon as possible."

"We'll do our best." Feehan held open the door for

Ella and Vadim and closed it behind him. "She seems like a nice woman."

"For someone who's desperately trying to protect her ass. She's got an influential political family breathing down her neck, which might affect future hospital funding, *and* she's got to stop any stories leaking to the media about Brad's stolen face." Ella turned to Feehan. "I bet she'll have Brad sedated. She won't want him talking about any of this."

She walked right into Vadim, who had stopped in the middle of the hallway. Feehan kept moving. "What's up?"

"I think I'll go back and see Brad and make absolutely certain he won't wake up and scare his parents."

"You can do that?"

He smiled. "Haven't you ever heard of Fae who can make humans sleep a thousand years?" He turned toward Brad's room. "Don't worry, I can bring him out of it too. I'll meet you in the parking lot."

Ella watched him walk away and followed Feehan down the stairs to the staff parking garage. Could Vadim really put people to sleep? What else could the man do? Sometimes it seemed better not to ask.

VADIM KNOCKED SOFTLY on Brad's door and waited until the nurse answered him. He gave her his best smile and she preened.

"I'm sorry to bother you—" he glanced down at her name tag "—Delia, but I need to return Brad's phone to him. Is that okay?"

"Sure. Do you want me to give it to him?"

"I'd rather give it to him myself. I don't want him to think I can't be trusted."

"That's fine. Go right on in."

When he approached the gurney, Brad's eyes were half-closed, but they opened when Vadim took his hand.

"Hey. Did you find out something already?"

"Not yet. I'm just returning your phone and wallet. I'll put them on the side here, okay?"

Even as he replaced the items, Vadim concentrated on tracking that small and ever-eroding stream of Otherworld magic that clung to Brad like cologne. One taste was enough for him to identify a creature's magical genes, his family, his connections and his power. After a moment, Vadim pushed more magic through Brad and waited until he fell asleep.

The nurse hovered at the end of the bed and Vadim nodded to her.

"Thanks for letting me see him."

"You're welcome." She walked him to the door. "You're not from around here, are you?"

"No, I'm originally from Russia."

"How cool is that?" She widened her eyes and leaned against the doorframe, arching her back. "I'd love to go there one day."

"You should. It's a wonderful country."

She glanced around and closed the door behind them. "I don't normally do this, but can I give you my number? Just in case you ever need someone to show you around town."

"That's very sweet of you, but—"

"But you're already taken." She sighed. "All the nice ones are."

"It was still a pleasure to meet you."

"Same here."

Vadim nodded and headed back down the hallway toward the bank of elevators, his thoughts focused on deciphering the myriad of messages from the Otherworld magic he'd sensed. When he first identified the power through Ella, it had felt vaguely familiar, and now he was sure of it.

He pressed the button and watched the lights of the elevator flicker downward to his level. He sensed Ella in the parking lot below him and concentrated on screening his thoughts from her. Of course, if he was right and the creature returned to seek his prey, he'd blown his cover completely, because like knew like.

The elevator arrived and he stepped in, his stomach sinking along with the descent. The magic stemmed from his bloodline.

From someone who was supposed to be dead.

THREE

"THERE YOU ARE, Liz. How are you?"

The last time Ella saw her friend, she'd been stuck between two Fae portals and ended up hospitalized in Otherworld. It hadn't been pretty.

"I'm fine. Luckily, the Fae heal super fast. How are you?"

"Good."

And that was the most Ella was prepared to say about the matter. She'd found Liz in the old conference room that used to serve as Vadim and Alexei's temporary office. Her new partner had been extremely quiet on the ride back to the office, letting her and Feehan discuss the case to their hearts' content. She didn't like it. He'd shut his mind to her completely. The moment she got him alone, she was going to find out what the hell was going on...

She refocused and noticed Liz was sitting in the middle of the floor.

"What exactly are you doing?"

"Nothing!" Liz jumped up so quickly that she almost fell off her impressively high heels.

"You're not mooning over Alexei leaving, are you?"

Liz made a face. "As if. Actually, I was looking for something." Her normally pale complexion was now as pink as her shoes.

"In here?" Ella turned a slow circle. "There's nothing except two tables and a ratty chair."

"Exactly." Liz tucked a strand of blond hair behind her ear. "Last night, Doug came to the office to pick me up, and because I had to work so late, the place was deserted and we, um, took advantage of the facilities."

"*Gross!*" Ella jumped away from the nearest horizontal surface. "Are you nuts?"

"Shut *up.* Doug has animal instincts, and there's nothing wrong with that. It's one of the things that attracted me to him."

"Anyway, so what did you lose?"

Liz sighed. "One of my antique diamond earrings."

"Damn. I'll help you look." She got down on the coffee-stained beige carpet and methodically searched the space. "Are you sure Doug didn't bite your ear in a surge of manly passion and eat the thing?"

"He would've choked. It's a big diamond." Liz continued to pat the carpet. "What did you want, anyway? I thought you'd be avoiding this place like the plague for a few days."

"Feehan called us in to deal with a new case."

"'Us'? Do you mean Vadim didn't go back to Russia with Alexei?"

"No."

Liz sat back on her heels. "That's a surprise."

Ella looked up at her friend. "He's been seconded here to work as my partner."

"The poor, poor man."

"He's not human, and he's definitely not a man, Liz. Don't waste your sympathy on him."

Liz raised her eyebrows. "Did you find out what he is, then?"

"Not exactly, but he does have some Fae Royal blood."

"Which family?"

"How would I know?" She tried to sound unconcerned.

"Find out, it makes a big difference."

"To what?"

"To how long he'll live, how strong his powers are and what exactly he can do with them over here."

"I'm scared to ask."

Liz studied her. "I would be too. He's like nothing I've ever come across before."

"That's not very encouraging." Ella moved her hand and hit something hard. "Look what I found!" She picked up the diamond and passed it over to Liz. "Jeez, it's *huge*. Here you go."

"Thanks a million. My Fae grandmother gave the earrings to me. She said that if I lost one, I'd be cursed forever."

"And yet you still wear them?"

Liz made an airy gesture. "There's almost always a way to get around a curse, you know that. Now what did you want to talk about?"

As they walked toward Liz's cubicle, Ella described Brad Dailey's situation. By the time they sat down, Liz's silver Fae-Web was already active and circling around her head.

"So have you ever heard of anything like this happening in our world before?"

Liz briefly closed her eyes. "I'm not sure. There are fragments of information, but most of the potential candidates die so soon after the event that it's hard to find a common thread."

"Do they die from their injuries?"

"No, they usually kill themselves."

"Damn." Ella let out her breath. "I wonder if that's what the creature wants? Maybe he thrives on that death. But what happens to the face of the victim afterward?"

"I've no idea. What I can do is type out the information I have and add any pictures through the printer. If I can get the sucker to work." Liz cast a dark look at the center of the office, where a bank of supposedly new printers sat. "Fae technology is crap."

"If you can't print them out, Morosov said to send the info to him. He can retain it."

"He can? That's useful." Liz cast Ella a speculative look. "So how are things going between you?"

"Ms. Walsh, where are you? I'm already in the car."

"I've got to run." Ella leaped out of her chair. "Morosov's waiting. We're heading down to the last bar Brad visited before he went home—well, the last one he remembers, anyway. I'll see you later."

"Coward!" Liz called after her, but then, Ella already knew that.

Vadim was in the underground parking lot that sat beneath the SBLE offices. She found him more by instinct than by design and paused to study the car he was driving. He opened the passenger window and angled his head so that he could see her. "Well, are you going to get in?"

Ella opened the door and slid onto the opulent leather seat. "When did you get this?"

"I had it delivered this morning."

She stroked the dark gray leather. "It's awesome."

"The seats are both heated and cooled." He closed

the window and backed slowly out of the parking space. "They also massage you."

"No way. Where's the button?"

"Down on the side of the seat. The bright green one."

"Oh, man. That's so cool." She shivered as the mechanism within the seat rolled up and down her spine. "It certainly beats my car."

"Everything beats your car." He emerged into the sunlight and tapped on the screen on the navigation system. "I've already programmed in directions to the Blue Flamingo, so we should be fine."

"What about Penny Jordan?"

"She'll be at the hospital in a couple of hours. I've arranged for us to meet her privately before her shift."

Ella hunched a shoulder and stared out at the crowded streets, where the tourists and office workers jostled for supremacy. "You're so organized. I'm not sure why you need me at all."

"Don't be childish. Pouting doesn't suit you." He looked to his right, then cut across the junction out onto Embarcadero. "It must've been difficult for you to walk away from Brad without easing his memories."

"It was, but I know we need more information before I can do that." Ella shook her head. "I just hope he can keep it together. He felt incredibly fragile."

"I agree."

She studied his flawless profile and wondered why she worried about anyone thinking they were mated. No one in his or her right mind would think she was in Vadim's league.

"You'd be surprised." He turned briefly to smile at

her. "Anyone with an ounce of magic in them can sense the connection between us right away."

"Don't read my mind!"

"If you mention me in such flattering terms, how can I help it?" He returned his gaze to the road and took a steep uphill street that reminded her of the climb up to the top of a roller coaster. "Haven't you noticed the looks we've been getting all day? Everyone magical at work can sense something is going on."

"Damn." She returned her attention to the street and the unlucky pedestrians who were struggling up the incline. Some of the San Francisco streets needed either a base camp halfway up or trained paramedics equipped with heart resuscitators. "I was hoping our shields were good enough to keep everyone out."

"I don't think we can do that. It's just something we give out as a mated couple. I'm not sure what it is, but I know it when I sense it."

"Well, it doesn't mean we have to admit anything, does it?"

A muscle flicked in his cheek, and she got the uncomfortable impression that her fake flippancy was starting to annoy him.

"No, but as I said earlier, your birthday is coming up next week, and then it will become obvious to even Feehan that something's changed."

Lampposts emblazoned with the Italian flag announced they were in the heart of Little Italy, with its closely packed bars, shops and eateries that spilled out onto the sidewalks even on cooler days like this.

"Oh, look, we're here." Ella pointed at an unlit neon sign at basement level. She wasn't discussing anything to do with mating. She had a job to do. "Can you find somewhere to park?"

"Naturally."

A parking space appeared to the right, directly in front of the Blue Flamingo.

"Now, that is one skill I'd really like to have. Can you tell me how you do it?"

Vadim reverse-parked the Mercedes in the tight space in one fluid motion. "It's quite simple. You just envision a space opening up, and it will happen."

"*Right.* You know, if magic was that easy, we'd all be doing it." She checked that she had her phone and got out of the car. The smell of garlic and baking bread tantalized her nose. "God, we have to eat while we're here."

He stepped onto the sidewalk beside her and inhaled. "Yes, we definitely should. Let's do the interview first, though."

She followed him down the steps to the front door of the Blue Flamingo, which was propped open with a beer crate. The usual stale smell of flat beer, disinfectant and urine wafted out. Inside, there were no customers, just one young guy behind the bar restocking the shelves and watching basketball on the flat-screen TV above his head.

He looked up as they approached. "Hey we're closed. Come back in an hour or two."

Vadim extracted his government ID card from his wallet and flashed it at the bartender. "We're from the SBLE. We just need to ask you a few questions."

Ella was always amazed at how quickly people accepted she was a bona fide government employee without checking her identity with a secondary source. It seemed this guy was no exception. He might be a bit nervous, but it wasn't because he feared them, which was definitely a mistake.

"You probably need to talk to the boss. He's not here."

"Actually, we want to talk to the person who was behind the bar last night."

"That would be me. I'm Mike. What's the problem?"

Ella pulled out a barstool and sat down, allowing Vadim to conduct the interview.

"We're trying to trace the movements of a Brad Dailey. We believe he was here last night."

"Brad? The blond-haired guy who got dumped?"

"That's the one."

"Did something happen to him? I made sure he didn't drive home. I called him a cab, and Adam, the other guy who was here, said he'd see him home to his apartment."

"The man's name was Adam? Did you get his last name?"

"Nope. I missed that."

"It doesn't matter. You did the right thing not letting Brad drive."

Ella sensed Vadim's magic enfolding Mike, making him more receptive to answering questions. It was a useful tool, and one she intended to borrow from Vadim's arsenal. It would complement her empath gifts nicely.

"Was there anyone else in the bar who conversed with Brad?"

"There wasn't anyone else here, period. It was a quiet night. Just Brad and his girlfriend—until she stormed out, and then just the two guys. They were here for about three hours until I had to shut up shop."

"Were they drinking heavily?"

"I wouldn't say, like, *heavily.* They switched from beer to shots after about an hour, and they were talking a lot more than they were drinking."

"Would you say either of them was intoxicated by the end of the night?"

"Brad was definitely a bit worse for wear, but Adam looked stone-cold sober. That's why I was okay with him helping Brad home." He opened the dishwasher and steam rose into the air. "Is the guy okay?"

"Brad's fine. We're more concerned about tracing the guy who helped him get home. Can you describe him to me?"

"Adam? He was probably in his thirties, well dressed in a suit and tie." Mike picked up one of the glasses from the dishwasher rack and polished it before putting it back on the shelf.

"What did he look like?"

Mike frowned. "It's hard to say. He was pretty average—brown hair, brown eyes, medium height, no visible tats or piercings, not buff or gay, just a regular kind of guy. It's weird…now that I think of it, I really can't picture him very well at all."

"If I sent someone from our office down here to make a sketch of him with your help, do you think you could do it?"

"It depends. He was just so *average*, you know?"

"It's okay, you never know what you might remember when you start working with the artist." Vadim handed over a card. "Call me if you have any further questions or information to impart."

"Will do." Mike tucked the card in his shirt pocket. "Is Brad going to be okay?"

Ella got off the stool and smiled at him. "I'm sure he'll be fine."

"How about Adam?"

"If we find him, we'll let you know. Did he mention if he was visiting the city, or has he been in here before?"

"I *think* he was here, like, for a conference, some computer thing, although he looked too well dressed to be a nerd, but you never know these days, do you?"

"Was he staying around here?"

"He did mention a hotel, but I don't remember which one." Mike shrugged. "I generally try not to listen to everyone's conversations, but it was a quiet night."

"We understand, and we're grateful you've been able to help us so much."

"You're welcome." Mike hesitated. "Did Adam, like, steal stuff from Brad's apartment or something?"

"He stole something, all right." Ella wrapped her scarf around her neck. "But we'll find him and make sure Brad gets everything back."

"Good luck."

She followed Vadim back out into the sunshine and walked into the nearest restaurant. She sat opposite him at a tiny table covered with a traditional red-and-white-check tablecloth. The table wobbled when she picked up her menu.

"Can you fix that?"

"The table?" He folded his paper napkin into a wedge, rocked the table for a minute and then shoved it under one of the feet. "Is that better?"

"Perfect. You don't have a magic fixing spell, then?"

"I'm more of a destroyer than a fixer."

"Funny." She grinned at him as the waitress placed breadsticks on the table, accompanied by a plate of olive oil and balsamic vinegar. "I'm starving."

"You always are."

"I can't help it." She dipped her breadstick into the oil and swirled it around. "I love to eat." Holding his gaze, she brought the bread to her lips and slowly licked the oil off the rounded tip. His eyes narrowed and the temperature around them seemed to increase by about a hundred degrees. Very slowly she sucked the breadstick into her mouth and bit down.

He shuddered and reached for her hand. She was scorchingly aware of his need beneath her own skin, of wanting to rip off his shirt and touch his bare chest, to reach lower and grasp—

"Are you ready to order?"

Ella jumped and turned to the waitress. "Yeah, I'll have the cheese ravioli with the Gorgonzola sauce, please."

"And for you, sir?"

"A green salad and a bowl of spaghetti with olive oil. No cheese."

"Thank you." The waitress scribbled on her pad. "Anything to drink?"

"Just some water, please."

Ella dragged her attention away from Vadim. "A soda. Any kind, I don't mind."

"There are about two thousand calories in that ravioli you ordered."

"So?"

"You're not going to die next week."

"We've already had this discussion." She picked up

another breadstick and pointed it at him. "What did you think of Mike the bartender?"

"He seemed to be telling the truth."

"That's what I got, too." She deliberately crunched her way down the breadstick, sending crumbs flying everywhere. "It fits in with what Brad told us, as well. Don't you think it's weird how this Adam guy hasn't left much of an impression on anyone?"

"I suspect that's part of his magic. A creature that steals other people's faces wouldn't want to draw attention to his own, now, would he?"

"True." Ella contemplated the plate of oil. "I still don't get what he wants with Brad's face, though, do you?"

"It could be for many things. A spell, an offering to a higher being, a collection of curiosities. Otherworld serial killers can be just as inventive as human ones."

She shivered. "I know."

He reached out and took her hand again. "We'll work it out."

"I'm glad you think so. I'm not so sure." She tried to ease out of his grip, but he held on and brought her fingers to his mouth. With exquisite care he kissed his way along her knuckles, his tongue always in evidence, his breath warm on her flesh.

"Don't play games with me, Ms. Walsh." He bit down on the fleshy pad of her thumb and her whole body came instantly to life. "You can't have it both ways."

"I don't know what you mean."

"Teasing me, and then talking about work."

"I didn't—" She bit back a moan as he bit and

then licked her. Damn, she was wet now, and he would know.

"*God, I know, and if I had a little less sense, I'd take you outside, back you up against the nearest wall and fill you up with my cock.*"

"*Shut up!*"

THIS TIME SHE did manage to pull out of his grasp. His gaze dropped to her open coat and the tight buds of her nipples, which were visible through her T-shirt.

He reached for the glass of water the waitress had placed beside him and drank it down in one long swallow. "You drive me insane."

"It's my fault now, is it?"

He looked at her indignant face, her flushed cheeks and soft fair hair. He wanted to shove his hands into her hair and bring her mouth to meet his, and then reintroduce her to other, more needy parts of his anatomy…

"*Stop it, you pig!*"

He took a slow inward breath and raised his head to look past her. The waitress was approaching with their lunch. Thank the universe for small mercies. Nothing ever got between his mate and her food. For once he was content to accept that. Except that this time, watching her enjoy her ravioli was akin to watching her orgasm. If he wasn't mistaken, her low moans were more suitable for being naked and in his bed than for a plate of cheese and pasta.

He eyed her speculatively. Of course, he could make her some pasta from scratch… He shoved his fork into his spaghetti and twirled it. He was behaving like a fool when he most needed to be on his guard. If he wasn't careful, Otherworld would have no problem dragging him back to face his fate, and Ella would be moaning over her pasta with someone else.

He finished his lunch and dabbed at his mouth with his napkin. "Are you ready to go? We need to be at the hospital."

Ella scowled. "Give me a minute. I'm still eating."

"Can't you get it to go?"

"What's eating your pants?"

Nothing, unfortunately. "I just want to avoid getting stuck in traffic."

"Fine, I'll get a box. This stuff deserves to be savored. I can have it for supper tonight."

He stood up. "I'll get you a box while I settle the bill."

The route back to the hospital was full of twists and turns, and streets of unimaginable steepness, but he kept his attention fully on the task and ignored his companion as best he could. She didn't seem to mind, having attempted a conversation, gotten pissed off when he didn't reply and then fallen asleep.

She snored.

He parked in the staff lot and got out of the car to open Ella's door for her. She smiled up at him and he almost snarled with lust. Tonight, unless she relented, he had to go back to his hotel room alone.

"Help me out, I'm still sleepy." She extended her hand and he just stared at her. "Morosov!"

He yanked her out of the car and into his arms and was kissing her before she'd even drawn another breath. She didn't fight him, just melted into him and kissed him back. Within seconds, his hand was on her ass, picking her up and molding her against his aching cock.

"*Morosov.*"

He kept kissing her and tried to ignore her voice in his head.

"*This isn't the right place.*"

"*It never is, with you.*" She bit his lip, driving him wild.

"*We need to talk to this witness, and then we need to talk, okay?*"

"*You're being the sensible one now? What the hell is wrong with you?*" He wrenched his mouth away from hers, breathing hard. "And how are we going to manage *that* when I'm living in the city, and you've banned me from your house?"

"I haven't *banned* you. How about I come and hang out with you at your hotel? We can have dinner and talk." She sighed, and looked into his eyes. "And have sex. Can we do that?"

He set her away from him. He'd never thought he'd be the one who had to beg for her time. With his powers, he could compel her to do anything he desired, but he wanted her to come to him willingly. He wanted her to crave him as much as he craved her. "All right."

She smoothed down her clothing, not that it made much difference to her appearance. She always looked as if she'd just rolled out of bed. "It's a deal. Let's go and meet Penny Jordan."

FOUR

"HE WAS JUST SO...immature, you know?" Penny Jordan glanced from Vadim to Ella, who nodded understandingly. "So full of himself that I couldn't trust him at all. He flirted with all my friends and lied to my face. I was sick and tired of it and finally broke up with him."

"In the Blue Flamingo bar last night?" Ella asked.

They were sitting in a small consulting room on the first floor of the hospital, near Penny Jordan's workstation. The space smelled of disinfectant and fear and made Ella's empath senses jangle like a toothache. She and Vadim sat on the only two chairs, and Penny perched on the side of the paper-covered gurney, legs swinging in her green scrubs. She was a slim, dark-haired woman with a sweet expression and a wide smile.

"Yes. I asked him to meet me there, because I hoped he wouldn't make a big scene in public."

"Had you been to that particular bar before?"

"Not with him. I chose it because it's a great place to pick up a taxi, and I wanted to make a quick escape."

"How did he take being dumped?"

Penny grimaced. "He smiled right in my face and said that he was okay with it because he'd already hooked up with someone else and was going to dump me anyway."

"Did you believe him?"

"It doesn't matter if I did or not, does it? It was just so typical of him to try and turn everything around and make it all about him. It actually made me glad I'd found the nerve to break up with him." She sighed. "No doubt he's telling everyone he dumped me."

"He's not saying much at all at the moment, actually."

"What do you mean?" Penny put a hand to her mouth. "He didn't go and do something stupid, did he?"

"To be honest, I don't think what happened between you had much to do with what's happened to him, other than that Brad was in the wrong bar at the wrong time."

"Was he mugged? I don't want to date him anymore, but I don't want him dead or hurt." She stared at Ella. "You don't think I did something to get back at him, do you?"

"It's okay. You don't seem the type to send someone to break his legs."

"So, he is hurt?"

"In a manner of speaking. From what we can make out, he stayed at the bar until closing and got drunk. Someone took him home in a taxi, and he didn't turn up for class this morning."

Penny shrugged. "That's a fairly normal night for him, so what else happened?"

"He was found in a distressed state this morning by the emergency services and brought into hospital for further observation."

"Did he use something illegal?"

Vadim sat forward. "Why would you think that?"

"Because he liked to experiment with stuff." Penny shook her head. "That was another reason why we argued. I've seen addicts come into the ER. I wouldn't want to end up like that. Brad should know that too. He's training to be a freaking doctor!"

"At this point, the medical team isn't quite sure what Brad took, or didn't take. All we know is that he is in a severely heightened state of anxiety."

"He's probably scared his daddy's going to cut off his money because he missed class again. I kept telling him he should just admit to his parents that he doesn't want to be a doctor, but he's too afraid of letting them down."

Vadim smiled. "I know that feeling. Do you really think he's scared of his parents?"

"Wouldn't you be?" Penny's faintly mocking smile disappeared. "He called them the Kennedys on speed. He was terrified of messing up." She hesitated. "Is Brad here? Do you think I could see him?"

"He's heavily sedated at the moment, Ms. Jordan, and not receiving visitors. But we will keep you informed of his progress, if you wish it."

"I'd like that." Penny rose and tossed her coffee cup in the trash. "He might be a jerk, but I still care about him. When he was nice, he was *really* nice, you know?"

"Oh, I know. The jerks always are." Ella held out her hand. "Thanks so much for talking to us, and as my colleague said, we'll keep in touch."

She waited until Penny closed the door behind her before sitting down next to Vadim again.

"She seemed way too nice to be going out with Brad."

"He certainly didn't come across as a very admirable or likeable character, did he?" Vadim stretched out and crossed his legs at the ankle. "I actually felt quite sorry for him."

"For Brad?"

"He's under a lot of pressure from his family to con-
form. It's hardly surprising that he's acting out and is
so immature."

"You can obviously relate. Was that your excuse for
getting kicked out of Otherworld?"

He considered her for a long moment, his expression bleak. "For my youthful behavior? No, although
the damage I caused was far more long lasting than
Brad's."

"What did you do?"

"Eventually I conformed." His mouth twisted.
"*That's* why I got kicked out of Otherworld." He rose
to his feet. "Do you want to go back to the office and
start looking for Adam, or stay and talk to Brad again?"

"Brad's in a fairy-imposed coma."

"From which I can awaken him." He stood by the
door and stared down at her. "What do you want to
do?"

"I suppose we should go back and tell Feehan what
we've learned so far." Ella groaned. "Liz might have
more information too. We can also check in with her
about the mysterious Adam."

"So let's go back." He held open the door for her
and followed her down the hallway. "Brad's probably
better off sleeping, at the moment."

FEEHAN OPENED THE door into the big conference room
and snapped on the fluorescent lights.

"Let's get everyone in here, shall we?"

Ella followed him in, glad to see that someone had
taken down all the horrific pictures and info about the
empaths the Siren had murdered, from their last case.

She was happy that he was dead, but it didn't bring back her fellow empaths, especially her best friend, Laney. She missed Laney like a sister…well, more than a sister. Ella's real sister drove her nuts. If it hadn't been for the Siren, she wouldn't have met Vadim and ended up mated to him, likely to live a long and happy life. Was she only allowed one special person in her life at a time?

"Sit down, Ella." Feehan pulled out a chair for her and hovered over her solicitously. "How are you feeling? I know your twenty-seventh birthday is coming up next week."

"I'm feeling good, boss. How about you?"

She gave him her best shark smile and he backed off and took a seat at the other end of the table. She supposed, being her superior, he had a right to inquire about the state of her mental health. Unmated empaths had a tendency to go nuts from psychic overload as their twenty-seventh birthday approached. And hers was next week. He didn't know she was mated to Vadim yet. No one did, although Liz had skated pretty damn close to working it out.

Not even her parents knew she was going to survive. She'd refused to consider choosing an Otherworld-approved mate until Vadim had practically forced her to take him on. She'd only done it then because he'd made it seem more attractive than death in an elevator shaft. If she was honest, admitting she was going to live after spending the last twenty-seven years deliberately pissing everyone off in the belief she would die young was somewhat embarrassing. She was still debating whether to mention it to them or not. She'd agreed to go to their house in the East Bay and eat birthday cake on the weekend. If she wasn't going out of her mind, that might just do it for her.

Vadim slipped into the seat to her left and Liz took the one on her right. A minute later, Andrew and Rich came in, accompanied by her trainee empath, Sam. As usual, they were arguing about something baseball related and barely stopped to acknowledge anyone else in the room.

"Here you are." Vadim put a cup of coffee in front of her.

"Thanks." She smiled at him and then noticed Liz was staring at them with a knowing look. "About time, too."

He merely raised his eyebrows and looked away. Liz nudged her. "He is so hot, Ella, I don't know how you can stand not jumping his bones."

She felt her cheeks heat. "Whisper that a bit louder, Liz. I don't think Morosov got it all."

"Oh, I heard." His low, amused voice held a hint of sex that sent little shivers up and down her spine. "For the record, I don't know how she resists me either, Liz."

Feehan picked up a pen and headed for the whiteboard.

"Now that we're all here, let's talk about the new case." He wrote Brad Dailey's name on the board, followed by the name of the bar and all the other details Ella and Vadim had given him. "What else do we know?"

Liz put up her hand. "I've been searching the Fae-Web for other cases like this, and as I was telling Ella, it's really hard to find anything concrete, because the victims tend to go mad or die fairly quickly."

"That's not good." Feehan frowned. "Can you share what you have anyway?"

Liz handed out some sheets of paper to the team. "I typed this out really fast, so excuse any errors. The Fae-Web refused to connect with our internet. I'm still waiting for some photographs of the victims."

Ella scanned the pages. "Have you come across any mention of a man called Adam?"

"Specifically?" Liz's silver Fae-Web unfurled over her head and started to shimmer. "Not that name, although from the fragments we have, most of the victims claim they did meet up with a helpful stranger just before their faces disappeared."

"A helpful stranger." Feehan wrote a question mark on the board. "Are we assuming that we're dealing with something from Otherworld?"

Ella nodded. "Both Morosov and I felt some residual magic clinging to Brad Dailey, so we assume that's the case."

She glanced at Vadim for confirmation, but he appeared to be lost in thought. She kicked his shin under the table and he jumped.

"Yes, after some discussion, Ms. Walsh and I came to the conclusion that magic was involved in some way. It would be easier if Mr. Dailey had left his face alone, so that we could've seen what he looked like."

"You mean we'd know if he'd been surgically interfered with rather than bespelled?" Feehan asked, his pen poised over the whiteboard.

"It's a faint possibility. Brad is a medical student, after all, so he and his friends have access to surgical equipment."

"But unlikely." Feehan noted Ella's nod. "So we're fairly sure this is Otherworld."

"Yes." She tried to catch Vadim's eye, but he was sipping his coffee and reading through Liz's report. Why was he so reluctant to agree that the perp was from his old stomping ground? "What is interesting is that none of the people who met Adam can describe him very well, so it's not as if he switches his identity with his victims."

Sam raised his hand. "It says here that last year, three people in the Bay Area were taken into medical care claiming to have lost their identities. All three of them committed suicide."

"That's terrible," Ella said.

"Maybe it's one of those legendary hunters from Otherworld—you know, like their dark-angel dude who brings justice and death to the wicked."

"In Otherworld, Sam, not here."

"But what if he was here?" Sam looked around, his eyes wide. "What if that bloodthirsty dude was in our world?"

"We have no way of knowing whether such a creature exists, or why he would murder innocent humans." Vadim cut across what Ella had been about to say, his tone cold. "I suggest we at least try and ground this discussion in reality."

"Sorry, Vad." Sam closed his mouth and hunched down in his seat. "I just thought I'd throw it out there. Otherworld has the scariest shit around."

"Then let's do our best to make sure we keep Brad Dailey alive and able to answer our questions." Feehan surveyed the team. "What can we do to find this man 'Adam'?"

"I'm going to check local conference records and hotels and see if anyone called Adam *did* register and attend anything in the city this week." Ella leaned back in her chair. "It's highly likely he used a false name when he met Brad, but you never know. If he's been successfully stealing faces for years, he might not be that careful."

"Okay, what else can we do?"

"I can liaise with Liz and work on extracting more information from the Fae-Web." Vadim appeared to have come out of his trance.

"That would be great." Liz smiled at him. "We can also extend our search criteria to the rest of the U.S.A. and the world, and see if there are any other cases to consider."

Feehan wrote busily on the board and then turned back. "Anything else? Do we need to contact anyone directly in Otherworld for help yet?"

Vadim shook his head. "It's too early. We need to have some idea what we're dealing with before we go charging in with our demands."

"And what do you think we're dealing with?"

"A killer with exceptional magical powers he can use in the human world as well as his own. That is quite rare."

"That's true." Liz agreed. "A lot of Fae magical powers are weakened when transferred to this realm. Only certain families have the ability to function fully here."

"Maybe Morosov can come up with a list of those families," Ella said. "He probably knows the bloodlines better than anyone. It would at least narrow the field."

"I'd appreciate that." Feehan smiled at her hapless partner and then turned to Andrew. "Maybe you and

Rich can check with the shape-shifting communities as to whether this Adam could come from them. It's unlikely, I know, but stealing a face could be a facet of shifting we just haven't come across before."

Feehan rambled on for a minute and then started gathering up his papers. His idea to involve the shape-shifters was an excellent one. Maybe he was growing into his job after all. It was about time. The look Vadim shot her wasn't entirely friendly. What the hell was chafing his ass? She'd promised to meet him later, *and* to have sex, so why wasn't he smiling?

She waited until everyone exited the room and then put her hand on Vadim's arm as he started to rise.

"Wait a sec." He subsided back into his seat. "What's up?"

"Nothing." Under her hand his biceps flexed and hardened as if he was considering fleeing. "I'm just thinking about the case."

"Morosov, as a woman, I already know that the answer 'nothing' means 'everything.' What are you worried about, and why are you so reluctant to get involved in this?"

"I am involved in it." His smile was distant.

"Then why won't you share your knowledge?"

"It's not that simple."

"It never is, with you. What's the problem?"

He turned to face her, his expression far too serious for her liking. "I suspect the man who calls himself Adam is involved with an ancient Otherworld sect."

"A sect? Like a cult or something?"

"I suppose that is as good a word as any. They... collect trophies."

"Like a serial killer."

"Yes, but this is for their amusement. They make bets with each other to see who can collect something that is hard to find like, say, a mermaid's tail or a unicorn's horn."

"Both of which don't exist, right?"

"They did before the Otherworld sect started hunting them." His smile was wry. "They don't care about the consequences of their actions. It's all about the hunt and the winning."

"And you think Adam is involved with them?"

"The magic he left behind held a certain signature I recognized." He met her gaze. "I've come across it before in Otherworld."

"When you were doing what?"

"Fulfilling tasks for the queen."

"Oh, damn. Why didn't you share this with Feehan and the rest of the team?"

He looked away. "Because I'm worried that if I bring this up, Feehan will immediately go to Otherworld and make this all aboveboard and public. If he does that, he and the rest of us will probably be killed fairly swiftly. The membership of the sect holds considerable power."

"Then why did you tell me?"

His eyebrows rose. "Because you're my mate."

Sometimes his honesty confounded her. Now she was the one to look away. "So, what can we do?"

"If we track down Adam and execute him ourselves, he will simply be out of the game. No one will care."

"That makes sense, but what kind of game is he playing? And if we kill him, won't someone else take his place?"

"The members don't compete directly against each other. It's more about how an individual *chooses* to interpret a challenge. His choice of prey, the way he kills and the way he displays his trophies count toward the eventual winner's score."

"That's macabre."

"That's Otherworld."

"So you're saying that a challenge could be, to find an interesting use for a human, and our guy could've interpreted it to mean let's steal their faces and make them into, I dunno, carnival masks?"

"Exactly."

"Gross." Ella shivered. "So how can we nail him?"

"The number three is a very powerful symbol to this sect. Did you notice Sam saying that there were three reports of similar deaths earlier in the year?"

"So you reckon Adam will be trying to add two more to his current collection?"

"I would assume that's his goal."

"But we still have no idea how to find him."

He sat back. "We'll find him. I know his scent now."

"How can you be so sure?"

"I'm trained to hunt prey." He smiled at her and his eyes glinted black. "I'm certain he'll return, especially if he knows I'm seeking him."

"Because we leave a trace of our magic at every scene, and if he goes back to check on Brad…"

"He'll find a trace of me."

"Will he want you?"

He rose to his feet. "Everyone wants me, Ms. Walsh."

Ella made a rude noise and grabbed her backpack. "Then maybe we'd better head back to the hospital right away."

SAN FRANCISCO GENERAL was its usual chaotic self, but Vadim had learned to ignore it. Since hooking up with his mate, he was finding it harder to deal with his emotions and the impact of other human minds. He wasn't surprised that most unsupported empaths went mad at the age of twenty-seven. His shields were constantly buckling under the pressure of the onslaught of feelings. Since joining minds with Ella, he'd come to respect her abilities quite considerably.

He was also glad she led the way through the maze of identical hallways to Brad's ward without faltering. Delia, the nurse who'd offered him her services as a guide to the city, was sitting outside the door, looking rather important. Flanking her was an enormously tall guy wearing dark shades and a suit cut to fit a bulky shoulder holster. He scanned the hallways like a pro and immediately tensed as Vadim and Ella approached the door.

He held up his hand.

"This room is secured. Please step back and then state your business."

Ella held up her badge. "We're from the SBLE. We're here to see Mr. Dailey."

"I have no instructions to admit anyone except approved medical staff and Mr. Dailey's immediate family."

Before Ella could get up in the man's face, Vadim stepped in front of her and smiled pleasantly. "I think you'll find that you are mistaken and that both Ms. Walsh and I are on that list. Please feel free to confirm that information with Ms. Phelps, the administrator dealing with this case."

"*Morosov, get out of the way. I can get in his head. I can make him let us in.*"

"*That's our next step. Let's try and do it the official way first.*"

Sometimes he agreed with her that it would be easier to blast his way through the obstacle, but since leaving Otherworld, he'd been attempting to cultivate more reasonable habits.

"*Why?*"

He smiled again at Delia. "Hi, how are you, today? How's Brad doing?"

After a swift glance at the security agent who appeared to be whispering into his mike, Delia turned to Vadim.

"Brad's grandfather is in there with him, but he's still sedated and unable to respond to them."

"Poor guy." Vadim shook his head. "Perhaps we'd better not disturb him, then." He turned to Ella, who wasn't looking very pleased. "Shall we go and find Ms. Phelps and get her up to speed?"

"I'd rather see Brad."

He took hold of her elbow and propelled her along the corridor. "We'll do that in a moment. Do you particularly want to go in there and face his grandfather? We can't answer a single damn question for them yet." She went to speak, and he kept talking. "It's not likely that Adam will get in there either, with Delia and that thug on the door."

"I suppose you're right. Maybe we should come back later."

"Let's do that. We can ask Ms. Phelps to call us when the ex-senator leaves."

She grimaced. "Okay, but I just have a bad feeling about this."

So did he, but he didn't want her to know that. "How about we catch an early dinner at my hotel and return this evening?"

"I suppose that would work. Look, there's Ms. Phelps." She walked over to the nurse's station. "Hey, we just got barred from Brad Dailey's room by some secret-service guy."

"You did?" Ms. Phelps took them back into her office and shut the door. She patted ineffectively at her blond bun. "I'm not surprised. That man was demanding I show him full security checks for every single member of staff and patient on this ward! If the ex-senator wants his grandson to have more privacy, he'll have to pay for a private room on a secure corridor." She lowered her voice a fraction. "It's not as if Brad is a VIP."

"How long is he staying?"

"The former senator is leaving in about two hours. He'll hopefully be taking his security detail with him. Brad's parents are due in tonight at around eleven. They are flying in from Florida. They were on their yacht."

"Nice," Ella said. "So will you call us just before the senator leaves? We need to talk to Brad."

"He hasn't been very responsive today at all." Ms. Phelps shook her head. "His doctor fears he might be going into a coma of some kind, his body signs are so minimal."

"Well, thanks for the heads-up. We'll do our best to get him to talk to us, but we'll understand if he can't."

Vadim held the door open for Ella and then followed

her toward the stairs and the elevator bank. She looked back at him over her shoulder.

"How much time do we have?"

"To get something to eat and get back here? Just under two hours."

She groaned. "At this time of day it's going to take us that long to get to your hotel in the commuter traffic."

"Not if we don't use the car."

"I keep forgetting about that." Her smile made his body come to life. "Can you take us right into your room?"

He could.

As soon as they materialized, he wrapped his arms around her and backed her up against the nearest wall, his tongue in her mouth, his hands roaming her jeans-covered ass.

"Morosov, what about my dinner?" She slid a hand around his neck. "I'm starving."

There were so many filthy things he could say to that. "Sex first, dinner after." He lifted her until her thighs hugged his hips and his cock ground against the seam of her jeans.

"But what about our talk?"

He scowled down at her far-too-innocent face. "After."

She rolled her hips against his hardness and he fought a groan. Why did she always wear so many clothes? He had her naked in a second and stretched out beneath him on the bed, her legs spread wide by his. With a sigh he bent over her breasts and licked one hard nipple into his mouth. She started to squirm and he increased the pressure, sliding his fingers over her swollen clit and into her welcoming warmth.

She climaxed almost immediately, and he added another finger, transferring his attention to her other breast. His cock beat an urgent pulse along with his heart, wanting to be in her, to be joined to her in every way possible.

"Morosov…"

Why did she insist on talking when he was busy savoring the delights of her skin and scent and texture?

"*Morosov, let me up!*"

He raised his head to look at her. "What?"

She blinked at him. "I want something to do."

"Then touch me."

"I can't reach the bit I particularly want to touch." She pushed on his chest, and he reluctantly allowed her to sit up. She immediately turned around until her mouth was a tantalizing inch from his cock, put out her tongue and licked a drop of clear liquid off the crown.

"Mmm, nice," Ella murmured.

He rolled onto his side, and her lips slid over his cock and took him deep. With a groan he returned his attention to her clit, using his tongue and mouth and fingers to bring her to another climax. Even while she still shuddered, he eased his shaft from her mouth and, reversing their positions, pushed her onto her back, spreading her knees wide with his.

She grinned up at him, her cheeks flushed, her blond hair escaping her haphazard braids. Something inside him tightened. She infuriated him, but he needed her as he needed oxygen. Something about her made him feel alive for the first time in years, made him want to protect her with every magical power he had inside him, good and bad. She was his mate. If it came to it, he would gladly die for her.

Words pressed on his lips. He wanted to slash his chest with his nails and bleed for her, have her lick his blood, give her everything...

"Morosov."

He opened his eyes and looked down at her again.

"Get on with it! I'm done waiting."

Without another word, he plunged deep inside her and felt complete, their minds in harmony, their bodies even more so. Every time they made love, the bond between them strengthened. Did she feel that? And if she did, would she ever acknowledge it to his face? This was when he knew her completely, and where he felt safe. He thrust deeply. Her hands tightened on his shoulders, leaving her mark, as he wanted to mark her.

But there was still some part of her that held back, that resisted him... Sometimes he wanted to take her to the edge and force her over the abyss into knowing him and the depths of his personal hell. She was right to be wary. He could destroy her with one breath. He yelped as she tugged at his hair.

"Pay attention! Stop thinking and just..."

"Fuck you?" He increased his tempo, driving shorter and harder. Her feet crept up to his hips and he worked her even higher, her knees over his elbows as she started to come and come and...with a muffled howl he joined her, spilling himself deep inside her.

When she pushed at his chest, he obligingly rolled off her and subsided onto the covers with a groan.

"Morosov."

"My name is *Vadim*. Can't you even call me that when we're naked?"

"Okay then, Vadim, although I doubt that's your real name, anyway. You didn't use a condom. Did you assume I was on the pill?"

He opened one eye. "I know you are."

"You've never asked me!"

"But I know *you*. If you were planning on leaving this life on your twenty-seventh birthday, you would never allow yourself to conceive a child."

Her hand came toward his cheek and he tensed, but she merely stroked him gently. "That's pretty observant for a guy."

"I'm your mate." He caught her fingers in his and kissed them. "However, you should also know that I could make any method of birth control fail."

She rolled away from him and sat up. "What the fuck?"

"Exactly." He smiled. "I really can."

"You wouldn't dare!"

Her scowl was tremendous but not intimidating at all, because he was staring up at her heaving breasts and tight pink nipples. It was nice to occasionally get the upper hand with his female.

"Morosov, look at me. You have to swear that you will never do that, or else that is the last time I'll ever let you make love to me." She climbed off the bed and started looking for her clothes, which he had folded neatly on the chair beside the fire.

He smiled slowly and put his hands behind his head. They were making love now rather than just having casual sex? That was progress. She stomped into the bathroom and the shower went on. While she was occupied, he ordered room service and then rose from the bed and followed her into the bathroom.

"THAT'S MY TOOTHBRUSH!"

Ella glanced back over her shoulder to see Vadim in all his naked glory, glaring at her. She spat slowly into the bowl and rinsed.

"I've put it back. Keep your feathers on. After the Fae public-health service announcement you just gave me, I'm entitled to be fricking annoyed."

She headed into the shower and allowed the steady drum of the water to soothe her tangled nerves. Her threat not to have sex with Vadim ever again was an empty one and he knew it. She could barely keep her hands off him at the best of times, and he wasn't much better. That had surprised her. Under that calm exterior he was as wild about sex as she was, and easily the best lay she'd ever had.

"Thank you."

"Don't read my mind!" He stepped into the shower behind her and wrapped his arms around her waist. She tried to stick an elbow in his gut, but he simply laughed and held her slightly away from him. "I'm not talking to you."

"Even here?"

She tried, but she couldn't shut him out anymore. "You have to promise you won't get me pregnant."

He nuzzled her neck and then her throat, and her knees went to jelly. "Not even if you wanted me to?"

A vision of a mini-Morosov danced inside her lust-driven brain, and she wasn't sure if he'd planted it there or it was coming from her. That was even more terrifying than the thought of being pregnant.

He bit down slowly on the tendon in her neck. "We would make beautiful babies."

"Shut up! I've only just realized I'm going to live beyond the age of twenty-seven. I haven't come to terms with having you around yet, let alone a kid!"

His chuckle reverberated against her wet skin, and his newly erect cock pressed against her ass. This time she did manage to get her elbow in his chest and spun around to face him. He looked quite breathtaking, his dark blue eyes narrowed in a combination of amusement and lust as water dripped down his perfect cheekbones to his perfect abs and his perfect...

She stuck a finger in his face. "You're messing with my head, aren't you?"

"I might be."

"Can you really make me pregnant?"

"Yes."

"But not without my consent."

He nodded. "Naturally."

"Do I even need to be on contraception, then?"

He shrugged. "It's up to you. You don't need it." He reached down and palmed his growing erection. "It's much nicer for both of us if there's nothing in between us."

"Like a nice fluffy towel, for example."

She stepped smartly out of the shower and shut the door on him. He kept smiling, his fingers gently teasing his thick shaft. She found it difficult to look away. She grabbed a robe and walked back out into the bedroom, rubbing her hair with a towel. Her stomach rumbled and she checked the time.

"We need to order some food."

"Already done. It should be here fairly soon."

He appeared in the bathroom doorway, a towel wrapped low around his hips. He strolled across to her and her stomach tightened in anticipation. "We still have a few minutes." He sat down, and before she could say anything, he brought her on top of him, his cock unerringly finding her wet center and driving home.

She pushed back at him, demanding control, and he gave it to her, his eyes half-closed, his hands riding her hips as she controlled the depth and frequency of his thrusts. He didn't even need to touch her clit to make her come this time. She loved it when he gave himself to her like this. It was like controlling a force of nature.

With a sigh, she rested her forehead on his shoulder and gulped in some much-needed air. His hand caressed the back of her neck, his thumb circling her spine. "See? Much better skin to skin."

She reluctantly climbed off him. "We still haven't talked."

"We can do that while we eat."

She headed back to the bathroom and heard the knock on the door that heralded the arrival of their food. The tantalizing smell of barbecue made her lick her lips and hurry to clean up.

When she emerged, Vadim was uncovering plates on the small table and setting out silverware and water glasses. He was fully dressed in his shirt, tie and pants.

"It smells good. What did you order for me?"

"Ribs, curly fries and beans."

"Really?" She smiled at him. "Does it come with a side of you lecturing me about my eating habits?"

"No, just eat." He shook out his napkin and sat opposite her. "You need your strength."

"What do you have?"

"Some grilled halibut, mashed potatoes and asparagus."

"Of course." She would've said more, but she was

too busy devouring the ribs, scooping up beans and eating fries with her fingers. She'd probably need another shower after this. Vadim would be amazed...

"How did you manage that?" She gestured at his clothing. "You love having a shower. I can't imagine you got dressed without one."

"It's an old Fae spell."

"Can you show me how to do it?"

"If you wish. But eat your dinner first. We're running out of time."

FIVE

"WE STILL HAVEN'T talked." Ella pushed open the door into the hospital and Vadim walked through beside her.

"It's difficult to have a conversation with someone eating ribs with such gusto."

She stopped and faced him. "Don't you want to discuss our relationship?"

He pressed a hand to his heart. "Words every male, both human and Otherworld, is just longing to hear."

"But you said you wanted to talk!"

He sighed. "And you've been avoiding me all day. Why now? What do you want, Ella?"

"It's more a question of what you want."

"I want you. That's it."

"But what about the logistics? What about where we're going to live, how often we see each other, what we tell our friends and family, or colleagues?"

His expression tightened. "You're so fucking contrary. At one moment you're pushing me away and telling me not to get in your space, the next we're setting up home together?" He shook his head. "You're the one who seems to have the problems with this, not me, so why don't you work it out? If you don't want me at your place in Tiburon, what do you want? Should I stay in the city and you can just join me at my hotel when you can't do without the sex?"

"That's not fair."

"Life's not fair, Ella. You know that." He started walking again, his last comment thrown over his shoulder. "When you work out how I'll fit into your life, let me know."

She let him leave, her heart stuttering, her breath uneven. Didn't he understand? She *never* made long-term plans. She'd never had to. Someone barged into her, and she moved to the side of the hallway and continued toward the stairs.

He was waiting for her by the door, his head lowered, his gaze averted.

"I'm sorry, Ella. I keep forgetting that for you this is an extremely difficult transition."

She stared at his blue-and-yellow tie until the pattern blurred into a swirl of dots.

After a long moment, he sighed and held open the door. "Shall we go up?"

She forced the words out of her mouth. "Will you come with me to my parents on the weekend?"

He hesitated, one hand braced against the frame. "If you want me to."

"Yeah." She swallowed hard. "You can use your charm to distract my mom from complaining about me."

His smile made her feel loved, which was ridiculous. "I'd be more than happy to do that. Let's go and check on Brad Dailey."

As VADIM APPROACHED Brad's room, his Otherworld senses came to high alert and he studied each person in the hallway with all his unique abilities. Beside him, Ella reached for her weapon. Delia sat by the door, but she didn't look up as they approached, her gaze seemingly fixed on some pleasant faraway memory. Vadim touched her shoulder.

"Delia?"

She didn't respond. The kick of Otherworld magic hit him hard.

"Ms. Walsh, get out of the way."

He didn't wait for Ella's indignant reply, just pushed in front of her and tried to force the door open. Dark magic shot up his arm, making him clench his teeth. If a human had touched the handle, the person would probably be dead now. He focused on the door and pushed the power back out, turning the spell on itself and blasting through it. Inside, someone was screaming like a wounded animal.

"Ella, call security!"

The room was in chaos, the bed halfway across the floor. Brad was no longer sedated or secured to the gurney. He stood on the windowsill, his scarred face free of bandages and contorted in agony.

Vadim held out his hand. "Mr. Dailey, calm down. Whatever is wrong, we can fix it." As he spoke, he sent calming magic toward Brad, but he appeared to be impervious to it.

"I'm a *freak!* My grandfather couldn't even look at me. I don't want my parents to see me like this!"

"It's not that bad. Your face can be altered again. We'll find the best plastic surgeons in the world to work with you."

He heard Ella and someone else approaching down the hallway and motioned for them to stay put at the door. He advanced toward Brad, still holding out his hand.

"Please get down, Brad."

"You're fucking lying! That SBLE doctor said plastic surgery wouldn't work! That I'd be like this forever!"

He swung his fist and it went right through the glass with an ease that surprised Vadim. Cold air rushed through the hole, and the rest of the window simply gave way, sending slivers of glass exploding in all directions. Even as he instinctively covered his eyes, Vadim was moving forward. He grabbed for Brad's skinny, tattooed ankle, but Brad slipped from Vadim's grasp, throwing himself forward into the night.

Vadim came down hard on his knees and shards of glass pierced his skin. Why hadn't he been able to keep hold of the man? What malign magic had held him at bay? From below came the sound of screaming and the wail of an ambulance. He pushed himself upright and looked out of the window. Brad lay sprawled on the unforgiving ground just in front of the ER, surrounded by a cluster of people who were either running around like ants or looking up and pointing.

"Are you okay, Morosov?"

He looked over his shoulder to see Ella advancing cautiously toward him.

"Stay over there, Ms. Walsh. There's glass everywhere."

She ignored him and came across to his side. She looked out of the window.

"*Shit*, that happened so fast!"

"I couldn't stop him." Vadim stared down at the scene below them, which was now being dealt with by the hospital staff and the authorities. "It was as if my magic bounced off."

"You're bleeding." She touched the corner of his

mouth. "Maybe it did. Maybe that dude Adam got to Brad while we were having dinner."

Vadim swore softly and walked toward the door, glass falling from him like raindrops. Two of the hospital security team pushed past him and surveyed the ruined room and began to take pictures. He paused by the empty chair outside the door.

"Where's Delia?"

"She seems to be in a trance. No one can wake her."

"Perhaps I should go and see her."

Ella grabbed his sleeve. "Hold up. You haven't told me exactly what happened here yet."

"Isn't it obvious? You said it yourself. Someone got in here and killed our patient."

"Did Brad say anything to you? I thought I heard him shouting when I was coming back along the hallway."

Vadim let out his breath. "He said an SBLE doctor told him he would never regain his true face even after plastic surgery."

"*What?*"

He got out his handkerchief and dabbed at the blood now dripping from his lip. "Someone got in here, convinced Brad his life was worthless and set him free to kill himself."

"And by someone, I assume you mean Adam." She took his injured hand and he sucked in a breath. "Come on, we need to see the security footage and get you fixed up."

"But what about Delia?"

"She's being guarded by SBLE security. I doubt they'll be quite as easy to fool. You can go and see her in a minute."

He allowed himself to be marched down to Ms. Phelps's office and sat in a chair while they waited for Mr. Feehan and the police. Jose came to check out the state of his hands and face and applied warm cloths to his skin and then a thin layer of white glue, which he peeled off after it set, bringing most of the tiny splinters with it.

"I think you'll be okay now, Vadim." Jose rose to his feet. "When you get home, take some painkillers and have a long bath. That should loosen any other pieces. If you see any reddish or swollen sites, come back. You might have an infection."

"Thanks, Jose."

"You're welcome."

He was quite capable of healing himself, but in present company, he didn't want to draw attention to his magical powers. Frustration boiled under his skin. He felt far too exposed. Had he spent so much time controlling his powers in this world that they wouldn't respond to him any more? Feehan arrived, his thin hair blown wildly around by the wind, a smudge of red sauce on his knitted sweater.

"Are you all right, Vadim?"

"I'm fine. I can't say the same for poor Mr. Dailey."

Feehan took the seat opposite him. "What happened?"

"The SBLE version, or the one I'm going to tell the police?"

"I'll handle the police. Tell me how you saw it."

"Someone got in to see Brad by bespelling the nurse and pretending to be an SBLE doctor. This 'doctor' told Brad his face was unfixable and that he'd always look like that. Brad believed him and decided to jump out of the window."

"Damn." Feehan shook his head. "This is not going to go down well with our head office or with the Dailey family." He hesitated. "Um, we don't have doctors in the SBLE, do we?"

"No." Vadim pressed his handkerchief to his lip again to stem the bleeding. "Where's Ms. Walsh?"

"I passed her in the hallway. She's gone to find the security tapes, or whatever they call them nowadays, for this floor. We'll bring them back to our office to review." Feehan patted Vadim's knee, making him flinch. "Let's hope we get an image of that so-called doctor."

The sound of an altercation at the door reached Vadim's ears and he looked up. Ella was toe-to-toe with one of San Francisco's cops.

"He's not ready to be interviewed. Can't you wait until we've cleared up our part of the investigation before you start on yours?"

"I'm okay, Ms. Walsh." Vadim waved the police officers over. "How can I help you?"

He told them the cleaned-up version of how Brad had been standing on the windowsill, threatening to jump, and that despite Vadim's efforts, he hadn't been able to reach Brad in time to stop him. The officers seemed okay with that, nodding as he described Brad's fragile mental state and his often-expressed desire to die. The hospital records would confirm his words. It was contrived, but at this point, it was in everyone's best interest to believe that the death was viewed as a suicide—everyone apart from Brad, his family and the investigating team of the SBLE, of course.

The police officers departed to check in with the

medical team in the ER, where Brad now lay. Vadim shoved a hand through his hair and dislodged another shower of shards.

"You look like the Christmas fairy." He looked up to see Ella standing in front of him, arms crossed over her chest, her expression fierce. "Are you really okay?"

Her mind tentatively touched his, and some part of him relaxed. "I'll be fine."

"Feehan wants us to go back to the office. Do you want me to put him off until the morning?"

Vadim got to his feet, aware of a thousand small pinpricks of pain stirring in his still-tender skin. He felt like an old man. "I'd rather get this out of the way while it's fresh in our memories."

"Then at least let me drive. Your car's still here, isn't it?"

He dug in his pocket and handed her the keys. "You don't actually use the key. The door will unlock when you approach the car. You start the engine by putting your foot on the brake and pushing the start button."

"Got it." She jangled the keys in her hand in a manner guaranteed to set his teeth on edge. "Do you want me to bring the car around to the front of the building?"

"I want to see Delia first, and then I want to see Brad's body."

"Sure. I'll come with you."

He halted, his hand on the back of the chair. "You don't have to follow me around."

"Yes, I do." She raised her chin to meet his gaze. "Let me show you where Delia is."

ELLA STUDIED THE nurse. Delia looked as if she were having an excellent nap. Only the fact that her eyes were still open gave a clue that it wasn't exactly a natural kind of sleep.

"Can you get her out of it, Morosov?" She still whispered, even though she knew Delia couldn't hear her.

"I'm not sure."

Vadim sounded exhausted. She had the strangest urge to pick him up, wrap him in a blanket and take him home to bed. Not that he'd be any use to her there, but at least she could hold him close and look after him…

"Ms. Walsh, what's wrong?"

Had her horror shown on her face? A ministering angel she was not. Damn Vadim for putting her in touch with her feminine side.

"Is she in a Fae trance?" She concentrated hard and found it impossible to penetrate Delia's mind. It was as if a thick fog surrounded her thoughts.

"Yes."

"And?"

"I'm not sure how to break the spell."

Even though the only other personnel in the room were SBLE, Vadim spoke as quietly as she did.

"But you can do everything."

"Not this time." He removed his hand from Delia's. "If she's not better in the morning, I can try something more radical. I just hope that whatever our murderer did will eventually wear off. He has no motive for killing her."

"As if that ever bothered the Fae."

"True." His smile was slight and looked painful. "Shall we go down to the ER?"

She nodded at the security team and shut the door behind them. It was quiet, as if the building held its

breath, waiting to see who would win the nightly struggle over life and death the hospital waged. They walked
back along the hallway toward the exit. She almost
bumped into Vadim when he suddenly stopped in front
of Brad's old room. She frowned. Shouldn't someone
be guarding this space?

He put his hand on her arm and she cautiously
opened her senses to the fractured magic around them.

"Is someone in there?"

"I don't know."

He pushed open the unlatched door and they both
viewed the scene. Everything looked the same. The
bed was still at a crazy angle, Brad's ripped-off bandages lay on the floor and everywhere there was glass
shining in the light coming through the broken window and the hallway.

She shivered. *"Can't they even board up the window?"*

Vadim didn't answer her. His attention seemed to
be riveted on the floor by the window, where the glass
was…

"Shit, it's moving around!"

His fingers tightened on her arm. Shards of glass
glittered and writhed on the floor. Tiny flashes of crim-
son—Vadim's blood?—joined the mass of movement
and formed into characters displayed against the floor.
She didn't understand the language. From the hitch in
her partner's breath, she reckoned he did.

"Is that Fae?"

He still didn't answer her as the glass swirled and
finally dispersed into a sea of dangerous shards.

"Morosov?"

He shook his head and walked out of the room, leaving her to chase after him. She poked him in the side.

"What was that all about?"

"Just a message from Adam."

"Saying what?"

"To back off."

"As if we would."

He stopped moving and looked down at her, his gaze shadowed. "Maybe we should just let him be."

"And stand back and watch his mutilate two more people on our watch? You're nuts if you think I'd go along with that." She practically stamped her foot. "What's wrong with you?"

His smile was wry. "Perhaps I'm scared."

"You? The big bad bird?"

"You can't win every battle, Ella. I'm living proof of that. Sometimes it's better to let something go, and avoid causing harm to even more people you care about."

"Everyone who works for the SBLE knows the risks of dealing with Otherworld. None of them are cowards. Do you really think that a threat from a secret sect would make them all run away?"

"That wasn't what I meant."

"But it's still the truth. If we let Adam get away with this, the next monster might want to take ten lives or twenty. Do we turn away from that, as well? Eventually we'll have nothing left to protect, and our world will be annexed. I'm not going to let that happen." She paused to stare up at him. "Are you?"

"You're a brave woman, Ella Walsh."

"Humph." She started moving again, and after a moment, he followed her down the stairs to the ER.

Brad's body hadn't been put in the morgue yet but was being guarded in a more private area in the ER. Ms. Phelps saw them approaching and told the security guards to let them through. She held a handkerchief to her mouth and looked to be on the verge of passing out.

"He's in there." She waved a helpless hand at the door. "Please forgive me if I can't accompany you."

Ella patted her shoulder as they went past. Even if you'd seen as many dead bodies as she had, they were never easy.

She waited until Vadim closed the door behind him and joined her beside the corpse. The smell already reminded her of a rotting apple or a compost heap. She carefully uncovered the body and stared down at Brad's now-motionless face.

"His body's a mess. Why isn't his face smashed in?"

Vadim put his hand out and passed it over Brad's skin. His magic resonated through Ella. "Because the face doesn't belong to him."

"Like it's not connected or touched by his death?"

"I assume so."

"Will someone, or something, come and take it back?"

"I don't know. If Adam wanted it, why didn't he just take it when he got in to see Brad?"

"Because he wanted him to die more than he wanted the face back?"

"I suspect that's part of it." Vadim pulled the sheet back up over what remained of Brad. "The magic feels the same to me. How about you?"

"Like Adam? Yeah, that's what I'm getting too. At least we can assume he's working alone."

"Apart from his affiliation with the sect."

"Which we haven't confirmed."

"Oh, he's connected. I'm convinced of that now." Vadim washed his hands at the sink, and she did the same. "We should be getting back to the office."

"I'm still driving." She dug out his car keys and steered him toward the stairs that led to the parking lot below. "You can heal yourself in the car."

THE LIGHTS WERE already on in the big conference room, and Ella headed there. Vadim was still complaining about her driving. She hadn't hit anything, had she? She heard him behind her and increased her pace, nodding to Liz, who was already seated next to Feehan at the table.

"How are you feeling, Vadim?"

Liz jumped to her feet and Ella bristled as she patted and cooed over poor, *poor* Morosov. He was fine! He'd magicked himself all better in the car and had still had time to criticize her driving. She had the most ridiculous desire to slap Liz's hands away and growl at her. Was that how Vadim felt when men looked at her? Was she turning into one of *those* women? It was incredibly uncool. She chose a seat as far away from her partner as possible, then kicked the table leg with the side of her boot until Liz finally sat back down.

Feehan nodded at Vadim. "I've given them the basics, but you were actually there. So can you tell everyone what happened?"

Ella waited for him to finish speaking, noting carefully what he said and what he didn't. There was no mention of the cryptic Fae message in the broken glass, but she'd half expected that. If Feehan thought Adam threatened them all, he'd be straight over to Otherworld, demanding that all kinds of shit happen, and he'd be dead.

"You couldn't break Delia's trance?" Feehan asked.

"Not easily. Each Fae's spell is unique to the individual and to his line. If Delia hasn't recovered by tomorrow, there are other ways of freeing her."

"More dangerous ways. The Fae don't like it when their spells are threatened or tampered with.'" Liz turned to Vadim, her eyes as silver as her Fae-Web, and her expression not human at all. "Be wary, the human mind is very frail."

"I'm aware of that."

"Of course, you bespelled Brad, didn't you?"

Ella shot a glance at Liz. "What makes you think that?"

"Just an educated, Fae-Web-assisted guess." Liz allowed herself a small satisfied smile. "The other patients were virtually impossible to sedate, and yet Brad was reported to be sleeping like a baby."

"I certainly helped with that," Vadim admitted.

"Then how did Brad break *your* spell and end up on the windowsill? As you just said, it's very hard to fracture a Fae dream spell because of the complexities involved in creating it."

"That's a good question. I have to assume that whoever we are dealing with has stronger magic than I do."

"I find that difficult to believe."

Vadim shrugged. "Why? I'm not invincible."

"But you are connected to several of the most powerful Fae bloodlines in Otherworld."

"Then this Adam, or whatever we want to call him, is obviously even more powerful and was able to override my magic and wake Brad up."

Liz sat back and stared at Vadim while the silver lines of her Fae-Web writhed around like a tornado.

He raised an eyebrow. "What is it, Liz? Do you think I broke the spell I placed on Brad, and caused him to leap to his death?"

"No, but—"

"Why would I do that?"

"This isn't getting us anywhere." Ella interrupted the staring contest that seemed to be going on between her mate and her best friend. "Can we focus on what we do know? What about the untouched nature of Brad's face? Were the other victims' the same?"

"I don't know." Liz turned to look at Ella. "I'm still attempting to download the pictures through that new Fae interface. It doesn't seem to work, which means I might have to go back to Otherworld to get the photos of the previous victims."

Ella shuddered. The last time she'd visited the records office at Merton, the Siren had tried to wipe her mind clean of all thought and bring her his version of empath peace, which meant her death and an increase in his powers. "Can't we just request them?"

"We can, but it will take a while. They're short-handed over there."

"And I bet they blame me for that too," Ella groused. "Anyone would think they'd be glad not to have a crazed empath in their midst."

"They *are* Otherworld. Apparently he did a good job."

"Killing empaths."

Feehan cleared his throat. "Speaking of going off topic, Ella, shall we focus on the matter in hand? Liz, you can request the photos by internal mail or send

Sam for them, as long as it's quick. Rich has been working on the security tapes and has isolated the time period we need. Do we all want to take a look?"

Rich opened his laptop and clicked his mouse. They all gathered round.

"Here's the hallway in front of Brad's room. The camera is facing that direction, so we should get some good shots of everyone who is going in and out of that door. I've gone back a few hours to where his grandfather, the ex-senator, came to visit and set his guard outside the door. This is just before they leave."

Ella pointed at the screen. "There's me and Morosov arriving and being told to take a hike." She inclined her head an inch. "Wow. My ass looks huge in those jeans. Why didn't anyone tell me? You look good in that suit though, Morosov."

"Thanks." Vadim was close behind her. "Delia looks fine here. Let's watch her when the senator leaves and see if anyone interacts with her."

There was silence as they all stared at the screen. Vadim's breath curled around Ella's throat and she inhaled his fancy aftershave and unique scent. The senator emerged looking suitably anxious, shook Delia by the hand and left. His security guard fell into step behind him, and they headed for the bank of elevators.

Nothing happened for a while. Staff walked by, some of them stopping to chat with Delia but most of them intent on their own tasks. Ella stifled a yawn. Behind her, Vadim shifted his stance and made it remarkably easy for her to lean back against him.

"Look." Liz pointed at the screen. "There's someone in a white coat. It's a shame we can only see the back of his head. Why didn't he have the decency to approach from the other side and make our lives easier?"

The man paused in front of Delia for a moment and then turned right, into Brad's room. Just before he opened the door, he lifted his head and smiled.

"Holy shit!" Sam said. "It's *Vad!*"

SIX

"DON'T BE FUCKING ridiculous, it can't be Morosov!"
Ella snapped.

"It sure looks like him," Rich said. Sam nodded
eagerly.

"But why the fuck would Morosov do that?"

"Just hold on a minute! Everyone shut up, and less
of the profanity, please, Ella!" Feehan stood and they
stopped talking. "There's an obvious place to start with
this. Vadim, is that you?"

"No, it isn't."

"He could be lying," Sam suggested.

Ella scowled at him. "It isn't him, you dumbass.
Look at the time on the screen. We'd left the hospital by then!"

"And you say you were with Vadim until you returned to the hospital?"

"Yes, we were catching an early dinner." She could
feel her cheeks going red. "At Morosov's hotel."

"Well, that's easy enough to confirm," Feehan said.
"The hotel will have a record of your check in the din-
ing room."

"We got room service. It was quicker." She glanced
over at Vadim to help her out, but he was still staring
at the screen, a frown between his eyes. Why the hell
was she the one who had to defend him? "We didn't
have a lot of time."

"Yeah, right," Liz murmured.

"Anyway, can you all please try and remember that we are dealing with a killer who can switch faces? Isn't it obvious that he did this to cause us to panic?"

"But Vadim still has his face," Sam objected.

"Well, maybe our perp can replicate someone's features as well as steal the whole thing! I don't know. I only know that Morosov was with me the whole time." She glared at Feehan. "I'll take a lie-detector test, if you don't believe me."

Feehan made soothing gestures with his hand. "That's hardly necessary. We are dealing with a creature that can manipulate faces, and what you suggest is highly likely."

"Did anyone else get the sense that he did it deliberately?" Liz asked.

"Did what?"

"Looked right at the security camera." She gestured at Rich. "Can you show that bit again? It's as if he wanted us to see him."

"Well, if he's wearing Vad's face, he probably did." Sam agreed. "That's, like, weird, dude."

Rich backed up the tape and slowed it down. Ella frowned as the doctor touched Delia's cheek.

"That's when he puts her under."

"Agreed," Feehan said. "She doesn't protest in any way when he goes into Brad's room, does she?"

In the next frame the doctor turned to look at the camera and Rich paused the image.

"He does look like Vadim, but there are some subtle differences," Liz conceded. "He's younger. It's as if someone took a picture of him ten years ago and used that." She turned away from the screen. "Do you have any relatives who bear a striking resemblance to you?"

"Not that I know of."

"Are you sure?"

Vadim shrugged, the epitome of cool unconcern. "I haven't been back to Otherworld for several years. I suppose there might be someone who has grown up to look like me."

Ella glanced at her partner. Despite his tranquil reply, he was not happy at all. Even worse, she was pretty damn sure he wasn't telling the truth. Was she the only one who could sense it, or was Liz picking it up too? It might explain why she had so many questions.

She stood up. "Well, if we've agreed it's not Morosov, can we all go home, now? We're not going to get anywhere tonight, and we have a lot to do tomorrow."

Feehan glanced at Liz, who gave him a slight nod.

"Sure. Ella, why don't you hang out with Vadim this evening and make sure he's feeling okay."

"*Me?* He's Fae. He doesn't need a human looking after him."

"You're his partner."

She stared at Vadim, who leaned back in his chair. "Would you like me to babysit you tonight, Morosov?"

"If that's what Mr. Feehan wants, I'm happy to oblige."

"Then come on, I'll take you home."

He stood too and said his goodbyes. In a few moments they were heading down to the basement parking lot. He held out his hand for his keys, and Ella reluctantly gave them up.

"Did you notice that no one else left?" Ella settled into the seat and Vadim shut his door.

"That's probably because they wanted to talk about me."

"You think?" She put on her seat belt. "I can't believe they think you had anything to do with it."

He backed out of his space. "I did put a spell on Brad."

"But that was for his own protection."

He grimaced. "But I interfered with Adam's trophy. It might've been enough to make him kill Brad."

"Morosov, all the victims we know about killed themselves. You weren't responsible for them."

"Thanks for believing in me." He glanced sideways at her and she kept her gaze fixed on the road.

"You're my partner. We've got each other's backs, right?"

"Right. My hotel or your apartment?"

"Your hotel is closer."

"Then let's go there, and I can get out of this glass-infested suit."

THIS TIME VADIM parked and walked through the hotel lobby like a regular human being, one hand placed on the small of Ella's back simply because he needed to touch her. He had a strange sense that he was being observed, but couldn't see an obvious threat. If Adam was around, there was nothing he could do about it except remain vigilant. He wished he had more time to prepare. He'd done nothing to help Ella accept her newfound magical powers either. She might need them, if the future turned out to be as awful as he feared.

"What's up, Morosov? You're like a long-tailed cat in a room full of rocking chairs."

"What the hell is that supposed to mean?"

"At least it made you pay attention. What's going on in your head? What did you think of that dude looking like you?"

"Can we wait until I've had my bath to discuss this?" He swiped his room key and the green light flickered on.

"Holy cow!" Ella dropped to a crouch and brought out her weapon. "What happened in here?"

His room was in chaos, drawers open, pillows ripped and his clothes strewn all over the floor... That wasn't even the worst of it. Sitting on top of his clothes was Rossa, wings neatly folded behind his head like some heavenly angel. He was naked, apart from a few strategically placed white feathers, and as beautiful as ever.

"Rossa! What the fuck?" Ella barged ahead of him and got straight in his cousin's face. "Why did you do this?"

Vadim shut the door. "Yes, why?"

"I didn't." Rossa glanced around the disordered space as if he'd just noticed it. "Do you want me to make it all better?"

"No, thanks." Vadim came to stand beside Ella. "I'd rather do it myself when you're gone." He wanted to taste the magic, to see if it was the same. "What do you want?"

"Just to tell you that there is a lot of interest in what you've been up to. Our grandmother wants you back, and your mother and father are arguing about it again."

"What's new?"

"It's more intense than it's been since you first left. I really think you'll be forced back fairly soon."

"And how are they are going to manage that, when I'm mated and entitled to stay here?"

"That's right. You're fucking her now, aren't you?" Rossa grinned at Ella and smoothed down the feathers on his chest. "Remember, they'll use whatever means possible."

Anger flooded Vadim's veins, and black feathers swirled around and over Rossa's head. He switched to Fae. "You can give them a message from me. If they lay one hand on my mate, I'll make them pay for it in blood."

Rossa stopped smiling and waved at Ella. "'Bye, gorgeous. Take care now."

Vadim took a deep, steadying breath and eyed the pile of clothes Rossa had been sitting on. Maybe he should get everything dry-cleaned or—better still—just destroyed. He'd like to destroy something. Preferably his cousin.

"Rossa is infuriating. And why did you start speaking in tongues for the last bit? You sounded quite menacing."

"Threats always sound better in Fae." Vadim picked up one of his shirts and shook it out. The scent of Otherworld magic entered his senses, and he knew exactly who'd been in his room. The question was why. With a flick of his hand, he restored the room to its usual clean state and went into the bathroom. Ella, of course, followed him.

"Are you going to tell me what you said?"

"I told him to fuck off."

"You always tell him to do that. So why did you speak in a language you knew I didn't understand?"

He loosened his tie and dropped it to the floor. "As I said, can I have my bath before the interrogation?"

"It's weird how you clam up whenever I ask you any questions, when you expect me to answer all yours immediately. I thought we were supposed to be in this together." She pulled a towel off the rail and threw it hard at his chest. "Enjoy your stupid bath."

For once he didn't have time to appreciate getting the upper hand. He was too bone weary to care. She didn't want him protecting her, and she was already suspicious. And she was right to be so. Adam's threat in the hospital had been far more specific than he'd let on to Ella. Because he was now mated, he was vulnerable. Every Fae knew that and wouldn't hesitate to strike. He growled low in his throat and his fangs pierced his lower lip.

But was Adam's attempt to involve Vadim personally in his crimes due to ancient grudges or to something more recent? Blood ties were a tortuous and complex thing, especially for the long-lived Fae. He needed to think up a reasonable explanation before Ella got fed up waiting and either told Feehan the parts Vadim had left out, or worse, decided to tackle Adam and Otherworld herself.

Eventually, he had to get out of the bath. He dried himself off, wrapped a towel around his hips and went back into the bedroom. Ella sat in a chair by the faux fireplace, boots kicked off and her feet curled up under her. If he wasn't mistaken, she was now wearing one of his T-shirts. She looked tired, and her hair was coming out of its braid. He thought about fixing it for her, but instead took the chair opposite. She'd closed the drapes, and the nighttime roar of the city traffic was slightly muted.

"Do you want me to show you that Fae trick for cleaning yourself up?"

She blinked at him. "Are you suggesting I need to take another shower?"

"If I teach you this spell, you won't need to."

"Ever?"

He leaned his head back against the chair and studied her. "That might be a stretch. Luckily, most Fae have an affinity for water."

"Okay, how d'you do it?"

"It's quite easy. You picture the thing you want to clean up and say these words, *geilan dah*."

"Gay Linda?"

"*Gey-ei-landah*." He repeated slowly. "If you forget to brush your hair one morning. You could fix the problem while you were driving to work without taking your hands off the steering wheel—not that doing that seems to bother you much anyway."

She sat forward. "Are you saying my hair is a mess?"

"I'm not saying anything. I'm just giving you an example."

"Fine. I should've known cleaning things would be your favorite spell." She sighed and closed her eyes. As he watched, her hair magically rearranged itself into two neat shining braids.

"Did it work?"

"Yes." His smile was enough to have her running to the mirror.

"I look like a Swedish tourist."

"Nothing wrong with that."

She returned to her seat, fingering one of her braids. "Now, if you've finished prevaricating, do you want to tell me what's really going on?"

"I think I've told you most of it."

"*Bullshit*, Morosov. I know how your devious Fae mind works. Even if I can't quite access all the important bits, I can still sense when you're hiding things from me."

She could?

Damn.

"What aren't you telling me?"

Perhaps it was time for the truth. "That you need to be on your guard, and that I would prefer it if we stayed together at all times."

She wrapped her arms around her drawn-up knees and rested her chin on them. "You're afraid for me?"

"You're my mate. Otherworld knows that. You will be used against me."

"Do you think I'd let myself be used?"

"Not intentionally."

"Well, thanks for that, at least." She considered him for a long moment. "What can I do to make myself less vulnerable?"

"You're taking this much better than I thought you would."

She shrugged. "Otherworld is your world. I'm a liability for you there. I don't want to be one, so I'd like to improve our odds."

"I appreciate that. With my magic, you aren't without power. You just need to learn how to use it."

"Can you teach me?"

"Not in time." He grimaced. "I fear that someone will come after me fairly soon."

"And when you say after you, you really mean after *me*, don't you?"

"You heard what Rossa said. Otherworld is interested in us."

"That's right, he did say that. Why are your parents fighting over you?"

"I'm something of a divisive force. The maternal line wants me back in Otherworld to carry out its wishes, and my father wishes me in hell." He held her gaze. "I'll do everything in my power to prevent you from being taken."

"I know that."

"It would also be better if you didn't go to Otherworld in the near future."

"Got it. Not that I want to go back to Merton ever again. I'll send Sam to pick up the photos tomorrow."

"Thank you."

"It's been a horrible day, and tomorrow isn't going to be any easier. How on earth are we supposed to know what kind of victim Adam will choose next?"

"Going by his previous behavior, it will be close by, and fairly soon."

She shivered. "Somehow this feels really personal." She glanced up at him. "Do you feel that too?"

"Yes."

Because it was.

He'd tangled with the sect in the past many times. But he wasn't in a position to reveal that to Ella yet. He hoped he never had to. It was going to be difficult to keep her safe while trying to solve his issues with Adam.

"Is there anything else you want to ask me?"

She uncurled her legs and stretched. "Loads, but I can't think straight."

"Then shall we go to bed?"

"Sure."

Her smile made him forget sleep and immediately think of sex. He rose to his feet and held out his hand, and she took it. He instantly felt better, more connected and safer. His mother always insisted that love was a cage. He could feel it all around him now, but somehow it was less frightening than he had imagined. If only Ella could see it that way too. But then how would she survive his inevitable death? He followed her into bed and held her close. Perhaps she was right not to allow anyone near her—especially him.

SEVEN

"WHAT THE HELL'S that?"

Ella looked up as Sam and Rich manhandled another desk in through her office door and dumped it right next to hers.

"It's for Vad." Sam beamed at her. "Now that he's your official partner, he, like, needs his own space."

"So do I," Ella muttered as the object of her ire sauntered through the door. "There isn't enough room for two of us in here."

"We can make room."

He pointed out exactly where he wanted the desk to be placed, and Sam and Rich obligingly moved it into position for him.

"I'll get your desktop and set it up for you. It won't take a minute."

"Thanks, guys." Vadim patted Rich on the back. "I appreciate it."

She gave up the attempt to work and watched as a parade of boxes and office equipment joined the desk and its smiling owner. Her phone rang and she let it go to voice mail. There was no way she'd be able to hear a thing, with the racket they were making. She tried to study the list she was compiling, but that proved impossible too. Eventually she looked up.

"Have you finished yet?"

Vadim gave her a charming smile. He looked remarkably well for a man who'd been covered in glass the previous day. She wondered if the cleanup spell he'd taught her worked on bumps and bruises…

"It can, but you have to be careful, or else you could overdo the power of the spell and end up looking like you've had plastic surgery or something."

"Thanks for the clarification. Now get out of my head."

Rich set up Vadim's desktop computer and phone line while Sam sat in his chair and spun himself around in circles.

Ella looked up again. "Don't you have somewhere else you need to be, Sam?"

He stopped spinning. "Not really, I was just waiting to tell you that Mr. Feehan wants us all in the conference room at eleven."

"Thanks. Maybe you could let Morosov try out his chair now?"

"Oh, sure, dude." Sam leaped to his feet and then swayed. *"Man,* I'm like, so dizzy right now."

Ella forced herself not to state the obvious and merely observed his unsteady progress out through the door.

"Idiot," she remarked.

"Me?"

"No. Sam. He's such a kid."

"Lucky him." Vadim had already assembled his half of the room into something that would feature on the front cover of *Office Weekly*, if such a magazine existed. For some reason, the space didn't seem to have shrunk too much after all. "Did you make any progress tracing Adam?"

"Not much. You?"

He checked his watch. "It's almost eleven. There's no point in repeating myself when we're just about to step into a meeting."

"Even for me?"

He held the door open for her. "This time there's only one version to tell."

Sam and Liz were laughing and comparing notes about the last wolf-pack party they'd both attended. Rich sipped his coffee and Feehan looked up as they entered.

"Good, let's get on, shall we?"

He added a couple of photos of Brad Dailey to the board. The pictures had obviously been taken after his death.

"Dude, that's weird." Sam sat up straighter. "His face is, like, beautiful. Like a mask."

"Which is exactly what it is." Ella agreed. "Even though he ripped it up before he died, Morosov and I reckoned, as it doesn't really belong to him, it didn't suffer the physical trauma of his death and reverted back to being perfect."

"That's creepy." Liz shivered. "It reminds me of that story with the guy with the picture in the attic that aged while he stayed young."

"*The Picture of Dorian Gray.*"

"That's the one."

"It makes you wonder what's happening to Brad's real face right now, doesn't it?" Feehan mused. "Or if that face even exists anymore. What else do we have?"

Ella held up her hand. "I've been attempting to trace Adam through the various conference-registration sites and hotels, but so far no luck."

"That's hardly surprising. How about you, Vadim?"

"Nothing here, either. I doubt our killer attended anything in the city at all this week."

Feehan's face fell. "Darn it. What else do we have?"

"Well, we have the security tape of 'Doctor Vadim' bespelling Delia and then going into Brad's room," Liz said. "By the way, how are we going to stop the hospital authorities from seeing that and immediately assuming he is the killer?"

"Simple, we just don't give them the tape back until we've found the real murderer," Ella snapped.

Liz blinked at her. "There's no need to be so defensive. I'm not accusing your partner of anything."

Aware that everyone was staring at her, Ella subsided into her chair.

"I do have some more evidence for us to look at." Liz glanced at Sam. "We got the before-and-after pictures of the last three victims from Otherworld."

She opened a large brown envelope and spread the pictures out on the conference table.

"They all ended up with fair hair, which is the opposite of what we've seen with Brad."

Sam put his finger on the closest picture. "And they all retain perfect features, even after killing themselves."

Ella contemplated the horrific differences between the happy faces of the "before" pictures and the death masks of the "after" ones. It was damned unsettling.

"Should we assume Adam is going for three blonds this time?"

"Seems likely."

Everyone looked at Liz and Ella.

Liz tucked a strand of hair behind her ear. "It's okay, we'll be careful."

"You'll need to be," Vadim said. "Even though you're half-Fae, you still need to be protected. I'm sure Doug and the wolf pack can take care of that for you."

"They will, but I'll be extra vigilant, I promise you."

"I'm all human," Ella noted.

"But I'm your partner, Ms. Walsh, and I don't intend to let you out of my sight."

The sincerity and purpose in his eyes was intense. Damn, he might as well be down on his knees proposing to her. No one would believe there wasn't something going on between them now.

"Um, thanks." She dropped her gaze and fiddled with her pen.

"We can't exactly protect all of the blonds in the San Francisco Bay Area from one man when we have no description of him, can we?" Feehan's shoulders slumped.

"He'll choose someone close."

Feehan turned to Vadim. "You sound very sure of that."

"The last three victims lived within ten miles of each other. I should imagine Adam has already decided on his next victim."

"I think you know more than you are letting on, Vadim." Liz turned to face him. "I sense a connection between you and this Adam in my Fae-Web."

A muscle flicked in Vadim's cheek. "I suspect Adam is connected to one of my family bloodlines. Unfortunately, I can't help that."

"You could if you asked your Otherworld family for more information."

"I'm not friends with anyone in my family. I left Otherworld on extremely bad terms."

Ella held her breath as Liz continued to stare at her partner. What was her friend seeing, and how would it affect the rest of the team's ability to trust Vadim? She didn't dare say anything else in case she put her big foot in it and made things worse. A thought occurred to her.

"Couldn't you ask Rossa?"

"No."

Fine, he wasn't interested in listening to her. She folded her arms across her chest and pretended to concentrate on the photos. There were two men and one woman. Was that significant too?

"What's the plan now, Mr. Feehan? Sit and wait for another crazy patient to show up saying he's lost his face?"

Feehan looked at her as if she was the most insensitive person he'd ever met. As long as it got everyone's attention away from Vadim and Liz, she didn't care.

"Unless we get more information, I suppose there isn't a lot we can do." He turned to Vadim. "I really would appreciate it if you could get some help from Otherworld as to what exactly we are dealing with. If you can't, I'll have to take the matter up with the SBLE head and his Otherworld counterpart, and that never goes well."

"I'll do my best," Vadim said. "After our last experience with Drew Spencer, I'm sure we'd all rather avoid him if we can."

Everyone agreed and filed out. Vadim followed Ella back to their office. She closed the door and leaned against it.

"You have to do something to stop Feehan going to Spencer. He's a dick. Last time he waltzed in here, he was quite happy to use me as bait to capture a serial killer. And he doesn't like you at all, does he?"

"Spencer doesn't like anyone in my family, apart from my father. I have to stop Feehan taking this *anywhere*, or he'll get us all killed." Vadim sat on the edge of his desk. "The question is, how much do I need to tell him to get him off my back?"

"Without mentioning the cult, sect thing?"

"Exactly."

"*Can* you find out anything about Adam?"

"That's going to be difficult."

"Why?"

He exhaled. "Because I thought he was already dead."

"*What?*"

"I'm beginning to wonder if Adam is simply impersonating this deceased person to draw my attention, or if he is the real deal."

"You mean he's come back to life?"

"It happens in Otherworld sometimes."

"Like a zombie or something?"

"Not quite. Most Fae are immortal, but under certain circumstances, and with certain weapons, they can be destroyed."

"I know that. So if Adam has been brought back to achieve a certain purpose, can he be killed again?"

"That's a good question." He glanced down at his locked hands. "Normally, I'd say yes, but in this world? I'm not so sure."

"Morosov, you're beginning to scare me." She advanced toward his desk. "Are you saying Adam is unstoppable?" He smiled at her and she went still. "What?"

"I told you that it might be better to let him have his way, didn't I?"

"And I told you what I thought of that stupid idea." She touched his arm. "What is it?"

He cupped her chin, his thumb skimming the corner of her mouth. "Just remember that as your mate, my first priority is your safety. I will do whatever is necessary to keep you alive."

"Why are you telling me this now, and why does it sound like a threat?"

"Because if we interfere with Adam's plans, we'll be putting everyone we know in danger."

"Are you trying to frighten me?"

He brushed a kiss over her mouth. "No, I'm just telling you the truth. I'll always put you first, Ella, never doubt it."

He released her and she stepped out of reach with an uneasy feeling in her gut. Why did he sound so convinced that disaster awaited them? She didn't like it at all, but she liked the idea of endangering everyone around her even less.

"Okay."

"Okay what?"

"Find out what you can about Adam and tell Feehan enough to get him off your back."

"Of course." He nodded.

The door opened suddenly and Sam appeared.

"Hey, Mr. Feehan wants you both to go with him to the hospital. Apparently, Brad Dailey's family wishes to speak to you."

"Oh, crap," Ella groaned. "What are we supposed to say to them?"

"Don't worry about it." Vadim stood up and shook

out the creases in his sleeves. "I'm sure Mr. Feehan will tell us exactly what he wants us to say on the way over."

IN THE HOSPITAL elevator, Vadim reached for Ella's hand and for once she didn't stop him.

"If the Daileys get cranky, you can wipe the memories, can't you?"

"Sure. But I always like to have a truthful conversation about what really happened first. It helps them deal with the subconscious aspects of the Otherworld experience."

"Does Feehan know this?"

"I'll tell him right now."

She cleared her throat. "Boss, if it's okay with you, we'll answer the Daileys' questions as truthfully as we can and then retrieve those memories and replace them with new ones that follow the more conventional version."

She realized she'd said "we." Was she really thinking of her and Vadim as a matched set now? Could he perform the same empath tasks that she could?

"That's my function as your mate. Seeing as you might be dealing with several people at once, I can at least bolster your powers with my own and stop you from becoming drained."

She smiled up at him. "I keep forgetting that."

"What?" Feehan was staring at her. Had she spoken out loud? Damn.

"I was just talking to myself. Are you okay with what I suggested, Mr. Feehan?"

"If it's necessary, please go ahead. I've never had to deal with a situation like this before directly."

"Don't worry, it'll be a breeze."

Ten minutes later, in Ms. Phelps's office, she was beginning to wish she hadn't been quite so confident. There was no sign of Ms. Phelps to help smooth things over. Instead, they'd been met by Brad's parents and grandfather, who were in no mood to listen to reason or Ella's Otherworld interpretation of exactly what had happened. Threats about lawsuits, medical negligence and government incompetence were flying around the room. No one was giving Feehan a chance to explain.

Eventually Ella held up her hand and raised her voice above the racket.

"Will you all shut it?"

Shocked faces greeted her loud pronouncement.

"Something terrible happened to Brad, something that is beyond normal human comprehension. Whichever world he hangs out in, we will do our best to apprehend the criminal. We will not stop until we have achieved justice for your son and closure for your family."

Mr. Dailey scowled at her. "You're right, this is bizarre. Your whole explanation is downright insane!" He glanced at Feehan and then back at Ella. "What kind of government employs idiots like you?"

"We wanted you to know the truth, Mr. Dailey."

"The truth?" He got in her face. "That my son's face was *stolen*, and he was left with someone else's? Bullcrap!"

Ella stared him down. "Yes, now step back, sir, or I'll let my partner at you. He really doesn't appreciate it when people aren't polite to me."

Mr. Dailey looked up and went very still. She sensed Vadim at her shoulder, emanating a sense of cold menace that would probably make Dailey wet his pants.

"Morosov isn't quite human, so don't think to appeal to his better side. He doesn't have one. He could probably kill you without even touching you."

Her adversary stepped back, his gaze still fixated on Vadim, who appeared to be making a low growling sound.

"Now if you will all sit down, I'll explain exactly what is going to happen next."

She waited until the three family members were seated and looking obediently up at her.

"Can you keep them calm for me, Morosov?"

"I'm already on it."

She took a deep, centering breath and focused on the turmoil of the three minds in front of her. Vadim's power blended smoothly with hers, and she began to extract the memories of the conversation, of the family's anger and disbelief, of their sense of horror... Other images—Brad as a sunny-natured little boy, a baby, a sullen teen—jostled with the ones she sought. She pushed those gently away and focused on only what needed to be removed.

After a quick check to see that she had everything, she opened her eyes and studied the vacant faces of the family. Usually she needed skin-to-skin contact to make the necessary connection, but with Vadim's help she could do without it.

"When you wake up, you will understand that Brad was an extremely unhappy individual who was afraid of letting you down by disclosing his lack of interest in a medical career. You will know that on his last night of life he unknowingly took some as-yet-unidentified new street drug and suffered a series of hallucinations that made him believe his face was not his own. Despite the hospital's best efforts, Brad was unable to recover from the effects of taking this substance and killed himself."

Mrs. Dailey's mouth quivered and a single tear ran down her cheek.

"You will feel shock and anger and grief over his death. You will insist on an investigation, which the hospital will offer you. It will become clear to you that no member of the hospital staff or the SBLE were responsible for your son's death."

She looked across at Feehan, who nodded, and then at Vadim.

"Good enough, Ms. Walsh."

She held out both of her hands, palms facing out, and gave a final push of power to set the new memories in place. The usual twinge of nausea and unsteadiness made her sway on her feet. Vadim was immediately at her side and led her to a chair.

"We can take it from here, can't we, Mr. Feehan?"

"Indeed we can. I wonder where Ms. Phelps has gotten to?" Feehan joined Vadim in front of the Dailey family, who were gradually coming out of their trances and staring up at the two men.

"Do you have any more questions for me, Mrs. Dailey?" Vadim asked.

"No, I...I don't think so, not at this moment." She wiped away the tear on her cheek. "It's just so sudden and unexpected."

"I understand." Vadim turned to her husband. "Mr. Dailey?"

"I'm not happy about this at all. My son was a fine, upstanding individual who never took drugs!" He stood up and brushed at the creases in his pants.

"You're probably right, sir. We don't know the circumstances. It is of course possible that another individual gave your son something illegal without either his knowledge or his consent."

"Exactly!" Mr. Dailey looked over at his father for a long moment, and the older man nodded. "We will be demanding a full investigation into this matter."

"As you should, sir." Vadim agreed. "I don't think the hospital should offer you anything less than a full public hearing."

The ex-senator cleared his throat. "A private hearing. My family has suffered enough."

"I'm sure they'll do whatever you want, Senator." Vadim handed over his card. "If you have any further questions or information for us, please call me or Mr. Feehan, and we will do our best to help."

"Thank you." Mr. Dailey took the card and studied it. "May we see Brad now? We'd like to say our last goodbyes."

Ella and Feehan stared at each other. Feehan cleared his throat.

"As to that—"

Vadim stepped forward. "It's not a problem. Mr. Feehan, I know you're expected at another appointment. I'll take the Daileys to see the body."

"If you're sure, Vadim."

"I'm happy to do so." He glanced at Ella. "Will you accompany me, Ms. Walsh?"

"Sure."

With a reassuring pat on Feehan's arm, she followed Vadim down to the ER.

"I'll need your help to maintain the illusion. Do you

remember what Brad used to look like? That's what I'm going to project."

"Got it."

She held the door open for the ex-senator and waited while they completed the necessary security checks to reach the body. Mrs. Dailey was the only member of the family who seemed genuinely upset by the tragedy. Ella was mainly picking up anger and disgust from the two men. It chilled her. Was that how they'd seen Brad? As some sort of pawn in their family empire, one that had disappointed them? No wonder he'd acted like such an insecure loser...

Vadim opened the door into the temporary morgue, and the Daileys filed in after him. She focused her attention on her partner, adding her emerging magical powers to his as he lowered the sheet and revealed Brad's altered face. How odd that they were using magic to add yet another layer to Brad's mask. Would Adam sense their spell and come looking for them?

Mrs. Dailey burst into tears and tried to reach for Brad. The two men held her back, their expressions remote and tinged with impatience. Mr. Dailey caught Vadim's eye.

"We should leave. There are arrangements to be made. When will you release the body?"

"You'll need to consult with the hospital authorities about that." Vadim replaced the sheet. "Hopefully it won't be too long. May I suggest you liaise with Ms. Phelps about drafting a statement to be released to the media? I'm sure she gave you her details."

Ella held the door open and waited until the Daileys had gone before turning back to Vadim.

"Where is Ms. Phelps anyway? Wasn't she supposed to be at that meeting?"

Vadim slowly raised his head. "Yes, she was."

"What's wrong?"

"I'm not sure."

"Dammit, she's blond, isn't she?" She ran for the door, only to have Vadim catch her arm.

"Hold on a minute."

"Why? She might be in danger!"

"*Wait.* Think this through. We've both got a good sense of Adam. Let's use our combined power to see if we can locate him."

"How?"

"Just close your eyes and use your empath abilities."

"But—"

"Ella, shut up and do it!"

She complied and forced herself to slow her breathing and turn her thoughts inward. Vadim's magic flowed along with hers, sometimes in parallel, other times so closely mingled that she couldn't tell where he ended and she began.

"*He's close.*"

"*Yes.*"

"*Now what do we do?*"

"*Concentrate on where you feel his power most strongly and find him.*"

She opened her eyes, and this time he didn't stop her leaving. Adam's power drew her on. He was in the hospital. He was close. She was standing outside Ms. Phelps's office, Vadim right behind her.

"She can't be here. We were just in here." She tried to turn the handle. "It's locked."

"Try it again."

A surge of Vadim's magic passed through her fingers and the lock clicked open. She drew her weapon and gently pushed open the door. Someone sat in Ms. Phelps's chair. She didn't turn or react to the opening of the door. Her eyes were wide open and she wasn't blinking.

"Holy cow," Ella whispered. "That's not how Ms. Phelps looked yesterday, is it?"

"No."

Vadim went past her. "She's in a trance."

"Maybe that's for the best." Ella moved closer. "If it *is* Ms. Phelps. Her face and hair coloring are completely different."

"It's her, all right. Can't you feel the magic? Remember, this was where Adam's power was most concentrated."

"Shall I call Feehan?"

"Yes, tell him what's happened and get him to send a second SBLE security team up here. I'll keep her under. You and I can take turns standing guard until they get here."

EIGHT

"ELLA, CAN I speak to you, please?"

She looked up to see Feehan at her elbow. "What's up?"

He nodded in the direction of the door. "Out here?"

She rose from her seat beside Ms. Phelps's bed, nodded at Vadim and headed out into the hallway. It was now dark outside, and the SBLE team had secured the private room where Ms. Phelps lay. She was still in a magical trance and had betrayed no trace of awareness of what had been done to her.

The smell of coffee lured Ella farther down the hallway to the nurse's station, where Jose obligingly handed her a cup.

"Thanks." She smiled at him. "I needed that."

"You're welcome. Where's lover boy?"

"Who?"

"You know, tall, dark and dangerous, who looks as if he wants to devour me whole every time I talk to you."

"Oh, him." Ella shrugged, then sipped at her coffee. "He's standing guard."

Jose leaned against the desk. "What's going on with Ms. Phelps?"

"She seems to have had some kind of fit."

"What kind of 'fit'?"

"They're not sure. That's why she's being kept in isolation."

"I saw her this morning at the staff meeting, and she looked fine." Jose shook his head. "Whatever happened, it sure seemed to come out of nowhere."

"I know."

"Ella?"

She turned back to Feehan, who was waiting patiently behind her.

"Sorry, boss. Emergency caffeine refueling." She nodded at Jose. "Thanks for the coffee."

Feehan walked her over to a seating area by the elevators and sat down beside her.

"I wanted to ask you something in private." He looked around and then settled his gaze back on her. "I talked to a couple of the staff on this floor earlier, and they told me the strangest thing."

"What?"

"That the last person they saw going into Ms. Phelps's office was Vadim."

"So?"

"Could it have been him?"

"Boss, you were with us most of the day. We only parted when we went down to the ER with Brad's parents. I was there the whole time with Morosov. He certainly didn't sneak away and do this to Ms. Phelps."

"Are you quite certain?"

"Sure I am. Do you think he bespelled me? He needed to be one hundred percent present in the ER to do the magic required to convince the Dailey family that Brad's face looked the same as it ever had."

Feehan scratched his thinning hair. "It does sound a little farfetched, doesn't it?"

"Look, whoever this Adam dude is, he wants Vadim

to take the blame for his actions. This is the second time he's pretended to be him."

"But why? Liz thinks—"

Ella sat up straighter. "What's Liz got to do with it? Is all this coming from her?"

"She's seeing a lot of connections between Vadim and Adam in her Fae-Web. *Serious* connections."

"So? He said they shared some of the same bloodlines. Doesn't that account for it?" Feehan studied her carefully and she felt herself blushing. "*What?*"

"She also insists that you and Vadim are, um, closer than you admit to being." He held up his hand. "I have to say I found that part a bit difficult to swallow, until I noticed how vigorously you've been defending him over the past couple of days."

"Do you think he's controlling me with his magic?"

"God forbid, just that you might be—" Feehan was beet-red now and struggling to meet her gaze "—*physically* intimate, and as you are close to your twenty-seventh birthday, you might not be reacting in an emotionally secure way."

"You think I'm like a sex-crazed teen who will do anything to protect her man?"

"Um, yes."

"Wow." She stared at Feehan for a long moment. "Well, that was ballsy."

"I know, I can't believe I said it. But, Ella, I'm your boss. I don't want this team imploding during an important investigation."

He'd impressed her. Who'd have thought it? Now she had to decide how to respond. There was only one answer.

"I suppose I should tell you something important."

"What's that?"

"Morosov is my Otherworld-approved mate."

"*What?*"

"I have the paperwork somewhere, if you want to check it out. I'm not infatuated with him, I'm mated to him. That means my empath gifts are working just fine, and I'm in no danger of going nuts next week. It also means I can connect with Morosov's mind, and he isn't the killer."

Feehan kept gawping at her.

She waved her hand in front of his face. "Boss? Are you okay? I'm telling you this in the strictest confidence, because I don't want you imagining all this other stuff is a problem. You know me, I wouldn't lie to you and compromise a case."

She supposed at this point she should vouch for Vadim's integrity too, but she didn't want to inhibit him. He definitely was hiding stuff. Hopefully she'd said enough to keep Feehan happy at least for a while.

He reached for her hand and awkwardly patted it. "Well, I'm very pleased for you—I think. Vadim is…"

"Well equipped to deal with me. I think that's what you're trying to say, isn't it?"

His smile was wary. "Something like that."

"Seriously, boss, Morosov and I want to solve this case. If I thought he was the murderer, I sure as hell would tell you."

"Then what do you think is going on?"

"I think this Adam guy is trying to draw attention away from himself and onto Vadim to confuse us. And it's working. But at least this time we're better prepared for when Adam comes back."

"He'll be back?"

"You have to assume he'll want to complete his task and force Ms. Phelps to kill herself."

"Hopefully we'll be able to stop that this time."

"Ms. Walsh, what the fuck are you doing?"

She slammed down her shields. "I'm sure we will. Shall we go back now?"

Feehan left her at the door to Ms. Phelps's room, and she braced herself for what lay within. Vadim was leaning back against the wall, arms crossed. His expression wasn't encouraging and his eyes were narrowed to icy blue chips. The temperature in the room dropped below freezing, and a couple of black feathers swirled in the air.

Oh, crap.

"Ms. Walsh."

"Morosov." She gestured at the bed. "No change here, then?"

"No."

She sighed. "For God's sake, stop sulking. I had to tell Feehan something. Between him and Liz, you were starting to figure as a shoo-in for the killer."

"So you told him we were *mated?*"

"It was better than telling him about your connections with Adam and the Otherworld sect, wasn't it? I had to choose the lesser of two evils."

"Our mating is an 'evil' now?"

"Don't split hairs, you know what I mean." She glared at him. "I thought you'd be pleased. You're the one who's always complaining that I don't take it seriously or want to tell anyone."

"You didn't share the news because you were *happy* about it. You shared it to get yourself out of an awkward confrontation."

She shot to her feet and advanced toward him, batting a few feathers out of her way. "I *shared* it to get *you* out of an awkward situation, you dumbass."

He stared down at her and she shook her head and turned away. "You're such an idiot sometimes, Morosov."

"Ella."

He reached for her, but she shook him off and marched right out of the room. She should have agreed with everything Feehan suggested and let Vadim sort it out from his Otherworld prison cell. She halted in the hallway. Where the hell was she going? She'd agreed to share the night shift with him.

She started walking again. He'd be fine while she got herself something nice and sugary to eat at the cafeteria. When she calmed down, she'd go back, and maybe, if he had any sense, *he'd* be the one to leave for a while…

The door to the janitor's office to her right opened and she instinctively went for her weapon.

"It's all right, Ella, it's only me." Rossa's head appeared around the door and he beckoned to her. "Come in here!"

She glanced around and then followed him into the small, crowded space, which smelled of disinfectant, damp rags and skin-stripping chemicals.

"What do you want?"

He blinked at her. "I got the impression you wanted to talk to me."

"From where?"

"You used my name."

"So?"

His smile was blinding. "You're family now, and I heard you. Now, what did you want?"

Ella studied his beautiful face. Up close he was even more stunning. His eyes were honeyed silver and his mouth begged to be kissed. She wanted to stroke the pure white feathers that covered parts of his skin. Mentally, she gave herself a slap. Number one, she knew better than to be taken in by Fae glamour. Number two, Vadim would probably kill them both if she laid a single finger on his relative. But Rossa was here with her, all nice and tight and up close in the janitor's closet, so she might as well make use of him.

"Do you know anything about an ancient Otherworld sect that competes to collect things?"

Rossa shifted his stance and his wings rustled, almost dislodging some of the bottles on the shelves. "What sort of things?"

"I think you know. They tend to collect groups of three."

His face paled. "I...don't know anything about that."

"If Morosov knows of them, I'm sure you do too. My question is, why are they collecting stuff in my world, and what does it have to do with my partner?"

"I have no idea."

She stared into his eyes for as long as she could. "If you're lying to me, all I have to do is take a peek in your mind and I'll know."

He flinched away. "Don't touch me, Soul Sucker."

"Then tell me what's going on. Does this have something to do with Morosov's family wanting him back in Otherworld?"

"Not all of them want him back."

"But those that do."

"It's highly likely his family are involved somewhere, but the sect plays by its own rules and doesn't listen to anyone."

"So the two things could be totally separate." Ella sighed. "You're not much help, are you?"

"I'm too afraid of your mate to be much help." He studied her face. "It's a shame he got to you first. I should imagine you are very creative in bed for a human."

"Well I certainly like sex."

Rossa grinned. "Cygnet is a lucky male, then. When he is executed, perhaps you will allow me to console you."

"Why do you assume he'll be executed?"

"Because one way or another they'll force him back to Otherworld to answer for his crimes." His smile faded. "And he won't be allowed to escape his fate a second time."

"Are you suggesting he's already a tried and convicted man?"

"Didn't he mention that? Crimes against the Royal blood, especially when it's your own line, are definitely frowned upon." He looked back at the door. "I have to go."

"Don't tell me Morosov's spotted you?"

"No, it's something worse than that. You're the one who sucks out emotions. Can't you feel it?" He shivered and all his feathers stood up on end.

"Just tell me one more thing. Do you know this Adam who is stealing human faces?"

"Is that what he's calling himself now?" Rossa started to disappear. "Whoever he is, I'm not staying around to see him."

"He's here? Rossa, wait!"

But it was too late, the Fae had already gone, leaving her in the closet alone.

"DAMMIT!"

After the door shut behind Ella, Vadim cursed as quietly as he could. Why was she so contrary? And why had she told Feehan about their being mated? He took a long, slow breath and contemplated the still figure on the bed. Ms. Phelps couldn't be left alone, so he couldn't even chase Ella down. Tentatively, he touched his mate's mind, but her shields held firm. He could get through them, but he didn't want to force the issue.

Especially when he'd made a complete ass of himself…

She'd told Feehan they were mated to protect him?

There was no other explanation, and he'd gone and made her feel bad about it. All this recent contact with the immorality of Otherworld was making him as paranoid as his parents. He wasn't used to dealing with someone who literally said what she thought and acted accordingly, whether he liked it or not. No wonder the whole of Otherworld was scared of her…

He leaned his head back and banged it on the wall. When he opened his eyes, Ms. Phelps was sitting bolt upright and staring at something at the end of the bed— something that shimmered and bent the air into different shapes.

Vadim held up his hand, and a shield instantly surrounded Ms. Phelps.

"*A little help here, partner?*" Politeness forgotten, he shoved the message into Ella's mind.

Coldness pushed at his magic, trying to find a way

in, and he strengthened the barrier. As he advanced toward the bed, the shape materialized into the distinct form of a man.

"You can't beat me in this realm, Adam, or whatever you are calling yourself these days."

Laughter rang in a discordant note that made Vadim want to cover his ears. "You're wrong, little cygnet. I've grown up."

"You're dead."

"Am I?"

"I killed you. Nothing I kill survives, so who are you really, behind that mask?"

"*I'm coming in.*"

Ella, just outside the door. "*Do it slowly.*"

He couldn't afford to look at her. His power was already being tested too much.

"What do you want, Adam?"

"My trophy."

"You can't have her."

"You can't stop me."

"Obviously, I can. Ella, do you see him?"

"Barely. What do you want me to do?"

"Can you access his thoughts?"

The bright image wavered. "Stand back, Soul Sucker. This is not yet your battle."

"Sure it is. You're in my world and you're killing my people." She took another step forward. "I've got a vague sense of him. He doesn't like you at all, does he, Morosov?"

"That's because I executed him. Can you find out who he really is?"

"If you want." She stretched out her hand toward the distortion.

"If she tries to touch me, cygnet, I'll—"

Ella staggered and almost went down. In that instant of confusion, Adam simply disappeared, leaving Vadim cursing in Russian, Fae and every other language he could remember.

"What the hell was that?" Ella gasped.

"Adam."

"God, when he touched me, it *hurt!*"

"I know. I felt it."

He helped her to sit in the only chair and knelt in front of her. "I apologize. I didn't realize he would affect you like that."

"It's okay. I'm fine now. I shouldn't have attempted to touch him." She cupped his cheek. "But, Morosov, what the hell? He does look like you."

"In this form, yes. That's why I wanted you to find out what lay beneath."

"Do you think he's after you as well as his trophies?"

"I have to assume so. Someone wants me involved in this case whether I want it or not. Why else would they use an image I'm familiar with?"

"An image of yourself."

"Close enough." He sighed and moved his head until his mouth brushed her fingers. "I wish I could say that was the end of this, but I'm sure he'll be back."

"Next time I won't try and touch him." She shivered. "I can still access his mind, though."

He stood up. "I should be able to do that by myself, now I've gained your skill set."

"It takes a while to get used to the idea, doesn't it? It's a bit like your power for me." She frowned. "We haven't had a lot of time to share our skills, though."

"Not really."

It was hard to believe he'd only known her for a few short weeks. He couldn't imagine his life without her now, and Adam had just touched her.

"Are you feeling okay?"

"Yes. I'm fine now, why?" Her expression changed. "Hell, he didn't take my face, did he?"

"No. He probably didn't have time."

Her hand flew to her cheek. "How can I keep him out?"

"He won't be able to overpower you as long as our minds are linked together."

"Are you sure about that?"

"Absolutely." He checked that the shield around Ms. Phelps was stable again and then went across and took Ella's hand in his. "You smell like Fae."

"Like Adam, you mean?"

He inhaled slowly. "No, Rossa. Was he here?"

"He might have popped in."

He raised her chin so that she had to look into his eyes. "You didn't tell him anything, did you?"

"Like what? He already knows the important bits."

"Don't trust him, Ella. Everything you say will be reported to Otherworld." She blinked and he forced himself to keep calm. "He might look like an angel, but he's as devious as the devil."

"I know that. What are we going to do about Ms. Phelps?"

"We'll just have to stay here and keep her safe."

"And stop Adam getting to her."

"Exactly." He kissed the top of her head and released her. "He won't be back for a while. Why don't you go down to the cafeteria and get us both some coffee?"

ELLA WOKE WITH a start and fumbled for her weapon.

"What's up?"

Beside her, Vadim was staring intently at the space around Ms. Phelps. It was dark in the room, and the unnatural play of light around the bed was startlingly obvious. Ms. Phelps was sitting upright, her mouth open as if she were silently screaming.

"Something's wrong."

"Duh."

"My magic's being attacked."

She could feel it now inside her, the insidious sense of being drained and squeezed dry.

"Then do something! You're supposed to be strong!"

"Too many forces are combining against me, all the power of the sect, I—"

Vadim crashed to the floor, his head in his hands, and Ella fought to reach him through the demons howling in her own mind. The room shuddered like the quiet center of a tornado. Why weren't the SBLE guards coming in to help? Ella tried to shout, but the sound was whipped away.

"Hold on!"

The shield around Ms. Phelps was thinning like the ripped silk of a defective parachute. Ella reached the bed and marshaled all her power to try and mend it, but nothing worked. Even as she watched, the Fae shielding spell was drawn inexorably toward Ms. Phelps's open mouth. Did she know she was inhaling death? Did she understand what was happening to her?

"No!" Vadim staggered to his feet, power shooting from his outstretched hand. "Leave her!"

Everything seemed to be suspended, and time moved so slowly that she could see the battle for supremacy being fought frame by frame. Even as Vadim's power roared through the room, it was already too late. The shield was gone, swallowed down by Ms. Phelps, who collapsed back onto her pillows.

As quickly as the storm had arisen, it subsided, leaving Vadim and her on the floor. The door flew open and one of the security guards nearly trampled her as he rushed in. She noticed for the first time that the drapes were ripped, the blinds askew and both the chairs were upside down.

"What the hell happened?"

She pointed at the motionless figure on the bed. "That happened. *Dammit!*" She crawled over to Vadim. "Are you all right?"

He snarled something obscene in Fae and shook off her hand. Without another word, he turned on his heel and pushed his way through the security personnel and medical staff now arriving at the door. She didn't bother to chase after him. She could find him anywhere, and someone needed to be here to tell Feehan the bad news.

As if he'd heard her thoughts, her boss appeared at the doorway, a cup of coffee in his hand.

"Ella, are you all right? I was just coming to check on you. I saw Vadim heading down the stairs. Was he looking for me?"

"He needs some space at the moment, boss. He's angry with himself for not being able to protect Ms. Phelps."

Feehan glanced over at the bed, where one of the medics shook his head. "Dammit. She's dead?"

"Yeah, and on our watch. We were literally right here." She stood up and shook her head, trying to ease

against you, against *us*. There was no way in hell that anyone could've withstood that."

"You don't understand. I'm not supposed to be vulnerable, I'm—"

"You did your best, right?"

He said nothing, his mouth a hard line as he returned his attention to the spectacular view.

"You told me that sometimes Otherworld power is diminished in this world."

"That's correct."

"Then isn't that what happened to you? You're still incredibly powerful. That's why they still had to send everything they had against you?"

"I should've known what they planned to do. I should've realized that Adam was testing the extent of my abilities when he first turned up."

"Hindsight's a wonderful thing, isn't it?" She poked him in the arm. "Let it go, Morosov."

"They killed her with my magic. That makes me responsible for her death." He shuddered and Ella poked him again.

"Don't be such a wuss. So they turned your own weapon on you. It happens. You still aren't to blame. What I don't understand is why they thought it necessary to demonstrate such power to achieve one death."

He sighed. "Because they're fucking crazy?" He stared out over the sea. "If I was in Otherworld, I could destroy them all."

"But if you go back there, you'll be executed."

He looked down at her. "Who told you that?"

"Rossa."

His mouth quirked at the corner. "That makes sense."

"Are you intending to sit here all night?"

"I'm not sure."

"Let's go home instead. There's food there, or at least I think there is."

"I don't have a home."

This time she punched him much harder. "Oh, for God's sake, lighten up, Morosov. Let's go."

She grabbed his hand, and the next minute they were in her kitchen, the lights were on and Vadim was delving into the fridge.

"You lied. There's nothing here to eat."

"Try the freezer."

He complied and she looked over his shoulder as he surveyed her collection of saturated fatty goodness with an air of horror.

"Come on, partner, let yourself go for once. A Hot Pocket won't kill you."

"How about I make us an omelet?"

"If you can make it quickly, go for it. I'm starving."

He took off his coat and jacket and loosened his tie. "Make some toast."

By the time they'd finished eating, it was almost five in the morning, and the sunlight was beginning to filter through the gray, foggy skies.

Vadim stretched and rubbed his eyes. "I left my car at the hospital. We'll need to get the ferry in the morning."

"Or use magic."

He almost smiled for the first time. "You like that mode of transport, then?"

"It's pretty cool." She waited until he set the dishwasher running and then took his hand. "We have to be at work by nine. If we use the ferry, we'll get much less sleep." She led him toward her bedroom. "We need our sleep."

He already looked exhausted. Had the struggle with the Otherworld sect drained him so completely? Or was it more a case of hurt pride? Ella pushed on his chest until he sat on the edge of the bed. She slowly unbuttoned his shirt and then knelt to unbuckle his belt. His hand covered hers.

"You don't need to do that. I can just…"

She bent her head and kissed the bulge of his cock. "I like doing it. Shut up."

He sighed as she slowly unbuttoned his pants and drew down the zipper. Underneath, he wore tight blue cotton boxers that now strained to contain his growing erection.

"Nice." Ella dropped a kiss on the crown of his wet cock, which had already escaped the waistband of his boxers. "Now, be quiet and let me concentrate."

She helped him ease out of his pants, socks and shoes and then returned her attention to his cock, sliding her hand inside his boxers at the back to stroke and cup his awesome ass. His hips jerked forward.

"Ella…"

There was a note of uncertainty in his voice that she'd never heard before. She kissed his shaft through soft cotton that did nothing to hide the length and girth of him, nibbled at the dampening fabric until his hand clenched in her hair, demanding more, trying to direct her mouth to more needy places.

"Patience is a virtue, Morosov."

His answer was a low growl in Fae that made her nipples ache and her lady parts ready for action. But this wasn't about her. It was about giving him some-thing she'd never attempted to give a man before...

Love, caring, support? She didn't want to name it. That screamed of some sort of permanency or security or *need* on her part. She just wanted him to feel better.

That was it. Sex made everything better.

She slid her thumbs down the sides of his boxers and pulled them off. A birthmark in the shape of a black crescent nestled in the lickworthy crevice where his hip met his groin, and she kissed it. With a happy sigh, she studied his cock.

"Lie back on the bed, Morosov." The hand in her hair tightened. "I mean, Vadim."

He lay back and she knelt between his thighs and studied the perfection of his abs, chest and beautiful face.

"I like it when you do what you're told." She bent and licked his cock.

"I noticed."

His eyelids were lowered, his voice a soft rumble of lust and need that made her want to start at his feet and kiss every luscious inch of him. She magicked off all her clothes except her bra and panties, which didn't match, but who the hell cared? The way Vadim was looking at her, for once, he certainly didn't.

"Let me touch you."

She shook her head. "No, this is all about you. Put your hands behind your head and behave yourself."

"If you insist."

The darkness was disappearing from his eyes and he was visibly relaxing—apart from the important parts that stayed impressively erect. She shook out her hair and then bent over his cock and sucked the first inch into her mouth. His groan encouraged her and she took more. He rolled his hips and she sucked on him hard, one hand cupping his balls as she worked her mouth and teeth along the length of his shaft.

His thoughts flooded hers, his desire for her a living thing that knew no boundaries and needed no words. She could tell when he was near a climax and ease off, or push him even closer… She teased and tantalized him until he was pleading with her, begging her to let him come.

With some reluctance, she released his cock and straddled him, the cotton of her panties rubbing against the base of his shaft. As he watched, she slowly removed her bra and cupped her breasts, teasing her already tight nipples to needy buds.

"Ella, let me, I—"

She smiled at him and rubbed herself and her swollen clit against his cock, the fabric of her panties wet from both his need and her own.

"*Please.*"

His stark request echoed through her head, and she disposed of her panties. Watching him the whole time, she slowly lowered herself over his cock, her groan joining his as his thick length pressed inward. She started to move on him. He helped her, thrusting upward into each down stroke, so in tune with her that every sensation was doubled and trebled and…

She climaxed and he followed her, bringing her hard down on him as he pumped upward. She nestled her cheek into the angle between his head and neck and sighed.

"That was awesome."

Tomorrow was soon enough to analyze why she'd

felt compelled to tend to Vadim's complex needs in such a way. Tomorrow was also soon enough to deal with the horrors of Adam and the Otherworld sect.

NINE

"So you're saying Ms. Phelps died from inhaling your magic shield." Feehan frowned. "Has that ever happened to you before?"

"No." Vadim glanced around the room at the rest of the team. "It was unprecedented. I do, however, accept prime responsibility for Ms. Phelps's death."

Ella shook her head. "I was there too, Morosov. There was nothing either of us could do against that amount of power. We just weren't prepared for it."

Feehan paced in front of the whiteboard. "If this thing is growing stronger, maybe it's time to call in the Otherworld authorities."

"I don't think Adam was acting alone this time," Vadim forced himself to say. "The level of power that was used against us was far too high and too complex to belong to one being."

"I agree." Liz's Fae-Web was busy lighting up over her head. "What happened wasn't normal. I've never seen anything like it either."

Before Liz could start asking awkward questions, Vadim spoke up.

"I'm meeting with a member from my family today to ask for additional information about Adam."

"Whom exactly are you meeting?" Mr. Feehan asked.

"A cousin of mine called Rossa."

"Rossa?" Liz grimaced. "I know him. He's a devious little shit."

He smiled at her. "You're right, but he's also afraid of me, and terribly indiscreet."

"Then you should learn a lot." Liz's smile disappeared. "But you also need to be careful, Vadim. I'm seeing you as central to this case, even more central than the poor victims."

"That's certainly worrying." He hesitated. "Would it be better if I removed myself from the investigation entirely?"

Everyone else in the room except Ella looked at each other. Mr. Feehan cleared his throat.

"We *did* think about that, Vadim, but Liz doesn't believe it will help."

So that was why everyone had already been in place when he and Ella arrived. What time had the nine o'clock meeting really started?

Ella snorted. "That's a nice way to treat a team member, boss. Aren't you the one who's always going on about us working together as a unit?"

"It's okay," Vadim reassured everyone. "I understand why you considered it."

Feehan shot him a grateful glance. "Thanks."

"Do we need to speak to Ms. Phelps's family?"

"She doesn't have anyone in the area. They've asked us to return her to Kentucky for burial in the family plot."

"What about her face?"

"We're going to seal the coffin and make it impossible for them to open it at their end by sending an SBLE team home with her." Feehan grimaced. "It's not perfect, but it's the best we can do for all of them."

"So all we have to worry about is victim number three," Sam said.

"*If* Adam returns. After that clash with Vadim and Ella, maybe he won't have the balls to come back."

"It might delay him for a day or so, but he'll be back," Vadim replied. "He's obviously a creature of habit, and he has a goal to accomplish." He put away his pen. "If that's all, I'll go and speak to Rossa right now and get back to you as soon as possible."

Feehan nodded. "Sure, go ahead. We'll finish up here."

Vadim deliberately didn't catch Ella's eye as he rose and left the room. She didn't need to be with him for this encounter. He had a few things he wanted to say to Rossa without an audience. Not that he'd shut her out entirely—that would make her too suspicious—but he could still shield some of his emotions if she wasn't breathing down his neck.

He went into their office and then immediately magicked himself to his hotel room. Rossa was already ensconced on the bed, watching porn on the TV.

"Hey."

Vadim turned off the TV and Rossa pouted.

"I was watching that."

"You can do it in real life. Why watch it?"

"True." Rossa turned toward him. "What can I do for you, cygnet?"

"I need you to take a message to my mother and grandmother."

"Okay…"

"Tell them that if Adam intends Ella to be his third victim, they have to stop him."

"And why would they want to do that? They don't

like your mate. If Adam killed her, it would make things all nice and tidy again."

"If Adam kills her, I *will* return to Otherworld and to my full powers. I'll demand vengeance for her death, as is my right as a bonded male."

"Um, that's not good, right?"

"It is for me. I've missed slaughter and bloodshed more than I thought I would. If my mate is involved, I strongly suspect my rage will have no bounds."

"You mean, you'd kill your own family?"

"If I had to." He paused for effect. "If I felt they had failed me."

Rossa's color faded. "I don't think anyone can stop the sect from completing their games."

"I've stopped them in the past."

"But only at great personal cost!"

Vadim held Rossa's silver gaze. "And I'll do it again, but this time I'll save my mate and take everyone who opposes her down with me. Tell them my terms."

"And what if they won't help?"

"If she is harmed, they'll be dead. It's quite simple."

"You can't—"

"I can, Rossa. You know I can, and so do they." He hesitated. "And if I'm killed, I'd appreciate it if you would look out for Ella."

"You're asking me? *Frakk*, cygnet, I'm probably going to get fried just for being your messenger."

"But if you survive, you will protect her?"

He shrugged. "Sure, I like her."

"Swear it."

Rossa sighed and placed his hand flat over his heart. "I will keep the faith until the sky falls upon me, until the earth opens and swallows me and until the sea rises and covers me."

Vadim nodded as relief swamped him. "Thank you. Now please go and deliver my message."

With a wink and a flash of light, Rossa was gone. Vadim slowly let out his breath and stared at the rumpled counterpane where his cousin had been sitting. Would it be enough to save Ella? Adam had touched her to show Vadim that he could. Luckily for him, she hadn't seen it as a threat, only as a near miss.

He got up and straightened the bed covers. Despite what he'd claimed, if the sect combined their powers again, they might have the strength to harm his mate. That was unacceptable. He hadn't been making empty threats to his family. For the first time in his long existence he was willing to lay down his life. Would they understand that? Would they act?

There was nothing else he could do at the moment to stop the inevitable battle between him and the cult. It was his destiny, one he'd tried to avoid by running away.

Ella would survive. He would make damned sure of it. She was worth dying for. Now he just had to find a way to convince her of that too…

"So you're okay about this."

Ella studied her companion as he drove across the bridge toward the East Bay and the joys of her parents' house in Walnut Creek.

"Are you deaf? I believe I've said that at least three times."

"I'm just worried. You know my mom will be all over you, right?"

"Yes."

"And my sister, Madison?"

"Yes."

"And you're okay with that."

"*Yes.* For God's sake, Ella, stop worrying."

"Madison can be difficult."

"I noticed that the first time we met."

"We used to get on okay, and then over the last few months, she's just shut me out again."

"Of course she's shutting you out." He glanced over at her. "For an empath, you can be surprisingly obtuse sometimes."

"What's that supposed to mean?"

"She's obviously scared about losing you again."

"So she treats me like shit?"

"Exactly."

She rubbed at a nonexistent spot on the glass. "I suppose that makes some weird teenage kind of sense."

"When she finds out that you're sticking around, she'll come back to you."

"Do you really think so?"

"Yes. And if she and your mother get too annoying today, you can soothe them with magic."

"Or stop them talking entirely. That might be fun." She smiled for the first time. "I'm going to have to tell them I'm not going nuts."

"I'm sure they'll be delighted."

"But that means I'll have to tell them about you."

"Which is also okay."

"She'll probably cry all over you."

"I have a handkerchief. Stop worrying."

She studied his handsome profile. He wore jeans and a tight black T-shirt that molded his biceps and muscled chest. She wanted to rip off his clothes and run her hands over his abs and tight ass...

"You can do that later. I wouldn't recommend trying it in front of your parents."

"I don't know, it might be fun." She patted his muscled thigh. "Mom already said we can stay the night if we want."

"And you *want* to have sex with me in your parents' house?"

She looked out of the window. "I've never done that before. I missed out on all that adolescent fun while I was at the empath college."

"You didn't get to go home a lot?"

"I never went home. My mom said it would be too much for her to cope with."

His hand covered hers and squeezed. "Then we'll stay the night. The shock should've worn off by then, and hopefully they'll leave us alone."

"You have no idea."

"Are your brothers coming, too?"

"I think they'll all be there for dinner at least."

"Great."

He didn't sound too rattled, but then he came from Fae royalty whose family gatherings were probably more terrifying and gory than she could even imagine. She stared out of the window at the rolling hills and the shady trees that covered them. By the summer, everything would be dry as dust and golden brown and ripe for a fire. Despite everything, visiting her parents was still an ordeal. How the hell was she supposed to have a relationship with the people who had dumped her in an all-year boarding school in Otherworld for empaths at the age of five? Sure, they'd done it to protect the rest of the family from the creatures who were magically drawn to her, but it still hurt.

And now she was bringing the Boy Wonder home with her...

"What do you want me to tell them about you?"

"What do you mean?"

"Should I say you're not human?"

"I am human."

"About one percent, right?"

"More than that." He clicked on his indicator and moved smoothly across the lanes toward the upcoming exit. "If you think they'll be okay with it, you can tell them the truth."

"I don't know the truth."

He glanced at her briefly, his black sunglasses shielding his eyes. "You know I'm related to Fae royalty. That's usually enough to make people happy."

"Maybe as one of your lame pick-up lines," she grumbled. "My mom isn't so easy to fool. She hates anything that's different. She certainly hated me."

"*Hate* is a rather strong word."

"What else would you call it?"

"Fear? Worry? Love? Some people find it difficult to express their true feelings for those they love."

She glared at him. "Is that a dig at me?"

"I thought we were talking about your mother."

"So did I."

"Well, let's see how it goes. Maybe she'll be so pleased to hear you're going to survive that she won't give a damn about me."

"Humph. I hate it when you're being nice." She subsided into her seat and crossed her arms over her chest. She wasn't sure what worried her most, telling her mom about her escape from madness or about her relationship with Vadim. If only they could avoid the party entirely…

"ELLA!"

Her mom opened the door, and Ella submitted meekly to an awkward perfumed embrace. Her mom's blond hair was short and spiky, her makeup perfect, and her velvet pantsuit emphasized her lean, well-exercised body. She always made Ella feel like such a frump. The house smelled of her mom's overpowering floral scent. It always had. Apart from the addition of a pool, the sprawling ranch house in the neat subdivision of Walnut Creek her parents had bought in the eighties to house their growing family remained exactly the same.

"Happy birthday tomorrow, darling."

"I brought Vadim. Is that okay?"

"Of course it is." She hesitated and whispered loudly, "Did the people at your work not want you to be alone at this crucial time?"

"Something like that." She left Vadim shaking hands with Darlene and headed down the hallway. "Where's Dad?"

She opened the door into the kitchen and family room and surveyed the glum faces. Apart from the removal of the horrendous purple flowery wallpaper and the addition of a flat-screen TV, nothing had changed much in there, either.

"This must be the party place. What's up?"

Her dad rose from the couch and hugged her hard. "Hey, princess, how are you doing?"

"I'm good." She buried her face against his shoul-

der and inhaled the familiar smell of beer and spicy
aftershave. Both of her brothers came over to hug her,
as did her pregnant sister-in-law, Julie. No one looked
happy. There was also no sign of her younger sister,
which was never good. Madison had a fondness for
drama that rivaled their mother's.

Vadim came into the room with Darlene at his side
and was soon busy shaking hands with everyone and
being reintroduced. By the time they were all seated
again, Ella noticed the pile of presents under the table.

"Hey, are they for me?"

Her dad patted her knee and passed her the first
present. "Yes, love. Happy birthday. We weren't quite
sure what to get you, but—"

"Considering I might be dead soon?" Ella grinned
at her dad. "It's okay, there's no need for anyone to get
all morbid and stuff. Hand it over."

She unwrapped the present and studied the pink
furry slippers. "Wow. Thanks, Dad, these are awesome! They'll look really good when I'm shuffling
around the empath mental health facility out in Santa
Rosa."

"*Ella...*"

She ignored Vadim and smiled brightly at Julie,
whose lower lip was already trembling. Julie handed
her a gift bag. Pregnancy hormones were obviously
an emotional minefield. Ella could pick up her dis-
tress far too easily.

"Is this from you and Scott?"

"Yes. If you don't like that brand, you can change it
to something else. The gift receipt is inside."

Ella unwrapped the tablet. "Cool! I've been mean-
ing to get one of these to read on for ages! Is this the

new mini?" Julie nodded. "Thank you. I can load up on books and games and keep myself busy."

"I'm so glad you like it."

She held Julie's gaze and sent her soothing mental images. Her sister-in-law relaxed back in her seat and leaned into Scott. "I really do. Thank you."

Her mother laid a big parcel across her knees. "This is from me."

Everyone watched as Ella carefully ripped open the wrapping paper.

"It's a quilt." She looked up at Darlene.

"Yes." She perched on the edge of the couch next to Ella. "Do you recognize any of the fabrics?"

Ella spotted a piece of neon orange cotton. "Didn't I have a pair of shorts made out of something like this?"

"You did."

"You *kept* them?"

Darlene traced another chevron of fabric. "Every year when the school sent back your outgrown clothes, I hung on to a few pieces. It was stupid, I know, but I found it hard to let go of them. Eventually your aunt suggested I make them into something useful, so I made this quilt."

"That's…" Ella stared down at the myriad of colors until they began to blur and dance before her eyes. Vadim took her hand and squeezed it.

"It's beautiful, Darlene."

"It really is. Mom, I—"

"I just wanted you to have something from home when you—" She moved away from Ella and returned to her seat. "—when you leave again."

"*How long are you going to let this go on?*"

She glared at Vadim. "*Okay, I'll tell them.*"

"This is all very nice of you, but I do have some news of my own to share—"

Before she could continue, Dave cleared his throat. "I didn't get you anything."

"That's okay. Seeing you is all the present I need."

He stood up suddenly and glared at her parents. Beside her Vadim tensed. "I thought you'd like to know that I got into that Otherworld class down at UCLA. I'm going to be a licensed medic in both realms by the end of the year."

Ella rose too, then hugged him hard. "And that's the best present ever. I'm so proud of you."

He shrugged out of her embrace. "It's the least I can do to make up for the rest of this family's neglect."

"Excuse me?" Darlene's voice rose on each syllable. "We've done nothing wrong. We're members of a close and loving family!"

"Ella could hardly be described as being close, Mom. She was stuck in Otherworld." Dave turned his full attention on their mother. "You sent her away and never even let her come back for vacations."

Darlene squared up to him. "I did what was best for us all!"

"No, you did what was best for yourself. You always do." Dave shook his head. "And it's too late to argue about it now, isn't it, when she's going to disappear on us again, this time forever. Do you really think a home-made quilt is going to make it up to her?"

"Well, that's just it, Dave, I'm—"

The door flew open and Madison sauntered in, her gaze drawn immediately to Vadim. She wore kitty pajama pants slung low on her hips and a bikini top. Her long blond hair hung straight down her back, and her makeup was perfect—if you liked teenagers looking forty.

"Sorry I'm late. Happy birthday, big sis. I didn't get you anything. I didn't see the point. Haven't you gone nuts yet?"

"I think I might start right now." Ella glared at her sister as she insinuated herself into the nonexistent space beside Vadim on the couch and cuddled up to him. "As I've been trying to say for the past few minutes, I'd like to thank you for the presents and the birthday wishes."

"You're welcome, Ella," her parents said dutifully.

Dave muttered something uncomplimentary and took another swallow of his beer. Vadim inched away from Madison's questing hands and kept his gaze fixed firmly on Ella.

"I never thought I'd live past my twenty-seventh birthday, but it seems I was mistaken."

"They found a cure?" her father asked.

"Well, not exactly." She took a deep breath. "I changed my mind and took the Otherworld Community Outreach Services mate offered to me."

The silence was deafening.

"You took a *mate?* You mean you have a *man?*" Darlene gripped her hands together until her fingers were as white as her face. "Where is he?"

Ella pointed at Vadim. "Right there. Why else do you think I'd bring him?"

"*Nice.*"

"*Can it, Morosov. Can't you see I'm nervous as hell?*"

"What exactly does it mean?" Her dad sat forward. "I know you mentioned it as an option years ago, but you seemed so set against it. What changed your mind?"

Madison waved a hand in front of her father's face. "Duh, *Dad*, have you *looked* at Vadim? He's *hot.* He's also, like, way out of her league. How could she say no?" She poked Vadim in the side. "The real question here is, why the hell did you saddle yourself with my sister?"

"He didn't. He was matched with me by the Other-world mating service."

"Like an arranged marriage?"

"I suppose so."

"Like, is that even legal in this country?" Madison demanded. "Look at the poor guy. He's still in a state of shock."

"*Morosov, help me out here!*"

"*I thought you told me to shut up and let you handle it.*"

"*Morosov…*"

He stood up, gently setting a clinging Madison aside, and took Ella's hand. "I'm delighted to have been selected as a mate for your daughter, Mr. and Mrs. Walsh."

Ella couldn't decide who looked more stunned, her mother or her father. "This is a good thing, right? I'm not going nuts anymore."

"But it's so unexpected!" Darlene glanced at her husband. "Why didn't you say something to us before?"

"I thought it was better said in person. I didn't want you to be shocked."

"Well, I am shocked!" Darlene pressed her hand to her bosom. "How could you do that to me?"

An all-too-familiar sense of anger rose in Ella's gut. "Mom, this isn't about you. Aren't you pleased?"

"Of course I'm pleased! I just wish you'd mentioned it before we bought you all these presents."

"The presents are great. It's still my birthday, isn't it?"

Vadim's calm voice slid over hers. "I was hoping to take you all out to dinner this evening to celebrate Ella's big day. Would that be acceptable?"

"That would be lovely," Ella's dad answered. "It will give us a chance to get to know you better, as well."

"Dad…"

Vadim kissed her cheek. "It's all right. I expect your parents have a lot of questions for me."

"I have one." Madison waved her hand in the air. "How long do you have to stick with my sister?"

He smiled down into Ella's eyes. "For all eternity."

"Oh, please…you don't have to lay it on so thick."

"You poor dude. But I suppose in her line of work, she might not last that long."

"Thanks. By the way, I don't think you can date your sister's grieving ex. That would be icky." Ella made a face at her sister. Why did she feel like a teenager again?

"I'm not being mean. I'm just stating the facts." Madison flipped her hair over her shoulder. "Empaths don't last very long, do they?"

"Only if they don't take a mate."

"It's not fair," Madison whined. "How come she ends up with *him?*"

Dave came across and shook Vadim's hand. "Welcome to the family. I'm glad someone will take care of my baby sister for a change."

"Oh, for goodness sake, Dave, can't you say any-thing nice?" Darlene faked a laugh. "Poor Vadim will think he's joining a family of freaks! Are you think-ing of getting married?"

"God, no." Ella turned to Julie, who had started to cry. "It's okay."

"I know, it's wonderful. Isn't it, Scott?" Her hus-band hugged her close.

"And you don't have to worry about naming your poor baby after me either." Ella winked at Scott, who winked back. He was a man of few words at the best of times. Stuck with his mother and his wife in the same room, he barely uttered a word.

Madison patted the couch next to her. "So, Vadim, tell us all about your family. Do you have any broth-ers or gorgeous male cousins?"

"Both my siblings are dead." He remained standing by Ella. "But I still have quite a large family."

"Ooh, are they local? Can you introduce me to some hot dudes?"

"*Madison!*" Darlene thundered. "You are hardly old enough to be dating anyone!" She turned to smile at Vadim. "Are your family from around here? We'd love to meet them."

She felt Vadim hesitate and replied for him. "No, they're not. He's Russian, remember?"

"Oh, that's true, I don't suppose that nasty govern-ment over there lets people out much." She waved at her husband. "Shall we have a drink to celebrate Vadim joining our family?"

"How about my survival, Mom? Isn't that worth celebrating too?"

Darlene patted her hand "But you wouldn't have

survived if Vadim here hadn't agreed to 'mate' with you, whatever that means."

"It means Ella and I are bonded physically, emotionally and psychically for life."

She glanced up at him while he was speaking. There wasn't a hint of mockery in his voice or his expression. When he said it like that, it sounded so…permanent.

"*It is.*"

"*Shut up!*"

"You might as well get married, then!" Darlene laughed. "Although I don't envy you having to deal with all that Otherworld stuff." She hesitated. "You *do* know about that, don't you?"

"Oh, he knows. Probably more than I do."

Darlene continued to ignore Ella and grill Vadim, while her father passed out glasses of champagne. "And you're okay with her being like that?"

"I'm fine with it. I wouldn't have volunteered to be an OCOS mate if I hadn't been."

Darlene patted his cheek. "You're obviously a saint."

Ella made a gagging sound. "Hardly that."

Darlene grabbed her elbow and steered her into the kitchen. "You should be grateful he took you on, Ella. Now that you have him hooked, try not to lose him too quickly, okay?"

Ella took the bag of peanuts her mom handed her and dumped them in a bowl. Several bounced out onto the floor. "Didn't you hear what he said? We're in this together for life."

"Men say these things, dear, but do they really mean them?" Darlene pointed her bread knife at Ella. "Let's hope he's not the kind to stray."

"Yes, Mom." She picked up the bowl of peanuts, aware of a strong desire to burst out laughing. How had her redemption turned out to be all about Vadim? "Let's hope."

She walked through into the family room and found Vadim in conversation with Scott and Julie. He looked up and she grinned at him. Within a second he was by her side.

"What's so funny?"

"This."

"Your family?"

"My mom just told me you would probably stray. Should I arrange to have you neutered?"

His smile was breathtaking. "You know you'd regret that."

"Will you stray?"

He held her gaze. "Never."

She swallowed hard as the echo of his spoken word reverberated through her mind. "That's kind of scary and reassuring at the same time."

"Will you?"

"Will I what?"

"Stray."

"Hell, no."

He bent his head and kissed her hard on the mouth. "Then what do we have to worry about?"

"Apart from crazy Otherworld sects, our dangerous jobs and your family? Nothing much." She shook her head. "In fact, when you think about it, my family is easy."

"Exactly, so let's just relax and enjoy the rest of the day."

MUCH LATER, SHE closed the door of the guest bedroom
and stared at Vadim. It came complete with pink roses
on the wallpaper and Austrian swag drapes. For the
first time in years she'd actually enjoyed an evening
with her family, and it was all due to Vadim. His attitude toward her and his excellent manners had almost
made them behave like a regular family celebrating a
normal family occasion.

"They still drive me nuts."

He appeared to follow her thoughts even as he
stripped off his T-shirt, displaying his flat stomach and
perfect abs. "Of course they do. They're your family."

"Is it true that both your siblings are dead?"

"Yes."

"That must've been horrible for you."

"Yes."

She raised her eyebrows. "That's all you're going
to say?"

"What would you like me to say?"

"Do you miss them?"

"Our relationship was…difficult. They were allied
with my father. My sister worshipped my brother and
hated me."

"Why?"

He shrugged. "Because I was the eldest?"

"That's stupid."

"Families often are. Your mother doesn't appreciate you at all."

"Because I disrupted her life."

"But that was hardly your fault, was it?"

He held her gaze and she hurriedly looked down at
the buttons on her dress. "I can't believe how she fawns
over you, though."

"I am rather spectacular." His smile was wicked as he unbuckled his belt and unzipped his jeans to reveal his already erect cock.

"You sure are. Spectacularly arrogant." Ella shrugged out of her jacket and dress. "Do you want to shower?"

"Let's do that later. I have to fulfill your fantasy first."

She paused. "Which one?"

"Having sex under your parents' roof."

"I was kidding."

"No you weren't." His gaze fastened on her bra and the tight buds of her nipples. "Maybe I'll make you scream when you come, so they'll hear you."

"And make my dad all awkward over his breakfast cereal?"

He advanced toward her. "Then you'll have to keep quiet, won't you? And I know how difficult that is for you."

He moved even closer until he was right in front of her. One gentle push on her chest and she was flat on her back, with him covering her. She couldn't help grinning up at him as he lowered his head. Who would ever have imagined sex could be so much fun?

"Now, lie back and enjoy, Ms. Walsh, and for God's sake, keep it down."

TEN

ELLA SAT UP in bed and scrabbled to find her weapon. It wasn't under her pink fluffy pillow. As it was still dark, she assumed something had woken her up, but what was it? Where the hell had she left her gun last night? Even as she thought about nudging Vadim, she froze, her attention on the end of the bed, where her naked mate was confronting something that gave off the strongest Otherworld vibe she'd ever encountered.

"Morosov?"

He didn't reply, and she crawled to the end of the bed. His attention was fixed on the shimmering image of the man she knew as Adam. Up close, the resemblance to Vadim was so startling, it was like seeing double.

"*Morosov.*"

She tried using her mind instead of her voice, but her thought bounced back from the strength of his shields.

"Tell her."

Adam's voice shuddered through her, breaking the silence and her fear. Her purse was on the floor and she lunged for it, bringing it up onto the bed, where she could finally retrieve her weapon. She fumbled to open the clasp.

"Hold on, Morosov. I've got it."

"*Tell* her."

She found her weapon and pointed it at Adam.

Vadim slowly turned to face her. His smile was cold, his expression pitiless.

"I'm leaving, Ms. Walsh."

"What?"

"I'm going back to Otherworld with Adam. He has convinced me that the only way we can meet and battle as equals is in my homeland."

"But you don't need to battle him anywhere."

"I do. I can't stand to be defeated."

"That's just stupid! If you go back, they'll kill you!"

He shrugged. "It's my destiny. I cannot escape it."

"Fine, but I'm going with you."

A muscle twitched in his cheek. "I don't need you, Soul Sucker."

"We're partners."

"You're human. In Otherworld you're also a liability. You'd slow me down and make me more vulnerable."

She swallowed hard at the harsh truth behind his words. "But—"

He sighed. "Do you really want to air your emotional laundry in front of Adam?"

"Why not?" She tried to push through his shields, to force him to let her sense his real thoughts, but it was impossible. "Your quarrel with him is obviously far more important than your partnership with me!"

"This is Otherworld business."

"This is *bullshit!*"

He averted his gaze. "I'm sorry, Ms. Walsh. I'll be far better off without your 'help.' Goodbye."

"Wait!"

It was too late. In a cloud of black feathers, Vadim disappeared.

Even as she registered his loss, she realized Adam hadn't gone anywhere.

"What the fuck do you want?"

His smile was so much like Vadim's, it hurt. "I think you know." He stretched out his hand. "Goodbye, Soul Sucker."

She fired at him, but wasn't quick enough to avoid his outstretched hand. With a cry, she fell back onto the bed and everything went black.

THERE WAS SOMETHING on her face. She lifted a hand and batted whatever it was away from her cheek. Damn feathers got everywhere. Who knew that swan shape-shifters molted so much?

Ella opened her eyes.

Black feathers.

Vadim.

She sat bolt upright and wrapped her arms around her knees. Had she dreamed him leaving her? His clothes were neatly folded on the chair, but there was no sound from the bathroom. Tentatively, she searched for him within her mind. There was nothing, just a horrible sense of loss like the whining static after an explosion.

He'd definitely left her.

"Bastard!" she screeched. "If anyone's going to kill you, it's going to be me! How dare he walk out on me? How dare he suggest I'm a liability?"

She stomped into the bathroom, just to make sure he wasn't hiding in there, and caught a glimpse of her reflection in the mirror.

Hell, no.

Black hair, blue eyes and cheekbones to die for.

Vadim in feminine form.

Had he sacrificed himself for her, or was this Adam's idea of a joke? She scowled at her beautiful new face. How long did she have until he came back to persuade her to kill herself? Would he wait until he finished off Vadim too?

She focused on her face and considered trying the spell Vadim had given her for cleaning things up. He'd said it might make her look like she'd had plastic surgery, but what could be worse than this?

"What was it again?" She said the words out loud and watched her new mouth shape them. *"Gey-ei-lan-dah?"*

Her face quivered like Jell-O and then reappeared in all its black haired, blue-eyed glory.

"Damn."

She threw Vadim's toothbrush in the trash and showered away all evidence of his lovemaking. He'd been incredibly gentle with her, bringing them to new heights of pleasure and a sense of being one that she'd never imagined existed. So why had he left her? It didn't make sense. She'd started to believe they were truly partners and that he trusted her. For years she'd been treated like an unstable bomb, and he'd changed that, had made her feel valued and *loved.* So why the hell had he lied to her and chosen to fight alone? Had he been saying goodbye? Her tears mingled with the water, and she let them flow. No one needed to know how she felt inside. Anger would sustain her through this time. At least she knew she could count on that.

She dressed and combed out her luxurious new head of hair and made the bed. Dammit, she was hungry.

She couldn't put off eating forever. With all her courage, she sauntered into the kitchen.

"Morning, Mom."

"Holy God! What happened to you?" Darlene screeched, and dropped her mug of coffee. It smashed into a thousand shards on the ceramic tile floor.

Ella mopped up the coffee and poured herself and her mom a cup. "I'm not sure."

"What do you mean?"

"Last night. Vadim disappeared, and I woke up looking like this." She shrugged. "Don't worry, I'll sort it out."

Darlene pounced on her father, who was coming into the kitchen with the newspapers under his arm. "Ned, look at her!"

Her father blinked and carefully put the papers down on the countertop. "New shampoo, love?"

Ella smiled at him. "Bespelled."

"Ah, that makes sense, then."

"Makes *sense?*" Darlene said. "Look at her! She's completely different!"

"She's still the same person inside. You don't have the same hair color or face you had when we met either."

"That's different, I—"

Ned patted her shoulder. "Not that I mind. If Ella was bespelled, there's not much we can do about it, is there? She's a big girl. I'm sure she can figure it out."

"I'll do my best, Dad."

"That's my girl."

Madison appeared in the doorway. "What's all the noise?" She stared at Ella. "Interesting look for you, sis. I like it." She dropped into a seat at the table and rested her head on her folded arms.

"Thanks." Ella topped up her coffee. "After breakfast, I have to be on my way. I've got to go and find Vadim in Otherworld."

"Why?"

"He's originally from there."

Darlene sat down narrowly avoiding dropping her second cup of coffee. "You said he was Russian."

"His human ancestors are."

"He's not *human?*"

Ella put two strawberry pastries in the toaster. "He's about five percent human. The rest is all Otherworld. Some of it is shape-shifter, some of it is Fae."

Madison lifted her head from the table. "Cool. Vadim's a big fairy. I knew there was something wrong with him."

Ella put her pastries on a plate and squirted them with frosting.

"What kind of shape-shifter?" Madison asked. "Is he a wolf, like Doug? I like Doug. He's kind of hot, but scary."

"Does it matter?" Ella chewed down on the sweet, sticky center of the pastry.

"I suppose not. I should've *known* there was something not right with him when he willingly took up with you." Darlene sighed and finished her coffee. "Do you want me to pack you a lunch?"

Ella paused to appreciate the moment, wanting to laugh and cry at the same time. Her family might drive her crazy, but who else would sit there and carry on as if nothing unusual had happened when their daughter's face had been bespelled and her newly found mate had disappeared?

"Thanks, Mom, but I won't need a lunch." She finished her pastries. "And thanks for not freaking out too much about everything."

Her dad raised his coffee cup in a salute. "Living with you, Ella, has been an education. After fighting off trolls in the closet and Water Fae in the shower when you were young, nothing fazes us at all."

"But you will be careful?" Darlene added.

"Of course I will." Ella slid down from her stool. "I'll be in touch. Thanks for a wonderful birthday."

She found Vadim's car keys in his jeans pocket and bundled the rest of his clothes in a deliberately untidy heap to take with her. The hint of his aftershave made her bury her nose in his T-shirt with a pang of what felt suspiciously like longing. Damn the man. She needed to be angry, not a moping fool.

The drive back to San Francisco was uneventful, the sky a bright uncaring blue, the sun warm on her newly acquired face. Every time she glanced in the rearview mirror, she was shocked by her appearance. It was worse than when she'd dyed her hair black and been a Goth. How long would Adam wait before he came back? Had he already fought Vadim? Wouldn't she know if her mate were dead?

Pushing her fears aside, she parked under the SBLE main office on Market and headed for the elevators. There was no one around when she walked into the department, so she headed for Feehan's office, knocked on the door and went straight in.

"Hey, boss."

He leaped to his feet, half a dripping tuna sandwich clutched in his hand. "Who the hell are you?"

She waved her ID badge at him. "It's me, Ella. Something's up with my face."

He grabbed his phone. "Security!"

"Boss, calm down. Adam got me last night after he got Vadim."

Feehan clutched the phone to his chest and stared at her. "Ella?"

She took a seat in front of his desk. "Yes."

"Are you sure?"

She patted her torso. "Same crappy attitude toward authority figures? Yup, I'm sure it's me." The door behind her burst open, and she turned to the two security guards. "Hey, Mitch, hey, Frankie, what's up?"

Feehan waved them away. "False alarm. Ms. Walsh has suffered some kind of magical accident. Can you ask Liz and Sam to come in here, please?"

After a long look at her new face, the guys departed and were quickly replaced by the rest of the special team. They all started talking at once.

"Everyone, sit down!" Feehan shouted. "Ella, shut the door and tell us what the hell is going on."

She told them the bare minimum of what had happened on the previous evening. For a change, no one interrupted her, their expressions ranging from horrified to appalled. Liz's Fae-Web hovered over her head like a billowing veil in a storm.

"So I need to get to Otherworld, find out what Adam's done with my face and get it back before he decides to come after me," Ella concluded. "I just wanted to let you know what was going on. I don't think I have much time."

"You don't," Liz said. "Adam is very sure of his victory."

"Not until I'm dead, he isn't."

Sam raised his hand. "What about Vad?"

"What about him?"

"Aren't you going to save him, too?"

"That idiot?" Ella snorted. "He went to Otherworld to prove what a big bad fairy he is. I'm not getting involved in his petty squabbles."

"Ella—" Feehan hesitated. "You might have no choice."

"Because of the mating crap? He's the one who left, not me. I don't owe him a thing."

"Hang on," Sam said. "You're, like, mated to Vad? *Dude!* That's awesome!" He tried to high-five her. "That's why you haven't gone nuts!"

Liz reached out and touched Ella's knee. "You have to save him."

"I damn well do not!"

"Whatever you think, he did what he did to save you. That's his primary goal. That's all I see."

Ella swallowed hard. "*Bullshit.*" She pulled away. "I have to go. Is the portal by the Bay Bridge still working?"

Even as Feehan was promising her backup, she left and magicked herself directly to the portal. She could probably get there without one, but this wasn't the occasion to be trying new things. Time sometimes moved differently in Otherworld. She might arrive and find Vadim hadn't even got there yet or that he'd already fought and died. Not that she cared. Not that the bastard owed her anything…

Then why was she so pissed at him? Because he

hadn't believed in her after all? She swiped at something wet on her cheek. Dammit, was she *crying?*

Had she really fallen for all his shit about forever together?

Apparently she had.

She checked her weapons and stashed a silver dagger in her back pocket. Didn't he know that saying about scorned women and revenge? She'd go to Otherworld, kill Adam and reclaim her face by herself. If she did see the slimy worm, she'd make him grovel and beg for forgiveness before she killed him with his own magic. Buoyed by this magnificent image, she stepped into the portal.

"Otherworld central, please."

Within a heartbeat she was stepping out into a wide paved square with a fantastic fountain set in the center of it. She'd arrived at this point in Otherworld once before, so was familiar with the layout. The sky overhead was a bruised purple and filled with storm clouds. Warily, she approached the statue, which depicted a male Fae dominating a female. She angled her head to study the face of the woman who appeared to be having an orgasm. Or was she? Clutched in the female's hand was the hilt of a dagger that had already pierced the male's side.

"Checkmate," Ella murmured.

"Indeed."

She spun around to see the still-beautiful-but-elderly woman she'd met briefly on her last visit to Otherworld. This time the Fae queen mother was unattended. Not that it mattered. Her power was immense. She wore a pale yellow gown made up of a thousand floating panels that shifted and mutated at will. Her dark hair was unbound and reached her waist.

"You are cygnet's mate."

"So he says."

"I am his grandmother."

"He already told me that."

The female raised her chin. "Did he also tell you who I am?"

"Don't you mean, what you are?" Ella studied the older woman. "You're wearing a crown, so I guess you're Fae royalty. Do you want me to curtsy? The thing is, I'm not in a curtsying kind of mood at the moment."

"Why are you here?"

"Don't you know?" Ella pointed at herself. "I want my face back. Where's the creature called Adam?"

"Where is cygnet?"

Ella grimaced. "What is it with you Fae not being able to answer a simple question? I have no idea where Morosov is, and I don't care. I *want* my face back."

"He is not with you?"

Ella pretended to look around. "Nope. He left last night with Adam."

A tiny wrinkle appeared on the queen's perfect brow. "That wasn't what we agreed."

"I don't actually care what you agreed. I simply want to find Adam."

The Fae queen studied her. "I'm afraid I can't let you meddle."

"With all due respect, it's not up to you what I do, is it?" She scanned the empty square and drew her weapon. "All I need to do is get a fix on Adam, and I'm off."

"No, Soul Sucker."

The Fae snapped her fingers and Ella was hur-
tled backward through walls and time and...oh, God,
she was going to puke. She landed with a thump on a
stone floor. Manacles slithered toward her and attached
themselves to her ankles. By the time she righted herself, all sense of the Fae queen had gone. She was alone
in what appeared to be a castle dungeon complete with
burning torches in sconces and an arched oak doorway
up a flight of stone steps.

"How very Disneyesque." She raised her voice.
"Where the hell am I?"

"Shh."

A familiar voice answered her from the shadows.

"Rossa?"

"*Shh!*"

"Can you get me out of here?"

"Not exactly."

"Then what do you want?"

He eased out from the darkness and crouched in
front of her, golden eyes wide. "Where's cygnet?"

"How the hell should I know? He disappeared off
with Adam."

He touched her cheek. "But your face! That wasn't
supposed to happen!"

He disappeared. Ella was left staring at nothing.

"Come back, you idiot!"

After a few more shouts, she stopped wasting her
breath and contemplated her options. Her gun had disappeared, but she still had her backpack. Did she have
anything sharp enough in it to cut through the chains?
If they were bespelled, which seemed likely, she might
be able to use iron to destroy them. She rummaged in

her backpack. Why didn't she carry an iron bar around with her? She really needed to be more prepared. She unearthed a small silver knife, but that proved totally ineffectual against the strength of the chains and merely blunted the blade.

"Dammit! This isn't how it's supposed to go."

The wall in front of her quivered and a man came through. He was tall, and blond like Rossa, but one hundred times more beautiful. His power flooded over her and through her, and she instinctively raised her shields.

"Soul Sucker."

"I prefer Ms. Walsh. Who are you?"

He leaned back against the stone wall and contemplated her, arms crossed over his bare, muscled chest. Thank God he had pants on, or from her viewing point she'd be getting quite an eyeful.

"I'm cygnet's father."

"Oh." That couldn't be good. Wasn't he the one who hated Vadim's guts and didn't want him anywhere near Otherworld? "What's up?"

"With me or with you?" He nodded at her chains. "You seem to be in some trouble."

"I'm good, thanks."

He smiled and for the first time she saw a hint of Vadim in him. "I can see why my son finds you so amusing, child."

"He doesn't anymore. He left me."

His smile disappeared. "So I hear."

"Do you know where he is?"

"I always know. He is my son and in some ways my creation." He sat down cross-legged on the floor and settled his massive shoulders against the wall. "You probably know I wish him ill, but not why."

"Um, you don't have to tell me anything. Families are hell sometimes, aren't they? You should meet mine." Ella gabbled away, with a horrible feeling that whatever came next wouldn't be good.

"Nevertheless, I feel you should understand the male you are bonded to for all eternity. The *monster* my wife's mother mated you with simply to fulfill her own selfish desires."

He half smiled. "Once upon a time, a male child was born from my loins. As is traditional amongst my kind, my kin were invited to celebrate his birth and bestow their various magical gifts on him, if they so chose."

She pretended to yawn. "I think I've heard this one before."

"As I said, amusing and *very* brave. After the guests arrived for the feast, a storm gathered overhead and disgorged another presence." His luscious mouth hardened. "A Fae of a different kind from the Dark Lord's court appeared. He insisted the child was marked in his master's name and that he was 'special.' When we examined the babe we discovered the mark on him and knew the Dark Lord's ambassador spoke the truth."

"So?"

Hell, she'd seen that weird mark just below his hip—kissed and licked it, actually. Was that the one?

"For every gift our Fae bestowed on the child, the Dark Court offered him another. For every positive, there was a negative."

"The gifts balanced each other out."

The Fae sighed. "If he had been left alone, then yes,

he would probably have been the most magical being ever created."

"Then what happened?"

"We couldn't allow him to be that powerful." He met her gaze fully for the first time, and it was like looking into a furnace. "I decided to train him as a weapon against the Dark Court."

"When he was a *kid*?"

"Of course. His instruction had to start immediately to instill the correct discipline in him."

"With what end in view?"

He shrugged. "As I said, as a defense against the darker elements of the Fae."

"You mean the ones who didn't agree with you, right?"

"I trained him to seek out evil and destroy it."

"At your command?"

"At first, but as he grew older, because of his gifts, he could sense discord and evil within any Fae and became the terror of Otherworld, the truth seeker, the bringer of death."

"The ultimate weapon." She shook her head. "Poor kid."

"Not at all. His power was immense."

"So what went wrong?"

"He began to defy my orders."

"And think for himself? Jeez, how ungrateful."

"It was certainly not acceptable."

"Because he was so powerful."

"Aye."

"What did you do to destroy his loyalty to you?"

He raised one haughty eyebrow. "Why do you assume I caused the fissure between us?"

"Because I know him. I'm his mate."

He laughed, the sound echoing around the dungeon walls. "You know nothing."

"Not true. You just told me a whole load of stuff about him, which in some weird way makes a ton of sense." She narrowed her eyes. "Why?"

"As his mate, you should know the truth?"

"I don't believe that for a second. I've never met a Fae who didn't put their needs front and center. You told me because you want me to do something either for you, or for him. And somehow, I doubt it's for him."

"He is too powerful to exist." The Fae stood and walked over to the door, his tattooed back to Ella. Whatever runes were inscribed on his skin moved and flexed with his moods, creating a fascinating pattern of discord. "I reluctantly agreed that he could stay in your world, but it seems he cannot keep away from mine."

"Adam made him come back."

"You don't really believe that, do you?"

She put all the conviction she had into her voice. "I saw how strong Adam and the sect were. I assume Vadim had no choice."

"That's impossible. His power is unassailable." He looked over his shoulder at her. "He *wanted* to come back."

"Are you afraid that when he's finished with Adam, he'll come after you?"

Invisible fingers closed around her throat and she gasped for breath, her own hand clawing at nothing. As quickly as the pain started, it stopped.

"Do not, as you say, push your luck, Soul Sucker. My motive in telling you about your mate's lies was pure."

Ella said nothing to that piece of bullshit, and he slowly walked back toward her.

"What do you want me to do?"

His smile was charming. "Persuade him to return to your world."

"And if he doesn't want to go?"

He studied her upturned face. "You have a unique bond with him. If anyone can make him leave, it will be you."

"And if I don't want him back?"

"We will bring him to trial for his crimes against his family."

She snorted. "If you can catch him."

"You could bring him to us, Soul Sucker."

"Why would I do that?"

"As you said, he deserted you. What better way to make him pay for his crimes than to betray him?"

"The way you Fae stab each other in the back so easily just amazes me." She shook her head. "If I want revenge on him, I'll do it myself, and not to make you happy."

"Then, there is another way." He opened his hand to show her a small dagger made from a dark reddish-brown metal that didn't shine at all. "Kill him."

She stared at the blade for a long moment. "How can I do that, when I'm chained up in the Fae queen's dungeon?"

"If you help me save Otherworld from your monstrous mate, I will order my wife, the queen, to release you into my custody."

"She won't do it."

He laughed. "You think she wants her little cygnet

to stay alive? You are mistaken. She will be as glad to be rid of him as I am. He is a threat to us all."

"Can I think about it?"

"While you think, things are progressing at a pace you cannot imagine."

"What about my face?"

He angled his head to observe her. "You don't like this one?"

"It's not really my thing. I look like Vadim's little sister, and that's just wrong, when you're mated to someone. Adam took my face. He usually makes sure his victims commit suicide fairly soon afterward."

"So that is your price?"

"Hardly. I'm just telling you the facts." She shrugged. "I don't need your help. I just need to get out of here, find Adam and that damned cult, get my face back and go home."

"Without my son?"

"He's not my problem. I can't make him come back if he doesn't want to. From the sound of it, he might have a few grudges to get off his chest over here."

"He *cannot* remain here."

"So you said."

His scowl shook the walls. "Let us be clear. In order for you to persuade my son to quit Otherworld you require—what?"

She ticked the list off her fingers. "My face back, Adam's death and the extermination of that secret cult. But as I've already mentioned, I can do all that myself, and I don't want your son back."

"Don't overestimate your abilities, my dear." He tossed the dagger at her, and she automatically caught it.

"Keep this anyway. If you do decide to execute him,

it is one of the few weapons that might actually do it for you."

"Is he so hard to kill?" The peculiar metal warmed against her palm as she wrapped her hands around the hilt.

His bitter laughter echoed around the cell. "He is practically invincible. I had to spend a fortune and go to the Dark Court to have that dagger made. There is enough power in that blade to kill three Fae Royal. Hopefully it is enough to pierce his black heart."

He inclined his head a regal inch and disappeared.

"I hate it when people keep doing that!" She shouted, but there was no one to hear her. What the hell was going on? Was Vadim really the monster his father painted him, or simply misunderstood? Despite all his bravado and the excellence of his shields, she'd felt the Fae's fear of Vadim's power. Was he really a toxic weapon that was out of control?

She sat down suddenly on the floor. Did it matter? She'd been feared her whole life, and it hadn't meant she was a bad person. Had Vadim had any more control over what he'd become than she had? The Fae king had tried to shock her into turning against her mate, but she wasn't convinced. Hadn't he left Otherworld to avoid all that? Hadn't he tried to change? Which was more than she had ever done. Unless he'd been deceiving her all along…

"Thank God, the king's gone."

It was Rossa again, a cloak over his usual nakedness.

"What do you want?" Ella demanded. "And why the fuck didn't you tell me about Vadim being the big bad fairy of Otherworld?"

"The king told you about that, did he?" Rossa pulled

a face. "Cygnet swore me to secrecy, and he's the more powerful being."

"You're such a wuss."

Rossa drew himself up. "I simply have a healthy respect for the continuation of my lifespan."

"So help me get out of this mess!"

"Here's the thing. I promised cygnet I'd take care of you." He glanced around the dungeon. "Believe it or not, this is actually the safest place for you right now. It's so heavily warded that neither Adam nor the sect can get in here."

"So what?"

"While you're safely contained, there's something else I need to tell you. The other night, cygnet gave me a message for his family that if you were a victim of Adam's, he would personally spill their blood."

"So that's why they're so desperate to keep me away from him and all chained up."

"Not exactly. The thing is—they agreed to do what he demanded. I took their message back to cygnet last night, but he'd already disappeared."

"And what about Adam?"

"He was supposed to agree to it as well."

Ella pictured her last sight of Vadim, the contemptuous smile sure to rile her before he'd disappeared. "The complete idiot!"

"Who?"

"Morosov of course! He must have…" She glared at Rossa. "Just get me out of here, please!"

"Don't be daft." His smile was sly. "I don't need to help you."

"What the hell is that supposed to mean?"

"You're mated to cygnet. You work it out."

And he was gone again. Ella shot to her feet and screamed just for the hell of it. This was why she hated Otherworld so much. Everyone talked in fucking riddles. She glanced down at the manacles around her ankles.

"Hold on a minute. I'm mated to Vadim, and he is the biggest, baddest dude in Otherworld, so…"

She stared down at the chain and focused her thoughts on it. With a strange noise, it shattered into a thousand pieces.

"Holy shit," she breathed. "I *can* do this!"

She blasted the other one and picked up her backpack. If Adam couldn't sense her inside the dungeon, she'd probably not pick up his trail either. Her first goal was to find him and get her face back.

Her reunion with the lying bastard could wait.

"WELCOME TO MY domain, cygnet, or should I call you Death Bringer?"

As the massive door swung open, Adam stood back and bowed, allowing Vadim his first glimpse of the stronghold of the Otherworld sect. It was as impressive as he'd suspected it would be—high towering ceilings, magnificent mosaics and paintings so beautiful they would make one weep. The sect's arrogance would demand a cathedral-like setting to worship the sordid achievements of a group of Fae who'd lived too long and lost all affinity for what was good and right.

He grimaced at the sanctimonious thought. And what was he? How many creatures had he killed in his egotistical assumption that his father's word was law? Since arriving in Otherworld, he'd dropped his human shape completely to reveal his true form. There was nothing to hide anymore. Death Bringer was not only his given name, but his bloody legacy. Every time he had to look at Adam, that message was reinforced. Had the male chosen his face with that in mind?

Of course he had.

The door shut behind him, and Vadim turned to Adam.

"Are we to fight here?"

"Oh, we're not fighting yet. I have something I need to do first."

Vadim smiled to reveal sharp fangs. In Otherworld, the swan wasn't the only creature he could shift into. In fact, he could become whatever species he wanted. "And if I don't agree?"

"You don't have a choice."

He drew himself up and felt long-forgotten power flood his veins. He flexed his fingers, felt the visceral tug of his claws. It was like receiving a blood transfusion. He'd been transforming ever since he set foot back in Otherworld. He wasn't quite at the full extent of his powers yet, but he was getting there. "I think you've forgotten whom you are dealing with."

"You won't want to destroy me just yet." Adam drew something out of his pocket, which hovered over his palm.

Rage coalesced in Vadim's chest, black feathers swirled in the air into a screaming tornado and the building began to shake.

"That is my mate's face."

"I know, so don't kill me. If you do, you'll never stand a chance of reclaiming it." He gestured with his other hand. "Would you like to follow me to the trophy room?"

Vadim forced himself to follow, each footstep distinct as he destroyed the delicate tile beneath his feet, but he didn't care. His rage knew no boundaries. His family had betrayed him. Everyone in Otherworld had betrayed him…

God, *Ella*…

He'd failed her completely. Was she even alive? In this threatening environment he couldn't even lower his shields to check the truth of that.

Adam approached the final golden doors at the end of the long hallway. Four trolls and two small black dragons guarded them. He held up his hand and the doors opened, releasing a waft of malignant power that almost made Vadim stagger. He forced his newly discovered empath talents to the back of his mind. He didn't need to be vulnerable to others' emotions when his own were threatening to cascade with the speed and ferocity of a national disaster.

The trophy room was well named. Beasts and races of all kinds adorned the crowded walls. He saw three extinct red dragons' heads and tails, the tusks of a mammoth and the horned skull of the Minotaur. On the shelves below were other "precious" objects. He could only assume Pandora's box and the Holy Grail were in there somewhere.

Adam held up his prize like a triumphant offering and headed for the farthest wall of the huge room. Vadim had no choice but to follow like a dumb beast. As they approached the wall, he recognized the ghostly floating features of Brad Dailey and Ms. Phelps hovering above two gold plinths. With a great deal of care, Adam leaned forward and carefully placed Ella's furious face next to the others. She obviously hadn't been

happy about Adam's face-stealing technique. The sight
of her riled expression cooled his temper somewhat and
made him able to think.

"There. My task is almost complete. All I require
now is her death."

Even before the words were out of Adam's lying
mouth, Vadim launched himself at him. Magic seemed
a poor substitute for the sheer pleasure of strangling
the male with his bare hands.

"If you kill me, she dies!" Adam squealed.

Vadim barely registered the words as a red tide of
rage colored his vision.

Pain shuddered through him as something attacked
him from behind. It felt as if he'd been caught in a net.
Manacles locked around his ankles, wrists and throat.
The smothering sensation of iron chilled his skin, making him feel heavy, his magic dull as it tried to reach
beyond the lethal cage.

Adam broke away and rolled out from under him,
his expression triumphant.

"We have him!"

Vadim was shoved onto his back and glared up at
his captors. He didn't recognize the other three men,
but he remembered the force of their combined power.

"I can still kill you, Adam. Unlike most Fae, iron
doesn't contain me completely, it just slows me down."

"But you won't be killing anyone, will you, Death
Bringer, while I hold the fate of your mate in my
hands." Adam smoothed his rumpled clothing. "Unless she kills herself without my input. She might do
that, I suppose, what with you abandoning her."

"You don't know my mate. She'll wait for you to
come after her, and she won't go down without a fight."

"So I hear."

He was hauled to his feet. The iron collar around his neck was choking him. He forced a thin bolt of power from his fingertip, and Adam backed away, cursing.

"I'll get free, eventually. Nothing can hold me forever."

"I'm counting on it, Death Bringer." His opponent smiled at the other men surrounding them. "When I kill him, I'll truly become the greatest collector of all time."

"You won't succeed."

"Why not? I thought you wanted to fight me."

"Oh, I do, and I shall." Vadim stared at the little weasel until the certainty faded from his gaze. "I'll enjoy ripping you limb from limb."

"We'll see about that." Adam nodded at the guards. "Take him below while we prepare the stadium for our battle."

In his present weakened condition, Vadim couldn't resist the concerted efforts of the four guards and the focused power of the sect, and was led down several flights of stairs into darkness, thick walls and the sounds of hopelessness. He was tossed ignominiously into a dark hole and left alone.

It took him several minutes to work out which way was up and where the door was. He leaned against the damp wall and took a quick survey of his current position. The sect had caught him before he attained his full powers. Coupled with Adam's threats to damage Ella's face, he hadn't stood a chance. With a groan, he considered what the hell had happened and what, if anything, he could do about it.

Who among his family had decided not to preserve

his mate's life? It could only be his father. But with what cause? Did he truly believe Vadim wouldn't turn against him? Didn't he understand his own creation? But what if it was worse than that? His fingers clenched into fists, his claws digging into his palms. What if his father understood him too well and had conspired with the sect to bring him down? That sounded far more likely.

And what of Ella? Was she slowly going mad, wearing someone else's face, or was she doing her best to pretend nothing was wrong while she waited for Adam to show up? He wouldn't put it past her. She wasn't going to make it easy for the face stealer. His heart ached. Had she believed him when he said he was leaving her forever? He damn well hoped so. Adam's last-minute offer to leave her alone if Vadim accompanied him immediately to Otherworld had seemed too good to be true, but he'd been willing to risk it if it kept Ella safe.

He swore softly and fluently in Fae. And what had he achieved? Ella's face was gone, and he was stuck in a dungeon. She'd be so proud...

Whatever happened, they would have to work fast if they intended to destroy him. He flexed his bruised fingers and imagined choking Adam to death again and finally revealing his real face. His power would overcome the deadly metal within a day or so, and he would be more dangerous than ever—and pissed off. Even though he was exhausted, he resisted the temptation to reach out to Ella. She didn't need to hear his woes. The last thing he wanted was for her to come running to save him. Hadn't he done his best to make sure she never wanted to see him again?

His smile faded and he listened intently to the magic-infused black darkness. His enemies might have forced him to play their games, but there was something they'd forgotten.

In Otherworld, he was invincible.

ELEVEN

ELLA HAD NO idea what time it was, only that since she was last outside, it had started raining and it was dark. As soon as she magically punched her way through the walls of her dungeon, she'd been returned to the square where she'd arrived. She loitered in the trees near the exit, concealed in the green shadows. Water continued to gush out of the fountain in a soothing refrain, but there was no sign of the queen or any of her guards.

That was weird.

Why *wasn't* anyone following her?

She checked around the square, using both Vadim's magic and her empath abilities. It was odd…the more she accessed his power, the stronger it seemed to be and the easier it rose to her amateurish commands. No wonder Vadim had been feared so greatly. She was only using a fraction of it, and it scared the pants off her. It was like being given the keys to a racing car after driving a tractor.

A shadow moved at her left. For a moment she wished she had her familiar weapon with her, but she had so much more in the tips of her fingers. Magic that was far more suited to Otherworld, as well. She needed to find Adam before the queen mother or the king found her. She attempted to clear her mind, but found it impossible as a clear sense of danger clouded her judgment.

"Dammit!" She walked toward the shadows, but instead of dispersing, they seemed to thicken. "What do you want?"

A guttural laugh answered her.

"What do you think, Soul Sucker?"

The advancing troll looked somewhat familiar. His heavily furred body was naked and his black eyes shone with hate. Behind him was a sniggering group of young Garden Fae.

"Do I know you?"

"You destroyed my nest and forced me back here." He raised his club. "Now you're going to pay."

He rushed her. Ella just had time to point her finger and shove magic at him before he cannoned into her and she fell to the ground. There was a *kaboom* and the acrid smell of burning fur. His screaming blocked out every other sound until an explosion of black blood made her gag, but at least stilled the screeching.

When she finally disentangled herself from the troll's soggy remains, she shuddered at the carnage.

"Too much power, Ella. Bring it down, girl."

She wiped at her face, which was sticky, and spat uselessly to rid herself of the unwanted taste of deep-fried troll. If any of the others had wanted to take a pop at her, her awesome display of power had sent them scurrying away. She headed back for the fountain so she could at least rinse herself off. How the hell did Vadim control himself?

She dipped her fingers into the flowing water and shivered. It was freezing. She suddenly remembered the spell he'd taught her and freshened herself up. The magic even repaired the holes in her pink jeans. Damn, it was useful. If only it worked on her face…

"Soul Sucker?"

She turned to see a woman standing quietly behind her. Even in the darkness, she registered the richness of the woman's dress and the sparkle of diamonds in her long dark hair.

"Let me guess. You're Morosov's mother."

"Indeed I am." The Fae inclined her head. "And you are my son's mate. I am so pleased to meet you."

"You are?"

"Of course. Why would you think otherwise?"

"Because everyone else in this batshit-crazy place, including me, wants to kill him."

"He is my son. How could I wish for his death?"

Ella scowled down at her boots. The apparent sincerity of the queen's answer made her feel like a loser who had given up on her mate way too fast. But the Fae were tricky like that. She shouldered her backpack.

"Is there something I can help you with? Otherwise I'd quite like to get on."

"Where are you going?"

"To find my face."

The queen drew closer. "You have been bespelled? I did wonder."

"Didn't anyone tell you? Normally I'm blond and blue-eyed. An idiot called Adam stole my face as his third trophy."

"But that wasn't supposed to happen."

She paused to study the queen's delicate features. The female looked about the same age as Ella was, and that couldn't be possible. It was also the second time someone had suggested Vadim had tried to protect her from Adam. "What *was* supposed to happen?"

"Nothing." The queen shivered. "Cygnet insisted that we stop Adam from taking your face."

"Well, it didn't work."

"But why?"

"Perhaps you'd better ask your husband and mother about that."

"We all agreed to it, as did the sect."

"Then someone didn't follow through, did they? You all wanted Morosov back here for your different reasons anyway. It's hardly surprising that my face wasn't enough to stop someone from getting what they wanted."

"Soul Sucker—"

Ella had to look away from the ethereal beauty of the queen, whose blue eyes were now swimming in tears.

"I understand that you are angry with us, but please consider what you intend to do."

She stared hard at the fountain and realized the figure of the woman was modeled on the queen behind her. *Awkward.* "I have to go. I intend to find Adam and get my face back."

"And what if he still has cygnet?"

"'Cygnet' is supposed to be the most powerful being in Otherworld. How could anyone 'have' him?" She glanced down at her hands. "I feel some of his power in me. I *know* how strong he really is."

"But what if his power is constrained?"

"By what?" Ella shook her head. "I'm so tired of everyone speaking around every subject. If he's so easily contained, why are you all so scared of him?"

The queen drew herself up. "His apparent weakness might not be our doing."

"So you're saying it's my fault?"

"You are mated to him."

"So what? It obviously means nothing to him. He walked out on me."

"There are many ways a male can show his love for his female, Soul Sucker."

"By buggering off to Otherworld to play at who's the biggest idiot? That's supposed to show that he *loves* me? I don't think so."

"Perhaps this time it is you who speak in riddles."

"What the fuck is that supposed to mean?"

The queen held her gaze. "He is your mate."

"So he's done all this for me, *right*."

"All I am saying, Soul Sucker, is that when you kill Adam, be very careful what you obliterate along with him. You alone have the power to destroy my son in many different ways, remember that." She inclined her head a regal inch. In the distance, the sound of voices rose. "I wish you well on your journey, and I urge you to leave right now. I will take care of the pursuit at this end."

"Well, thanks."

"Goodbye, Ella Walsh."

Ella had no time to reply as she focused on Adam and sent herself hurtling through Otherworld, landing with a bump outside a heavily fortified wall complete with security cameras and troll guards. Why were cameras even necessary in magic-centric Otherworld? She rubbed an elbow that had contacted hard against the wall.

"Ouch."

There was no cover around the perimeter of the wall, so she backed off until she reached the surrounding forest and sat down with her back against a tree.

Her whole body was shaking. Experience told her that there was no way she could move forward until she'd conquered her hunger and fatigue. She took off her backpack and opened it up. Inside were her emergency supplies. Two juice boxes, one of chocolate milk, three energy bars and two Pop-Tarts. A meal fit for the gods, as Feehan had always joked.

She paused for a moment to imagine what was going on back at the SBLE office. Would she ever see her colleagues again? Feehan had promised backup, but what could he do against the combined might of the sect and Vadim's family?

Not a lot. She was basically on her own.

She opened the first energy bar and a cranberry-apple juice box and alternately chewed and sipped her way through them. As she ate, she watched the wall to see if anyone was coming in or out of the one main gate, but all was quiet. Was Vadim in there with Adam? Did the sect know that she was there? She assumed they did.

The Fae queen had a point. If Vadim could kill anything in Otherworld, why wasn't Adam dead already? What was stopping him? Was he really trying to protect her? But why? He hardly knew her. She started on the second bar.

That wasn't true. He knew her better than anyone else in the world.

But then, he'd also told her he was hers for all eternity.

The rat.

She stopped chewing. Would she kill to get him back? It was something she had to consider before she charged in to get Adam. Everyone needed a plan. Did retrieving her face mean more to her than Vadim's life? She had more power in her than she'd ever imagined existed, and it was a huge responsibility. How did he deal with that on a daily basis? How had it felt to be the executioner of the Fae?

She stared out into the darkness, her appetite diminishing with every breath. Exhaustion threaded through her. In her present state, getting into the sect stronghold was beyond her. She'd be unable to control her power and would kill everyone in sight, or she'd implode and be dead in a second. The thought of another fried troll made her want to puke. Better to sleep for a while and then plan how to take down Adam and retrieve her face.

She closed her eyes and resolutely refused to think about Vadim. One problem at a time. That was all she could cope with right now.

SHE WOKE UP feeling cold and automatically grabbed for the covers. Which weren't there. Opening one eye, she remembered that she was in the middle of Otherworld, her head pillowed on her backpack and her clothes her only covering. Thank God she'd been wearing jeans, even if they did have a few new holes in them, despite her magical repairs. The smell of coffee floated past her nose and she abruptly sat up.

"I thought you might need this." Rossa handed her a jumbo-size cup. "I got it in your world."

Ella made an inarticulate sound of extreme gratitude and gulped at the scalding brew. After a few minutes she opened her eyes and regarded her companion.

"Don't you ever get cold?"

He glanced down at his superb physique and literally fluffed his feathers. "Not really. Why didn't you magic yourself up some blankets last night?"

"Because I keep forgetting that I can!" Ella glared at him. "I'm also terrified that I'll ask for a sleeping bag and conjure up a tree house complete with elevator and servants to plump my pillows."

"Magical power can be a very scary thing if you don't learn how to control it." Rossa settled himself comfortably across from her. "The main thing is, always treat it with respect."

"That's such a cliché. Did you bring food?"

He grinned at her. "What is your wish, fair lady?"

"A toasted egg-and-bacon muffin would be awesome."

"Then do it yourself. Just try and focus down, or it will be raining buns or something." She glowered at him and he shrugged. "It's good practice before you go in there with all guns blazing."

She thought lovingly about her egg-and-bacon muffin, pictured it in her mind and sent the smallest lick of power through the image. Her greasy, fatty treat appeared in her hands, wrapped in paper, and she actually squealed.

"I did it!" She devoured it in less than a minute. "Now I just have to work out how to harness the power of the muffin to the enormity of the task ahead." She nodded at the exterior wall. "Have you ever been inside this place?"

"No one has."

"That's stupid. Adam obviously has. I sensed him in there, and he's not alone."

"That's because cygnet's there, too."

"Are you sure?"

"I heard Adam brought him in yesterday."

Ella cautiously raised her shields. "I can't feel him." The emptiness was chilling. Even her anger wasn't big enough to conceal the loss of her awareness of her mate.

"That's probably because he's being held somewhere that's magically warded."

"But can't he get out of anything?"

Rossa looked critically at the walls. "It depends what they did to him. If he's totally encased in lead, Han Solo style, even he might find it hard to get out of that."

Despite the heat of the coffee, she shivered. "Surely, I'd know if he was dead..." She raised her head. "*Can* he die?"

"All Fae can die, given the right circumstances, you know that."

"But Morosov's different, isn't he?"

"He certainly is." Rossa sipped at his own coffee, his expression uncharacteristically somber. "But now that he has you, it's certainly possible he could die."

"Why?"

He sighed. "I told you he threatened to dismember his own family if they allowed Adam to take your face?"

"Yeah."

"What I didn't tell you was that he also said he'd take them all down with him if it meant that you survived."

She forced a laugh. "He's such a drama king."

"That wasn't his intent. He meant what he was saying, so *technically*, he could choose to sacrifice his immortality to save you." He winked at her. "Ah, the power of love."

"Don't say that." She hunched a shoulder at him and finished her coffee. "If I'm the source of his death, I want to be the one to hand out the sentence *and* execute it."

"That's funny, Soul Sucker."

She bared her teeth at him until he stopped laughing. "It wasn't a joke. Now how are we going to get into this place?"

He recoiled. "*We're* not going anywhere."

"You're not coming?"

Rossa stood up. "Of course I'm not! What do you think I am, suicidal?" He bowed elaborately. "You have all the power you need to get into this stronghold and save your prince."

"Thanks for the support." Ella finished her coffee and handed him the empty cup. "Can I ask you one more thing before you desert me?"

"Certainly, my lady."

"Now that we're both in Otherworld, when Morosov and I are *communicating*, can anyone else hear us?"

"In your thoughts, or did you mean something else entirely?" He winked lasciviously.

"I meant in our thoughts, you perv." She frowned at him. "Sometimes I can catch other people's internal conversations here."

"Like the way I can communicate with you?"

"Exactly."

"There's definitely a familial link, but I've always been told that the bond between a mated couple makes those conversations impenetrable for anyone else. A family member might know that you are speaking to each other, but not what you are saying."

"That's a relief."

"You're welcome. Good luck!"

He disappeared, grinning broadly, and she was alone once more. She hadn't really expected him to join her, but it had been fun watching him charm his way out of it. She returned her attention to the task in hand. There had to be a way to get through the walls without going through the main gate. Surely there had to be a service entrance somewhere.

With that in mind, Elia walked around the perimeter of the wall, stopping every so often to scan the stone face and identify any other entrances, magical or not. Once or twice, when she detected a change in the surface, she attempted to magic herself through it, but nothing seemed to work. It was a tedious business, not helped by her awareness that she was being watched and that time was running out. Whenever she used Vadim's magic, she was certain she was sending out a big fat "come and get me!" signal. She'd gathered so many enemies in Otherworld already, she was surprised she wasn't being hunted down by a mob. But perhaps because she was Vadim's mate, they were scared of her as well? It might answer the question as to why she hadn't been killed on arrival.

She halted opposite the main gate again and studied the movement of the four guards from the shade of the trees. Would it be easier to simply walk up to the gate, ask for Adam and go right in? By the time the alarm was raised, she reckoned she could take most of the opposition out. She didn't even need to see him. All she had to do was find where he kept his grisly trophies and take her face back.

How she was going to reattach it was another matter...

Well, it was pointless hanging about. She had to do *something*.

"Rossa? Come back here immediately!"

"*What?*" He reappeared, his expression grumpy. "I was just about to take a swim in a lake full of nubile young Water Fae."

"They can wait. I need you."

His smile widened and he placed his hand over his heart. "I've dreamed of you saying that to me. Have you decided to let fate take its course and follow your true destiny to have endless sex with me?"

"Not quite. I *need* you to help me create a diversion outside the main gate while I figure out a way to get in."

He took a step back. "No way."

She batted her eyelashes at him. "Oh, come on, Rossa. If you help me, I'll tell Morosov not to kill you when he executes all his other relatives."

"But if I *don't* help you, he'll die in there anyway."

"Do you really believe that? I don't think Adam has a clue what he's taken on, do you?"

Rossa stared pensively at the gates. "All right, I'll help as long as I don't get caught…"

TWELVE

"JUST KEEP AN eye on that fire and don't let it get out of control!" Ella yelled back at Rossa as plumes of thick black smoke billowed into the air. "Two of the guards are coming over!"

She ran headfirst into the magical smoke, using her hands to push it ahead of her like a shield. Her vision blurred, but she kept her sights on the gate and the two remaining guards. No one had seen her yet; they were all too busy staring at the fire she'd started. She sidestepped one of the remaining trolls, who had deserted his post, and slammed right into the massive door. Luckily, with all the noise, no one heard her, the bang or her muttered expletive.

Dammit, the door was locked. *Duh.* She closed her eyes and concentrated on exhuming its secrets and its weaknesses. Even as she searched, the timber groaned and shivered under her hand like a living being.

A snap of light whizzed past her nose as the smoke began to clear. Could they see her? Rossa had tried to help her with an invisibility spell, but she wasn't sure she had the ability to maintain it.

"Watch out!"

He was bellowing in her head. On the road behind her, she saw a figure approaching on the back of a horse, long blond hair flowing in the breeze, a hand raised to cause magical mayhem. If that wasn't Rossa ratting her out, it had to be Vadim's father.

Another blast of deadly power hit the door, bounced off, and buried itself in her left shoulder. It also weakened the integrity of the door. To her complete surprise, her desperate spell worked. She fell flat on her face on the other side and looked up into the unwelcoming black eyes of yet another troll, his long spear an inch from her nose.

"Hang on!" She got to her feet, arms raised, and ignored the horrendous pain in her shoulder. "I didn't mean any harm. I was just getting away from the smoke."

He didn't reply, just gestured at her with his weapon to move off. She didn't argue, and let him walk her down the narrow corridor. When he grunted, she paused obediently before a locked door. As he reached past her to unlock it, she brushed against his hand, pushing the smallest amount of power into him. Without a sound, he crumpled to the floor.

Using all her strength, she bundled the troll into one of the empty rooms and shut the door on him. She had no idea whether she'd killed him or not and didn't have time to check. At least he hadn't exploded all over her. A quick glance back at the entranceway confirmed her fears that Rossa and the fire's usefulness had ended and that the guards were once again mustering at the door. Would they sense her presence? Had the Fae king seen her escape through the smoke, or had he simply been attempting to get into the castle himself?

She didn't have time to care. With her current luck, she'd be captured before she even had a chance to look for her face. She could pick up no sense of Adam, so what should she aim for? An image of Brad and Ms. Phelps came into her head, and she focused on that instead. If she followed their empathic signals, she would hopefully find hers.

Carefully reciting the invisibility spell Rossa had hurriedly tried to teach her, she locked the door, gathered herself and ran toward the back of the massive building. Bits of her eluded the cloaking hex, so she caught the odd glimpse of her arm, her boot and her jacket like pieces of an ever-changing kaleidoscope. It was quite bizarre. Even though she was in a rush, she couldn't fail to notice the beauty of the place. It was a monument to the work of the sect, like a treasure seeker's private paradise where they could come and gloat about their cleverness.

There was another long hallway and, at the bottom, two huge gold doors, which were guarded. That had to be the place. Flattened against the wall, Ella spared a moment to touch her shoulder, and discovered the cloth of her jacket was still smoking and seared right through. Her skin was broken and discolored and radiated a weird metallic glaze. What the hell had the king fired at her? Molten lead? She stuffed one of Vadim's old handkerchiefs over the wound and used magic to repair the damage to her jacket. It would have to do.

After a deep, steadying breath, she sauntered down the hallway toward the two guards, her hands at her sides and her expression pleasant.

"Hey, what's up?"

The guards glanced at each other and then barred the door with their crossed spears. Ella flexed her fingers.

"I need to get in there, and you two are in my way.

I'm giving you this warning, because my magic is a lot stronger than my control, so I might *accidentally* fry you both." She raised her eyebrows. "So if you want to leave right now, I won't tell anyone, okay?"

The taller troll hissed at her in his own language and brought his spear up, nearly taking off the top layer of her new face.

She wasn't even aware she'd brought her hand up. "Don't say I didn't warn you." Power sliced from her, and the nearest troll screeched and fell to the ground. She swung to face the other one, but he was already running in the opposite direction, no doubt to raise the alarm. She stepped over the smoking body and pushed open one of the golden doors. Dark power streamed past her and through her, strengthening her magic.

She drew the door shut behind her—there didn't appear to be any way of locking it—and walked toward the furthest end of the vast cathedral-like room. The ceiling was domed and painted, the walls covered in trophies. It was also silent in the vast space, as if someone held their breath.

There.

Already aware of a huge commotion behind her, she ran toward her goal, her gaze fixed on the smiling face of Brad Dailey, the agony of Ms. Phelps, and her own familiar features.

"Thank God," she breathed, and reached out her hand to claim her prize.

Agony hit her hard and she staggered and held on to the nearest shelf. Looking down, she discovered her ankle was clasped firmly between the jaws of a small black dragon with eyes like rubies. Blood dripped from his jaws, and she knew it wasn't his.

"Oh, holy crap. No one said there would be *dragons*."

Before she could even think of retaliating, blackness engulfed her. She collapsed onto the carpet, aware of claws scrabbling at her legs, and then no more.

HIS CELL DOOR opened, and Vadim winced at the glare of the torch. Adam appeared, silhouetted against the light. He threw something at Vadim that hit him hard on the chest and came to rest on his lap.

"Bad news, Death Bringer. Now you have every reason to stay and fight."

He left the torch in the sconce by the door, giving Vadim some light, and withdrew. Still half-constrained by the leaden chains, he stared down at an all-too-familiar blue-and-red backpack.

Rage and grief coalesced in an unstoppable crescendo. He roared his fury at the top of his lungs, making his prison shake and the torch go out, leaving him in darkness with madness his close and dearly desired companion. Pain flooded his senses, tearing down his carefully constructed barriers. Inwardly he screamed for her, not willing to expose her precious name to his captors.

Slowly he came back to himself, his breathing ragged, his claws and fangs extended to their fullest, more beast than man, more filled with bloodlust than love. He forced himself to think through his instinct to simply destroy the world that had destroyed her.

A growl escaped him and he shut his eyes.

Think.

If she were dead, there would be no reason for him to do anything but annihilate Otherworld.

Adam wouldn't want to provoke that.

Would he?

Treacherous hope stirred in him. But if she wasn't dead, she was being held captive, her survival subject to his good behavior. If Adam expected him to fight, he obviously had to offer him an incentive to do so. Vadim took a deep steadying breath. If Ella was in Otherworld, he would find her, and be damned to anyone's expectations of him playing nice.

He reached out a shaking hand, grabbed the backpack and brought it to his face, inhaling Ella's scent. Beneath his tightening grip, the fabric started to tear, and he forced himself to relax. She felt close, but was that an illusion created by his need or was it reality?

Dammit, he was *touching* the backpack. His hands were free of the chains… His rage had fueled his power to new heights and he was recovering far more quickly than Adam might have anticipated. Vadim smiled into the darkness. Luckily, the attempt to undermine him had simply made him stronger. If Ella was near, he was going to find her and then let loose hell…

ELLA SAT UPRIGHT as a burst of magical power shook through the building, and more importantly, right through her. That had to be Vadim, but what was up with him, and where was she? Her head pounded and she was thirsty. Dammit, she was tired of waking up and not knowing what the hell was going on…

Her leg hurt.

Looking down, she couldn't see the damage the dragon had inflicted on her ankle, because someone or something had bandaged it up. Were dragon bites infectious? Would she need a shot? Where the hell would she get that?

She was in a small room with just a bed and a sink, rather like a monk's cell. There was a window, but it was set high in the wall. She didn't think it faced the outside, because the light was wrong. Tentatively, she searched for Rossa in her mind, but he wasn't there. All she could feel was Vadim, and even he felt *different*.

Her backpack had gone, which meant she had no food. Her stomach rumbled in protest. Maybe they knew that after twenty-four hours without coffee and donuts, she'd be willing to tell them anything they wanted. She couldn't sit here and wait for that to happen. With as much care as she could manage, she lowered her injured foot to the floor and immediately winced.

Would the cleanup spell work on wounds? It had certainly worked on clothes. She had to suspect that the words Vadim had given her were rather more complex than he'd let on. Or was it the power of Otherworld that enhanced them? She didn't know, and as long as it kept working, she wasn't going to second-guess herself. She felt her left shoulder, which was still throbbing like a bad tooth. Would it work on that too? Sounds beyond the door made her lie back down on the bed and close her eyes.

The door opened a scant inch, and a troll looked in on her.

"She's still unconscious, sir."

"Good. Leave her, then. The master wants to see her when she awakens."

The *master?* Ella wanted to snort. Adam obviously thought a lot of himself, but then power-crazed individuals usually did. The door shut, and she was alone again. She counted to five hundred and then cautiously got up and went over to the door. There was no sound from outside, but that didn't mean much. One of those stupid dragons might be curled up right on the threshold.

She turned back to the window. Surely that was the better option? Vadim had been a whiz at opening locked doors and getting through stuff, so she assumed she would be too. Unfortunately, she was pretty sure her ass wouldn't fit through the space. Maybe she could be like Alice and minimize herself a bit? She'd managed to do that at the front door without even thinking about it. Or could she walk through the wall?

She tried that first and ended up with a bump on her head and a bruised right knee. So the wall was out. How about the window? What would happen if she got stuck halfway? She sat back on the bed and considered her options. Another wave of raw power shook the building. Her heart rate sped up in response. Vadim was seriously pissed about something. Did she dare try and contact him? Did she want to? She took off her boot and threw it toward the open window. It bounced back off some invisible barrier.

She shoved her foot back into the boot and stood up. There was no time for finesse. *Fuck it.* She had to get out right now. From her position by the bed, she raised her hands and blasted power at the door. It blew outward and crashed against the door opposite with a horrendous crash. She didn't wait to see the reaction from her captors, but tried to magic herself back outside the complex. Nothing happened. In desperation, she started to run along the corridor in the hope of finding her way to the exit.

Her mind seemed to know where she was heading, so she followed her instincts, aware of pursuit but more than willing to kill to reach her goal. She reached an inner covered courtyard with a Japanese-style koi pond, miniature temple and a covered glass ceiling, her breath loud in her ears. The only other sound was the tranquil stir of the fountain.

"*Ella!*"

She clapped her hands over her ears as a possessive roar crashed over her senses.

"*Keep it down, Morosov!*"

"*ELLA!*"

Something huge and dark appeared on the other side of the space, and she forgot how to breathe. The creature was massive, with black wings, clawed fingers and sharp, wicked-looking teeth.

"Um, *Morosov?*"

The thing glared at her and then spoke, its bellowing voice beating against the walls like a drum.

"Who are you?"

"It's me, you big feathered dummy!"

She didn't have time to say more as the creature leaped forward, picked her up and shot upward, shattering the glass ceiling as they soared above the complex. Wind rushed through her hair, and she clung onto his massive shoulders as they climbed higher and higher. Had she ever mentioned to him how much she hated heights? She buried her face in his feathered chest as they plummeted back to earth, and kept it there until her feet touched something solid.

"Morosov, what the hell—?"

His mouth was on hers, his fangs grazing her lip until she opened to him. He backed her up until she was braced against a wall, or a tree, or something. She didn't care as long as it held her up and he continued to kiss her. His mouth devoured hers, and her hand tightened in the feathery softness of his long black hair. It was Vadim, but it wasn't. She probably should've been afraid.

He picked her up until her knees rode his hips and pressed himself against her hidden core. He didn't need to say anything; the thick ridge of his erection was driving her wild. It was only a couple of days since she'd last seen him, but it felt like forever. She magicked off her own jeans and panties and felt him there, hard and throbbing, needing her as much as she needed him.

Bigger everywhere, bigger there too, but she took him inside inch by inch and started to climax before he was all the way in, which made the last few thrusts even easier. She kept coming and he took everything, his clawed hands moving carefully over her, his mouth kissing hers, sliding down her throat to sink his teeth into her soft skin as he finally came hard and deep within her.

"Don't cry."

His voice resonated inside her, raw with emotion and saturated with power.

Was she crying?

What the hell was going on?

He held her close; his face buried in the crook of her neck, his cock still inside her. In that first confused moment when he saw her altered face, he'd almost killed her… The shock of it still reverberated through him. He hadn't expected her to be that close.

She bit down hard on the side of his neck and he flinched.

"Get off me."

Reluctantly he released her, found her pants and handed them back. He didn't want her to put them on just yet. He wanted her again.

She struggled into her purple panties and then her pink jeans. Even though it was difficult, he couldn't stop staring at her face.

"It is uncanny. You look like my sister."

"And you look like a bad Big Bird." She glared at him and then touched her face. "I know, it's creepy, isn't it? I wonder if Adam did it deliberately."

"I'm sure he did."

Vadim walked away from her and sat on a nearby log. They were in a clearing high up in the uninhabited mountains to the north of the sect's stronghold, a place only his immediate family knew about. The feathers on his wings caught the slight breeze, and he barely resisted the urge to unfurl them and shake out his tension. He'd hoped Ella would never have to see him like this, but it was too late to change back into what she was used to.

"What are you doing in Otherworld, Ms. Walsh?"

She folded her arms across her chest. *Never a good sign.* "Don't worry, fathead, I wasn't looking for you."

He tried a neutral smile. "You seem to have found me anyway."

"I was at Adam's because I wanted my face back. That's the only reason why."

She was definitely mad at him. Was that a good sign or a bad one?

"What happened to you, anyway?" She waved a hand at him.

He looked down at his body. "This is my true form. Does it offend you?"

"It's nothing to do with me, is it?"

He sighed. Perhaps it was better to give her an open target for her pent-up rage. "It's going to be like this, then? You having a major hissy fit over nothing?"

"Nothing?" She stalked over to him and stuck her finger in his face. "Don't you dare fuck with me, Morosov! You waltzed off to Otherworld, telling me to stay put like a good little girl and insisting you didn't need me anymore. Why should I care what becomes of you?"

"You're here, aren't you?"

"As I said, and as I've already told your family more than once, I came to get my face back, not to baby-sit you."

Diverted from his true purpose, just as she had probably intended, he couldn't help asking, "You've met my family?"

She counted on her fingers. "Your grandmother stuck me in a dungeon to keep me out of the way, your father wanted to blackmail me into taking you back to San Francisco and your mother practically cried all over me to save you."

He focused on the most dangerous part. "You saw my father? What else did he say to you?"

She finally looked at him. "You don't want to know."

"He said I'm a monster, didn't he?"

She shrugged. "Something like that."

"Then I understand why you aren't pleased to see me." He had to look away. "I can't defend my past."

She didn't even attempt to contradict him. An iron band closed around his heart. "What do you want from me, Ella?"

"To help me get my face back and bring Adam down."

"That's all?"

"I haven't decided about the rest, yet."

"But we're mated."

Her unfamiliar blue eyes shot sparks. "And you walked out on me!"

He grabbed her hand and held fast. "You know why I left." She tried to pull away, but he wouldn't let her. "I had to try and protect you. You're not dumb, I'm sure you worked that out for yourself."

"That you're such a hero?"

"No, that despite everything, you mean more to me than anything else in my life." Something hot fell on his skin and he realized she was crying. "Ella—"

"I don't need this right now, Morosov, all right? I just want to get my face back. If you can't help me with that, go away."

He released her hand and stared down at the trampled grass. Perhaps he had misjudged her. Her fear of rejection and abandonment ran so deep... Perhaps his father's words had made her hate him beyond reason, and even beyond their mated state. He wasn't surprised. Who would want to be mated to an executioner? There was still one thing he could do for her...

"There is a way for you to regain your face."

She looked back at him, her eyes still full of tears. "There is?"

He slowly stood up and bowed. "I would be more than willing to help you achieve your aim."

Hope blossomed in her eyes. "Thank you."

He nodded. "Perhaps after you've rested for a while, we can discuss how we mean to go on."

SHE WOKE UP feeling warm, for once, and slowly opened her eyes to discover she was in a sleeping bag with a proper pillow under her head. Trust Vadim to have all the right camping gear. Despite the fact that she was out in the middle of nowhere with a no-good shape-shifting Fae prince, she felt remarkably safe. The clearing was in darkness, only the light from a small fire breaking the gloom. She sat up and scanned the area. The high peaks of mountains and pine trees surrounded them, and the air had an icy freshness to it that literally caught at her breath.

Behind her, in the forest, she could pick up the presence of smaller woodland Fae and other species. Nothing approached the fire or the solitary male who sat facing it. She'd never thought of herself as a coward, but part of her wanted to turn over, go back to sleep and pretend none of this had really happened. Something about the rigid set of his shoulders made her get up and walk toward him.

He spoke before she reached him.

"There's coffee keeping warm by the fire."

"Cool." She went forward and poured herself a cup of the fragrant brew. "Thanks." She stood and looked out over the clearing. "You should've woken me earlier."

"There was no need. It is too late to start back for the palace. Adam will not find us here."

"Did you ward the clearing?"

"It is always like this. Only those of the Royal blood can get through the shields. It's a place of refuge."

She got the sense that he'd been there a lot. She looked down at her boot and kicked a stone. "Thanks for the sleeping bag. That's the first decent nap I've had since I got here."

"You are welcome."

She kicked another stone, which thunked against the log he was sitting on. God, this was awkward. Why the hell was she feeling sorry for him?

"Did you think I'd come to save you?"

She caught a hint of a smile. "No one needs to save me, Ms. Walsh. I'm Death Bringer."

"So your father said."

His expression went blank. "Do you want something to eat?"

So he didn't want to talk about that. What a surprise. "Of course I do." She held up her hand. "But I know how to do that stuff myself now." She concentrated on the image of a triple cheeseburger and fries, but nothing happened. "Damn, I had it the other day."

"It's not your fault. The wards around this space are extremely powerful."

"Can't you get through them, either?"

"Not unless I want to bring my entire family down on us, but I have something better." He held up her backpack.

"Where did you get that?"

"Adam gave it to me."

"Why?" She took it from his outstretched hand.

"To mess with my head?"

She sat down beside him and rummaged in the backpack. "I have a couple of juice boxes if you want one, and some protein bars."

"That would be wonderful."

He was being terribly polite, which meant that underneath he was as pissed off as she was. When she handed over his share, she risked a joke. "How the mighty have fallen."

"Needs must, Ms. Walsh."

"Why are you calling me that?"

He ripped open his protein bar using his teeth. "I thought you'd prefer it."

"Would you like me to start calling you Death?"

"Not really."

"Then Ella will do nicely." She struggled to open the foil packaging of her bar. Vadim reached across and slashed through the foil with one long claw. "Thanks. Since when did swans have talons?"

"In Otherworld I can become anything I choose."

"You're full of surprises, aren't you?"

"Most of them unpleasant, as you've no doubt discovered." He finished his bar and started on his juice. "I noticed you were limping earlier. Is there something wrong with your ankle?"

"I was bitten by a dragon."

His head snapped round. "What kind?"

"Does it really matter? Aren't they supposed to be extinct?" He continued to stare at her, and she sighed. "Fine. It was small and black, with red eyes and sharp teeth. Does that help?"

"You got as far as the trophy room?"

"I got as far as reaching for my face, and then that damned dragon closed his jaws around my ankle, and I lost it."

"May I see your ankle?"

She stuck out her booted foot. "Someone bandaged it up for me while I was out of it. I was going to try that cleanup spell you gave me on it, but I didn't get a chance."

"Let me see."

He gently maneuvered her foot onto his thigh and removed her boot and striped orange sock. She winced as he folded back her jeans to reveal her bandaged ankle.

"Is a dragon's bite poisonous?"

"It can be, but if someone went to the bother of treating the wound for you, I suspect they wanted to keep you alive."

"To use as bait."

He looked up into her eyes, his own faintly amused. "I was already caught."

"You were?"

"I have to thank you, actually." He started to unwrap the bandage. "My rage at your capture allowed me to slough off the effect of my shackles with greater speed than my enemies expected."

"Well that's cool, because your rage woke *me* up and helped me make the decision to escape. How's that for anger management?" She flinched as he finished uncovering the wound and touched her skin.

"I can see the tooth marks, but there isn't any infection. Is it still sore?"

"A little."

"I can fix that." Warmth flowed from his fingers into her skin, and slowly the ache disappeared. "Is that better?"

"Much." She had to get his hands off her before she launched herself into his lap and covered him in kisses.

Being close to him was so confusing. She was never sure if she wanted to slap him or fuck him. God forbid she ever got up the nerve to do both. In his current form he'd probably love it. "Thanks."

He hesitated, his broad shoulders blocking out the light from the fire. "There is something else hurting you."

There was no point in prevaricating. She touched her upper arm. "My shoulder. When I was trying to find my way in the main entrance earlier, I got caught by some sort of magic pulse rebound."

"You broke into the palace?"

"Yeah, did you think Adam dragged me in by the hair?"

"I *assumed*—"

"Well, we all know what that makes you, don't we? I broke in by myself." She glared at him. Yeah. It was so much easier to feel mad than sorry for him. She did mad *so* well. "I am perfectly capable of evading capture and executing my own plan." There was no need to tell him that five seconds after getting through the door, she'd been captured again. She certainly wasn't telling him that she owed most of her success to his powers and Rossa's help. "I'm not stupid, you know."

"I never thought that."

"You said I would be a liability in Otherworld."

"I *said* what I needed to say to keep you safe."

"And then waltzed over here by yourself and were immediately captured."

"I—"

"Just because you were dumb enough to get caught, doesn't mean I had to be too."

He breathed out carefully through his fangs. "I

didn't get caught. I allowed Adam to bring me to Otherworld."

"Oh, that's right. Your noble gesture to save my pretty face."

"Who told you that?" His question was sharp.

"Several people. Apparently there was *supposed* to be a pact to prevent Adam from taking my face. A pact brokered by you." He shifted in his seat but remained silent. "Aren't you going to defend yourself?"

"I thought you said you didn't want to discuss our relationship."

"This isn't about us, this is about you threatening your entire family if they didn't do what you wanted. Who the hell *does* that?"

"Death Bringer does." He scowled at her. "And this isn't about my family. You're pissed because I left you. Can't you even admit that?"

She drew herself up to her full height. "I thought *that* was too obvious to mention. Why would I care that you deliberately tried to alienate me and kept me in the dark about your true purpose? Who the fuck would mind that they were deemed *useless?* Why the hell would I even give it a second thought?" She realized she was shouting and that he was regarding her with a faint smile. "Don't you dare laugh at me!"

"I'm not laughing. You've expressed your lack of concern for my welfare many times before."

She hated the way the light had gone from his face and that she was responsible for it. "Do you want them all to loathe you?"

"If it brings results, why not?" He shrugged. "They made me what I am. Perhaps it is time that they learn to fear what they can no longer control."

There was a hardness to him that she hadn't expected, a grandeur and arrogance that fitted the immense power of his true form. He'd always seemed strong, but now he was truly frightening. He stood up and walked away, presenting her with a fine view of his wings and the tight, high curve of his ass.

"You're saying you'd kill everyone who loves you, just for me?"

He swung around to face her. "They don't love me. They are afraid of me and wish to control my power."

"Which is why you left Otherworld in the first place."

"Yes."

"If we can retrieve my face, would you stay in Otherworld or go back to San Francisco?"

"That's up to you, isn't it?"

This time she was the one to look away. Damn the man for demanding certainties she wasn't yet prepared to give him. She was no therapist, but didn't he understand that his desertion had activated all her fears of abandonment and betrayal? She hadn't expected that, hadn't ever wanted to feel like a bawling five-year-old kid left at an institution again. She'd spent years learning to protect herself from the hurt, putting up barriers to keep herself safe. Why should she let him know that seeing him made everything right in her world? Why give him the ammunition to destroy her again?

"It's getting late. Do you want to take a look at my shoulder, or not?"

He regarded her steadily for a long moment. "Still hiding, Ella?"

"I'm not hiding anything."

"Liar."

He flowed toward her; the beauty of his movements made her think of sex and entangled limbs and kisses. "For a female who prides herself on speaking her mind, how is it that for me, your *mate*, the male who shares your thoughts, you have nothing but deception? Is what you feel for me too 'honest' to be shared?"

"As I said, it's getting late."

"Then show me your wound." His tone was impersonal and polite again. It made her want to sink her teeth into his flesh.

"*Be my guest.*"

Ignoring his suggestive intrusion into her mind, she eased out of her jacket and then her rose-covered blouse to reveal the handkerchief that covered her shoulder.

"Is that one of mine? I can never find any of my handkerchiefs. What the hell do you do with them?"

"I had to pack it with *something*, and it's not as if you have any pocket to put it in here." She carefully removed the folded cotton.

Vadim's breath hissed out. "*Ddwu.*"

"What?"

She awkwardly turned her head to stare down at her shoulder, which appeared to be glowing with a dull red light.

"That's not good, is it?"

"No."

"Can you fix it?"

"It's difficult. Where did the spell come from?"

"I'm not quite sure. As I said, I was trying to get into through the main door when someone started shooting spells. One of them rebounded and hit my arm."

"Was it one of the guards?"

"No, it was some guy on a horse." She hesitated. "I did wonder if it was your father."

"That might explain it." He sat back. "If it was him, I suspect he wasn't aiming for the door."

"Then make it better!"

"I can stop the pain and slow down the spread of the poison, but I can't remove it completely."

"Back up." She grabbed his hand. "What poison?"

"Perhaps that was a bad choice of words. The substance in your arm means that my father can always find you. The spell is like his personal brand."

"Why would he want to do that?"

His smile wasn't pleasant. "You tell me."

She stared right back at him. "I told you. He was very keen for me to take you away from Otherworld."

"And what did he promise you in return for that small service?"

"He offered to get my face back."

He took his hand away. "No wonder he wanted to put his mark on you."

"You're such an idiot, Morosov. I didn't accept his terms. I told him I was quite capable of achieving what I wanted without his help."

"And how did he take that?"

"Not very well, obviously."

"And yet you are still alive."

"I'm not stupid—I didn't outright tell him no. I said I wanted to think about it."

He shook his head. "Sometimes your gall amazes me, Soul Sucker. There are not many people on the earth who argue with my father and survive."

"You did."

"And look where it got me." His faint smile disappeared. "Right back where I started."

"That's not quite true, is it? You're no longer under his control, and you have me."

"I thought you'd disowned me."

"I said I needed some *space.* I didn't say I was running out on you. I'm still a professional. You're my SBLE partner."

He stared at her for a long moment. "You just can't say it, can you? You just can't admit that I mean anything to you at all." He returned to kneel at her feet. "Let me do what I can for your shoulder."

As he worked, she looked down at his bowed head and admired his long silky hair and the curve of his spine. Even if he disagreed, she thought he was beautiful in his true form. She reached out and touched the back of his neck with one finger, stroking the soft down. His folded wings quivered.

"Ella, stop it..."

She stroked down his spine and he went still.

"Are you finished with my shoulder?"

"Yes."

"Can I touch your wings?"

In answer, he spread his wings wide. He continued to kneel like an angel at prayer as she went to stand behind him. Using both hands, she started where his wings emerged from his shoulders and traced the long line outward. The span was too great for her to encompass by herself. She leaned in close, her hands spread wide and her breasts pressed to his spine. He shuddered.

"You look so threatening, and yet up close, you're

soft and feathery." She buried her face in the crook of his neck.

She slid her hands around his chest and felt the frantic beating of his heart. He might look different, and so did she, but at their core, nothing had changed. They were both outsiders in their worlds. It was a hard truth to swallow, but she still wanted to jump his bones.

"Stop thinking about sex."

"Why?" She found his nipples and used her finger and thumb to shape them.

"Because you said—"

She bit his neck. "I said I wanted time to think about our *relationship.* This is about sex."

"Isn't that my line?"

She bit harder, and he winced. "Indulge me, Morosov."

"And if I don't want to be used as a sexual convenience?"

"Then say no. Take your little fluffy pillow and sleeping bag and go over to the other side of the fire. I promise I won't come after you."

Underneath her hands, his massive body tensed. She closed her eyes and nuzzled his throat. "Vadim..."

"I am your mate." He sighed, the sound echoing in the quietness of the glen. "I'll take whatever you have to offer me, Ella. You know that."

She closed her eyes against yet another attack of unwanted emotion and wrapped her arms around him. Sex was so much simpler. A meeting of bodies and an exchange of pleasure, a way to show him what she couldn't say. Didn't he get that? Or perhaps he did and was allowing her the opportunity to share how she really felt.

She groaned. God, this caring for someone was *so* confusing.

VADIM SLOWLY DREW his wings in, their tips brushing Ella's side until she was almost enclosed. She stepped back and he turned around and drew her against his chest. In his true form, kneeling down, they were almost the same height. He stroked the side of her cheek, his thumb angled under her jaw, and tried to remember the real face that lay beneath the mask.

Closing his eyes, he let even that image go and saw her truly, his thoughts marching with hers and their needs entwined. Everything she hadn't been able to say flowed over him and through him. Why didn't she have the words? Would she ever admit how she felt out loud?

"It's all right," he murmured, and kissed the side of her mouth.

"It isn't. I *hate* crying and I'm being a wuss."

"You've had a difficult day."

"I sure have. I've been bitten by dragons, imprisoned, pursued by trolls, shot at—" He stopped her talking by taking control of the kiss. She continued in his head "—*flown away by winged creatures to magical glades…*"

He skimmed his hands down her sides and rested them on her hips.

"I frightened you?"

"Only for a second, until I realized who it was."

"I'm glad."

She kissed his forehead. "I'm not sure why everyone else is so afraid of you, really. You're like a big fluffy marshmallow."

He slid his hand around the back of her neck, trapping her. "Only with you."

She held his gaze. "Is it true that you can kill anything in Otherworld?"

"Yes."

"Even immortal Fae?"

He nodded. Why did she think he was an outcast?

"Wow. That's some responsibility." She kissed his nose. "Will you sit down?"

"I am."

She smacked his shoulder. "I mean cross-legged."

"If you wish, Soul Sucker."

She fixed him with her more usual intimidating glare. He didn't mind it so much now; in fact he'd even begun to miss it.

"It wasn't your soul I was thinking of sucking." Her gaze dropped to his groin and his already erect cock. "It's a good job I'm not allergic to feathers, isn't it?"

She leaned forward and rubbed her face against his flat stomach, her tongue sneaking out to lick his already-wet shaft. He placed his hands flat on the ground, taking more weight on them as his hips jerked forward to meet the demands of her mouth. He wanted to grab her and pull her down over his aching flesh, but he'd already done that once tonight. It was her turn to dictate and his to endure.

And she made the most of it, teasing and learning his new body, making him wait and making him beg for her. When she finally shed her clothes and lowered herself over him, he was shaking with need. He wrapped one hand around her hips to hold her close and surged upward, enjoying her every climax along the way until she screamed and came again, dragging him with her in huge pumping waves of need. She collapsed over him and he held her tight. Did it matter that she couldn't say the words out loud? That she insisted it was just about sex? He knew her on a subliminal level that no other being would ever achieve. He knew everything…

Was it enough? He wasn't sure, but he'd do anything to keep her safe. He eased her over onto her side, placing his sleeping bag underneath them both. She grumbled something and clung to him. In truth, if he managed to help her retrieve her face, it might be the last thing he ever did for her.

A tremor in the shield caught his eye and he sat back up, pushing Ella behind him.

"What is it?"

He didn't bother to answer her, all his attention fixed on the male who was materializing in the glade.

"Death Bringer." The Fae king bowed. "I apologize for intruding on such a tender moment, but needs must."

Vadim rose to his feet. "What do you want?"

"Dear me, such hostility. Didn't your mate tell you about my offer?"

"She told me she'd met you."

"And not the rest?"

His father strolled closer. He wore a flowing red cloak and low-slung leather pants with a silver belt. His hair touched his shoulders and gleamed like spun flax in the moonlight. Power radiated from him, and Vadim automatically raised his shields. It had taken him years to learn how to keep his father out of his mind. It was a lesson once brutally mastered, never forgotten. Of course Ella ignored his efforts to keep her safe and stood shoulder to shoulder with him. At least she'd put her clothes back on…

"Soul Sucker, why didn't you relay my message?"

"That you want him gone from Otherworld because you're scared of him? I think he knows that already."

His father's assessing gaze swung around to Ella. Inwardly Vadim groaned. Sometimes his mate's ability to piss people off was a real liability.

"You've forgotten what I offered you so soon?"

"I haven't forgotten anything, because I didn't agree to anything. You disappeared in a huff before I could make up my mind."

"Ella—please, shut up."

Something of the urgency in his voice must've got through to her, because she paused and looked up at him. "What's wrong?"

"I think he's trying to remind you that I am Fae royalty and that I'm not used to being treated with such disrespect."

Ella raised her eyebrows. "What are you going to do? Set Morosov on me? He won't harm me."

Vadim looked at his father's face and saw it then, a hint of fear quickly masked. He steeled himself as his father's golden gaze swung back toward him.

"Death Bringer, all is not as it seems."

"In what way, Father?"

"Your mate has not been telling you the truth."

"I doubt that." He reached out a hand and grasped Ella's arm, holding her close. As long as they were linked, he no longer thought his father was strong enough to beat them. "Mates cannot lie to each other."

"She intends to do you harm."

"And you don't?"

His father ignored the question, and pointed over at Ella's backpack.

"Search her possessions."

"Hey, that's my stuff. There's nothing in there that could hurt a fly." Ella lunged for the backpack as the king sent it flying toward them.

"She lies, Death Bringer."

"Ella, let it go, he's just—"

She leaped for the backpack separating herself from him, and everything seemed to slow down. His father's magic swept between them, cutting her off from him and immobilizing her in midair.

"Don't you wonder why she wants her backpack so badly?"

"Let her go, or I will retaliate."

"She has my mark on her. Shall I let her die of it?"

Power sizzled between them, scorching the grass. A void opened in the shield and several Fae guards stepped through.

"What do you want?"

His father drew himself up. "Justice?"

"For what?"

"For those you killed?"

"You were my master, I killed where you bade me!"

"Not at the end."

"What are you saying?"

"I want justice, Death Bringer, for Ciaran and Nia."

"No!" Vadim took a hasty step forward, but it was too late. The guards surrounded him.

"Don't fight them, and I'll keep her alive to watch you stand trial."

His last sight was of his father standing tall in the clearing, his predatory smiling gaze fixed firmly on an immobile Ella.

THIRTEEN

"WHERE'S MOROSOV?" THE moment the spell lifted, Ella started speaking.

"He's quite safe." The Fae king looked up from the scroll he was reading. "You will see him presently."

She was sitting in a chair in what appeared to be an old library. Her backpack had disappeared again. She tried to get up but was unable to move.

"I'm starting to hate this place."

Just to make a point, she focused down, found the spell and blew it away. Standing up, she stretched and headed toward Vadim's father. Her ankle felt fine, although her shoulder still throbbed.

"Very clever, Soul Sucker. It seems as if you are developing some magical talents of your own." He turned toward her. "But there is no point in running away or seeking trouble. Your evidence will be required very shortly."

"Evidence for what?"

"Death Bringer's trial for murder."

"Oh, that." She frowned. "But what about the sect? Don't they have priority?"

"Over a trial for the wanton spilling of Royal blood? I don't think so. They will be content to wait for our verdict."

"So Morosov will get off, then, and live to fight another day?"

The Fae king smiled. "You are so amusing, my child. Just remember that if you want your mate to live long enough to stand trial, you must behave yourself."

A bell began to toll and he stood. "The trial will be starting very shortly. Come with me."

Unfortunately, she couldn't think of anything to do but follow him. Four Fae guards fell in behind her as they marched along a series of hallways and down the wide stairs. As soon as her feet hit the ground floor, the guards closed around her and she could see nothing but their broad shoulders and armor. They continued to move forward and eventually came into a less crowded space, which smelled of old books, ink and dust.

Above her head there was an ancient hammer-beam ceiling, the beams darkened with smoke. The floor was wooden planks and scratched and dulled with age. It reminded her of photos of the thousand-year-old Westminster Hall in London, where the English parliament used to sit.

"Sit here."

She did what she was told, aware that Vadim's life was currently in her hands. Was that what they were hoping? That she'd accidentally lose it and give the court the excuse they needed to execute her mate? *Could* they execute him?

While she waited, she surveyed the scene. Slightly raised on a platform, a long oak table with five chairs dominated the end of the room. In front of the table was a stand, and on either side of the stand were two smaller tables, just like a regular courtroom. Behind her were several rows of benches, currently unoccupied. She looked around for the Fae king, but there was no sign of him.

"Hey, you." She nudged the nearest guard. "Is this trial open to the public?"

He looked down at her from his considerable height. "No, Soul Sucker. It is a matter for the blood Royal to determine alone."

She winked at him. "Thanks, handsome."

He tried to look stern but failed and had to look away from her. Somewhere trumpets blared. The guard slid a hand under her elbow, bringing her to her feet.

"All rise."

A door opened to the right of the long table and several figures emerged. Ella recognized Vadim's grandmother, mother and father, but not the last guy.

"Who's the dude with the white hair?" she whispered to the long-suffering guard.

"That is a representative from the Dark Court."

The two males took the seats on the left, and the females sat on the right. The door opened again, and someone Ella unfortunately recognized all too well came out.

"Oh, crap."

"Did you speak, Soul Sucker?"

"Not to you." She focused her gaze on the smiling face of the man she knew as Drew Spencer, the head of the SBLE in North America and possibly the rest of the known universe. She hadn't liked him the first time she met him. He hadn't really taken to her either.

"Why is Drew Spencer here?" she said loudly.

The Fae king looked over at her. "He is knowledgeable about both our world and the SBLE. Therefore he was acceptable to all present as an impartial judge."

"I bet you didn't consult Morosov about that."

The Fae king ignored her and turned his attention back to Drew Spencer, who waited patiently by the dais.

"You may proceed."

Spencer bowed, took his place at the center of the table and addressed the four occupants. He wore a long white robe that made him look vaguely clerical and completely judgmental.

"I will call each witness and allow you the opportunity to ask as many questions as you wish. Then, if necessary, we will hear from the defendant. After all the evidence has been presented, I will retire to consider my verdict and then present it to the court."

The older queen nodded and clasped her hands together in front of her on the table, her head bowed. None of them appeared to have noticed Ella's presence, although she was certain they were all aware of her. She glanced around the otherwise-deserted courtroom. Was she the only witness?

"Bring in the accused."

A flash of light and Vadim was there, enclosed in a silver cage of pulsing energy. She attempted to touch the power source with her mind, but it seemed determined to rebuff her. If she needed to get to him, how the hell was she going to get through something she couldn't analyze and defeat?

She stared at her mate, who was doing his best imitation of a faultless hero going to the guillotine, his face immovable and his mouth stern. Was she going to rescue him? Had that ever been in doubt?

There was a gentle cough beside her, and she turned to see Feehan and Liz sliding into the seats next to hers.

"Guys!" she whispered. "Am I glad to see you!"

"Is that Vadim?" Feehan said in her ear. "He looks… different."

She couldn't help snorting. "He certainly is."

The guard cleared his throat warningly, and Ella stopped talking.

Spencer looked down at the parchment he held in his hand. "Death Bringer, you are accused of the worst crime a subject can commit in Otherworld, the spilling of Royal blood. Your *own* blood. Do you wish to enter a plea?"

"What's the point?"

Spencer sighed and looked beyond Vadim at the guard beside Ella.

"Please escort Mr. Feehan to the stand."

Feehan went forward, smoothing his brown spotted tie over his rounded stomach as he passed Vadim. The Fae king stood up and bowed.

"Mr. Feehan, I understand that you are an employee of the SBLE."

"That's correct."

"I also understand that the accused came to work for you this summer."

"Yes, he did, but not looking like that."

"How did he present himself to you?"

"As a member of a Russian SBLE team who was an expert on empaths and serial killers."

"So he lied to you."

Feehan shrugged. "Not really."

"What do you mean?"

"My team is a secretive lot. They've had to deal with a lot of prejudice in our world. I don't blame them if they wish to hide their pasts and their talents."

For the first time since she'd met him, Ella wanted to give Feehan a big fat kiss.

"When did you begin to suspect that the accused was not being completely honest with you?"

"As I said, he never tried to hide his Otherworld abilities, so he was hardly being dishonest. When they were needed, like when he saved Ella from the Siren, he used them. When I asked him to take on certain tasks in the current investigation, he volunteered the information that he had contacts here in Otherworld who could help us out. So I knew he had powers."

"But didn't you begin to suspect he was lying to you?"

Feehan fiddled with his tiepin. "When we saw the first clear image of the killer and he looked just like Vadim, we did get a bit worried, but we cleared that up."

"You mean he managed to deceive you as to his true purpose?"

Feehan turned to Drew Spencer. "I thought I was here as a character witness for Vadim, not to incriminate him. He isn't on trial for anything he's done while in my employ, is he?"

Spencer nodded. "You are correct, Mr. Feehan. I believe your questioner was trying to establish that Death Bringer is untrustworthy in all aspects of his life."

"Which Mr. Feehan didn't actually say." The interruption came from Vadim's grandmother, who smiled at a blushing Feehan. "In truth, I gather my grandson was an excellent and valued employee of yours."

"Yes, he was...I mean, he is." Feehan risked a glance over at Vadim. "Despite him turning into...that."

"Thank you, Mr. Feehan."

"You're welcome."

Spencer glanced at the other occupants of the table. "Does anyone have any more questions for this witness?"

No one replied, and he inclined his head toward Feehan.

"Thank you for your input. You may leave now."

He turned sharply on his heel and was escorted out after giving Ella a wink and a thumbs-up.

"Please call Ms. Liz Goddard."

"Wish me luck!" Liz whispered.

Vadim's father stood and nodded at Liz.

"Ms. Goddard, you are the Fae-Web liaison in the SBLE special team?"

"Yes, I am."

And what percentage Fae are you, roughly?"

"About thirty-five percent."

"Can you tell us about Death Bringer and his suspicious involvement in your last case?"

Liz raised her eyebrows. "That's hardly an unbiased question, is it? Who are you, exactly?"

"I'm his father."

"Oh, right." Liz blushed and looked at Spencer. "Are you okay with me sharing classified SBLE information here?"

"Please go ahead."

"Whenever I attempted to connect up the evidence for the latest case, *Vadim* showed up in my Fae-Web. I was uneasy that he seemed so central to the issues and shared those concerns with my team." She glanced over at Ella. "Well, initially with everyone except Ella. She was firmly on his side, and that's understandable."

"Are you suggesting that Soul Sucker was aware of

the accused's actions in this case and was helping him conceal his true motive?"

"That's stretching it a bit. I knew Ella wasn't quite being her normal self because of how she felt about Vadim."

"Did you at any point confront the accused?"

"Sure, but there wasn't a problem. When I asked him publicly what was going on, he was more than willing to help. He offered to get us any information we needed from his contacts in Otherworld."

The Fae queen spoke up for the first time. "So, in fact he offered to help you with the investigation, not hinder you?"

Liz turned gratefully toward the queen. "Yes, that's exactly it."

"But, Ms. Goddard," the king interrupted. "Are you saying your Fae-Web was wrong? I didn't believe that was possible."

"My Fae-Web reached a series of conclusions that are always open to interpretation. Once I was assured that Vadim intended to help us chase down the face stealer, I knew the issues would be resolved."

"And were they?"

Liz hesitated. "To a certain degree."

The Fae king bowed. "Your loyalty to your team and its members does you credit, Ms. Goddard, but even you aren't prepared to lie for him completely. The accused's offer to help you might have allayed some of your fears, but I bet it brought up a hundred new ones."

He turned to address Spencer. "Let me recap. In essence Ms. Goddard is saying that despite her desire to believe that 'Vadim' meant well, her Fae-Web chose not to trust him, and placed him squarely in the center of the case."

"*She* said she believed him. Does that count for nothing?" the Fae queen said quietly. "Fae-Webs can be wrong. And what does this current SBLE case have to do with the charges laid against my son today?"

It was the question that was bothering Ella too. She looked at Vadim, but he appeared lost in a trance, his brow furrowed, his gaze inward. This was one crazy trial process, when the prosecutors could ask loaded questions and the overall judge was a man who'd shown open dislike for Vadim when they last met. What chance did he have for a fair hearing?

"Thank you, Ms. Goddard."

Liz waved as she passed Ella but didn't get to stop and chat.

The Fae king continued to stand and stare at his wife. "As to your question, my queen, all will be answered in good time."

"Yeah, right," Ella muttered.

"Call Rossa."

The blond Fae appeared in front of Ella, blew her a hasty kiss and strolled over to the stand, where he bowed to the assembled line of Royal Fae.

This time it was the older Fae queen who started the questioning.

"Rossa, you have been my appointed guardian for my grandson since he left Otherworld."

"I have."

"Do you believe he sought this latest conflict with Adam and the sect?"

He considered her. "No, actually, I don't think he did. In fact, he was absolutely furious about it."

"And why was that?"

"Because his life had changed. He was mated, and able to live in the world of the humans for as long as he liked."

"So you don't believe this was an elaborate plot to return to Otherworld to avenge his wrongs?"

"Not at all. He only came back to stop them getting his mate." His gaze scanned the table. "You all know that. I told you."

"Yes, you did, with your usual ability to play both sides." The king looked across at his mother-in-law. "He was working for me, too."

"I knew that. He is also in the pay of the Dark Lord."

The white-haired man nodded. "The dark king likes to keep an eye on his progeny, as well. After the rift developed with his family here, the king was rather disappointed that Death Bringer didn't bring his outstanding talents straight to him." He looked over at Vadim. "The offer still stands, my boy."

"Over my dead body," the Fae king snapped. "I've spent my entire existence keeping him out of your foul realm."

Spencer held up his hands. "Can we resume? I have a question for Rossa myself, if I may."

"Of course." Rossa was all smiles again.

"You believe Death Bringer will do anything necessary to safeguard his mate?"

"Naturally."

"Would he kill for her?" He glanced down at his notes. "Is it true that he threatened to annihilate his entire family if Adam was allowed to complete his task and steal Ms. Walsh's face?"

Rossa's smile disappeared. "Adam went back on

our agreement, so technically Death Bringer is in the right if he wishes to claim vengeance. But I don't see him carrying out his threat yet, do you?"

"That's because he's been restrained since he got here."

"I suspect he's just allowing you to restrain him until he gets what he wants."

"Which is?"

"His mate's safety."

"Which brings us back to the point of this trial, the deaths of other family members who stood in his way, Nia and Ciaran." Spencer paused. "So if, as you state, Death Bringer is prepared to execute his entire family to defend his mate, killing off a couple more of them wouldn't be a big deal to him, would it? Thank you, Rossa."

Rossa gave Ella a slight apologetic shrug as he walked past, and she glared at him. It was no wonder there hadn't been anyone pursuing her. Rossa had been spying for everyone. She'd been merrily entertaining her keeper all by herself. She glanced impatiently over at Spencer. Were they going to call her as a witness, or was she just supposed to sit around and watch them annihilate Vadim? It was hardly fair.

"The court calls Adam."

"What the hell?" Ella blurted out.

She sat up as her least favorite person in the world appeared in front of the judge. A hand clamped down on her shoulder and she glared up at the guard.

"Adam, I believe you have evidence that is relevant to this trial."

"I do, sir. I am also confident that anything that is revealed within these walls will stay here."

"As we agreed." Spencer smiled. "Then please continue. Why were you hunting trophies in the human world?"

"It's nothing new. We've been hunting there for centuries."

"But why did you involve my grandson?" the old queen asked.

"Because of the nature of the request."

"I don't understand."

"I was required to find three faces."

"You were specifically requested not to take the face of Death Bringer's mate."

"That is what I was originally told, yes." Adam hesitated. "I must admit, I was surprised at the change in plans. When I met with Death Bringer at the hospital, I realized it had been a mistake after all."

"You refused to carry out a direct order from Fae royalty. Doesn't that make you as much a traitor as my grandson?"

"Not when he was the one to retract the demand."

Vadim looked up for the first time, and Ella evaded her guard and shot to her feet. "That's ridiculous!" She stared at Spencer. "Why are you even listening to this crap? This idiot stole my face! Make him give it back!"

"Please be quiet, Ms. Walsh. You will have your opportunity to speak later. Adam is not on trial here." Spencer pointed at her seat. "If you can't sit down, you will have to leave the courtroom."

The queen raised her hand. "I will ask the same question, then. Why would my son allow you to steal the face of his mate?"

Adam waited until everyone was quiet again. "Because he wanted an excuse to return to Otherworld and complete his destruction of his own bloodline."

Spencer stared at Adam. "Why on earth should we believe you?"

"He was using her to get back here." Adam said patiently. "Doesn't it make a perfect kind of sense? Look at my face and look at his mate's. Whom do we resemble?"

"Nia and Ciaran." The king's expression darkened. "Are you suggesting that Death Bringer chose those faces *deliberately?* Isn't that the decision of the sect?"

"Not in this case." Adam looked faintly regretful. "We were 'persuaded' to help Death Bringer. I assume he intended to make a point."

"By making us look upon the face of his murdered victims, his sister and his brother?" The Fae king slammed his fist into the table. "Why are we even holding this trial? Isn't it obvious that we are dealing with a monster who cares for nothing and even taunts us with his pathetic victories?"

Ella's gaze fell on Vadim, who was watching his father, his expression inscrutable.

He'd killed his sister and brother? She felt as if she'd been punched in the stomach. Something was very wrong here. From his sadness, she'd guessed Vadim was hiding something from her, but not that.

She sat back and tried to make sense of the incredible pile of crap Adam had just spouted. Like hell, they'd allowed Vadim to persuade them to work for him. She'd seen them in action, and they were way too powerful and arrogant to play nice with anyone, especially a rival of Vadim's magnitude. If the sect liked tidy sets of three, then why hadn't Ms. Phelps and Brad been made to look like Vadim's siblings, and not her? If Adam were correct and Vadim was gunning for a third victim, presumably his father, wouldn't she be wearing *his* face? He was blond. He would've been the perfect third victim for Adam, so how had she ended up getting involved?

Unless… Her gaze traveled from Adam to Vadim, and then back to the Fae king.

Adam was still talking. "I *assume* that Death Bringer realized he had to allow me to take his mate's face so that he had an excuse to descend on Otherworld in all his righteous wrath. You would all be afraid of the repercussions of not carrying out his wishes, and he would have a perfect excuse to execute every one of you."

"By God, he's right!" shouted the Fae king. He pointed at Vadim. "I want to hear him defend himself against these inarguable truths."

The silver bars around Vadim thinned until they resembled silken strands of silk. Ella focused all her empath ability on her mate and the cage as the Fae king stalked toward him.

"Do you deny that you murdered both your brother and your sister in cold blood?"

"Aye."

Vadim sounded far too composed for Ella's liking.

"You came back to finish what you started, didn't you? This whole elaborate charade was simply to get yourself back into a position of power. Thank God Adam revealed your perfidy in time."

"I didn't set out to kill my siblings."

"You were seen!" He threw a pile of parchments onto the table. "We have witnesses."

"I was defending myself!"

"You are the strongest power in Otherworld. Why would you have to defend yourself against those who are weaker than you?"

Vadim's chest heaved as if he'd sucked in a much-needed breath. "When they are my *siblings!* They wanted my power, Father. They were prepared to kill me for it. Should I have let them? Should I have let my love for them make me weak?"

"Why not? Perhaps they would've used your power more wisely."

"I have a unique set of gifts. You taught me how to use them. Doesn't the blame lie with you too?"

"Don't be ridiculous." The king picked up a handful of the pages. "All these witnesses saw you raise your hand and murder your brother. He died instantly. Your sister wasn't so lucky and died raving and out of her mind, grieving for her lost twin."

A muscle twitched in Vadim's face, and for the first time Ella got a sense of the immense control he was exerting on himself. With the barriers thinned, could he sense her too?

"As I said, I didn't intend to kill him. He gave me no choice."

"So you admit it, then?"

"He died at my hand but only after extreme provocation. His magic was corrupt, Father. He and Nia were—"

The Fae king turned his back on his son and walked over to the high table. "I've heard these excuses before. You deliberately took my favorite son away from me out of spite and malice."

Vadim briefly closed his eyes. "I did what your

training taught me. I found a source of evil and destroyed it. That was my function. That was what you ordered me to do. Why should the fact that it was your son make a difference? Are you not able to see his flaws? Should those of Royal blood be above the law?"

Ella saw the answer in the Fae king's face and held her breath as he slowly turned back to face Vadim.

"You are the only person who considers himself above the law, Death Bringer."

"Which is why I left Otherworld. Can't you see that?"

"Leaving death and disaster behind you? You can't escape your destiny."

"Why now, Father?"

"What do you mean?"

"Why force a trial now? The deaths happened many years ago, when I was only just coming into awareness of my full powers."

"Because your foul scheme to come back to Otherworld has to be stopped. You are mated now. You might believe your powers are enhanced by your association with the Soul Sucker."

Holy cow. She hoped no one took him up on that. Ella met Vadim's gaze and raised her eyebrows, but he didn't respond.

"All you've done, Father, is exploit my desire to protect my mate. You've used her against me to force my return."

"See how he shifts the blame so easily." The Fae king shook his head. "Why would I want this monster back? It's quite extraordinary."

"If I am supposedly in league with Adam, why hasn't he given Ella her face back? He had the opportunity when we were both at his castle. Why were we both imprisoned rather than treated as honored and welcomed allies?"

"I have no knowledge of this."

"But you were there, Father," Vadim insisted. "Ella has your mark on her."

Spencer beckoned at the guard. "Bring Ms. Walsh here, will you?"

"He doesn't need to bring me anywhere. I'm quite capable of walking by myself, you know." Ella stalked over to the high table and shrugged out of her jacket. She unbuttoned her shirt sufficiently for the Fae to see the glowing wound on her shoulder.

"You did mark her." The Fae queen glared at her husband. "Remove it *immediately.*"

"But he's using it to keep Morosov in line." Ella ignored the Fae king's frown. "It's the only reason my mate allowed himself to be captured."

"Remove it, Fergal."

"With respect, dear wife, I'll remove it when she leaves Otherworld. It isn't safe to let her wander around by herself." He glared at Spencer. "Isn't it time for you to make a decision about this matter? It's fairly straight-forward. Death Bringer admits he killed his brother, and by extension his twin sister. Now you must pass sentence."

"If I might make a suggestion?"

Adam stepped up beside Ella. She gave him her best death glare.

"Of course," Spencer said.

"If this court is unable to ascertain the guilt of the accused, there is another way he can be tested."

"And how is that?"

"In a battle to the death with me."

Silence greeted his calm statement. Spencer was the first to recover. "I don't understand."

"Death Bringer came back to Otherworld not to face his accusers in this court but to fight me for stealing his mate's face. If you hadn't interfered, that's where he would be right now."

"Are you suggesting your petty conflict with my son is more important than the deaths of his siblings?" the Fae king demanded.

"No, my king. I'm saying that death by combat would be a fitting end for a creature that considers itself the strongest power in Otherworld. Wouldn't you like to see that, sire? Your son finally overthrown, his power stripped from him and his life ended?"

The king hesitated, his gaze going between Adam and Vadim. "It isn't my decision. It is up to the court."

"But would you be willing to consider it?" Adam turned to the others at the table.

"I would enjoy seeing a fight to the death." Not surprisingly, the Dark Lord's representative looked suitably excited by the prospect of blood and mayhem. "If the court permits."

Spencer turned to the two Fae queens, who were quietly conferring. The older woman looked up.

"We have no objection to this fight, as long as it is clear that if Death Bringer wins, all charges against him, including those regarding Nia and Ciaran, are dropped completely."

"Hold on," Ella said. "What about what I think? He's my mate. Don't I get a say in anything?"

Spencer looked down his nose at her. "I hardly think

you have anything of interest to add, Ms. Walsh. This is an Otherworld matter."

"What about Vadim? He might not want to face Adam."

"I am more than willing to face him, Soul Sucker." Vadim's voice carried clearly across the room to her. "I would only ask that if I lose, your face is returned to you, and you are allowed to leave this world unharmed."

Adam nodded. "That is agreeable to me."

"And you speak for the whole sect?"

"I do."

"Like you think they'll keep their word." Ella scowled at the lot of them. "You're all a bunch of idiots."

Spencer gathered up his papers. "Then there is no need for any further deliberation on my part. If all parties are content with Death Bringer being held to account in a battle to the death, so am I. This case is adjourned."

Even while he was speaking, Ella took the opportunity to edge as close to Vadim as she dared.

"*Can you hear me?*" His cool blue gaze flicked over her. "*Do you want me to break you out of there?*"

"*Why would you want to do that?*"

"*Because there's something fishy going on here, and I need to talk it through with you.*"

There were sounds of movement behind her, but she didn't dare look back. "*Didn't you get that bit about our combined powers? I bet we can do anything we want.*" She held out her hand. "*Are you game?*"

"*Of course I am, Soul Sucker.*"

She focused her thoughts and reached through the

thin web of power to take his waiting hand. Shouts echoed behind her, but they meant nothing, because as her power met Vadim's, they were suddenly and impossibly free.

"THAT'S RIDICULOUS."

Vadim paced back and forth in front of his mate, who was regarding him with a somewhat aggrieved expression.

"No, it makes perfect sense. Adam steals my face, you come back in a rage, threatening to wipe out your entire family—either way he wins."

"You think this was all set up to destroy me?"

"Why else would the sect be so desperate to get hold of you? Think about it. Think about their obsession with patterns!"

"And killing me would be Adam's ultimate triumph."

"*Yes!*"

He considered the spectacular view over the forest. The sun was setting and he sensed their pursuers were not far behind. Ella still bore his father's mark. They would be easy to track.

"We have to go back."

"I know."

He walked over to her and cupped her cheek. "*I* have to go back, you do not. If you wish, I can help you find your way home."

"But I'd have this face, and at some point, if Adam is still alive, he'll come after me to reclaim his prize and end the contest."

"I will do my best to kill him for you before I succumb."

She attempted a grin, but it was a pitiful sight. "You're so freaking noble."

"No, I simply want you to survive more than life itself."

She grabbed his wrist. "Do you want me to go?"

"I don't want you to see me die."

"That's hardly an answer."

"Ella, I want to live out my life with you for all eternity." She made as if to break free, but he covered her hand with his own. "I need you." It was so much easier to express himself in his true form, so much *simpler* when he didn't have to worry about exposing his dark side. Ella knew all about him now, and she still hadn't walked away.

"And I don't want to leave. I can't do that to you. Whatever happens, we should face this together."

He let out a slow breath. "In their supreme arrogance, that's one thing they haven't thought about, isn't it? Your power added to mine brings a whole new dimension to their ability to bring me down."

"I can help you."

"I know that." He kissed her hand. "It's going to be difficult to prove what you suspect."

"I suppose it doesn't matter, if you kill them all anyway."

"But it does. It matters to my family. I'd rather obtain a confession first."

"Why should you care? None of them have exactly stood up for you, have they?"

"My mother and grandmother have supported me to the best of their ability, but the charges of killing Nia and Ciaran were enough to shake even their faith. They believed I'd become a danger to everyone." He sighed. "If what you suspect is true, my death will simply enhance the power of the sect."

"If Adam really has delusions of ruling Otherworld."

"We can't allow that to happen." He glanced over at the hills, where an ominous cloud was forming. "They are coming. Are you sure you want to go through with this?"

"Absolutely. If anyone is going to kick your ass, Morosov, it's going to be me, not a bunch of crazy old Fae."

"I love you, Soul Sucker."

She rolled her eyes at him. "*Dude*, don't say that. Wait until the end of the movie. If you start getting all emotional now, it means you'll never make it."

"But what if I never have the opportunity to say it again?" He hesitated. "What if they succeed in killing me?"

"They will, if you go in with such a defeatist attitude. What's wrong with you?" She smacked his upper arm. "You're the most powerful being in Otherworld! Get a grip!"

Her ability to simultaneously see through his doubts and make him feel like a complete dork made him want to smile. She was maddening, but God help him, he couldn't imagine a world without her. If only she would say the words to him. He would carry them into battle like a medieval lady's favor and become invincible.

He stepped away from her and swept an elaborate bow. "As my lady wishes."

Guards appeared all around the small clearing. Adam materialized and nodded complacently at them both.

"I assume you are ready now, Death Bringer?"

"Damn right, he is." Ella strolled up to Adam and

smiled at him. "There's something else you should know."

"And what is that, Soul Sucker?"

Ella flicked a glance over her shoulder at Vadim. "He's not as smart as he thinks he is, and neither are you."

Adam's expression hardened. "I don't like your tone."

She laughed, and behind her, Vadim growled a warning. "Having seen what he's like in this world, do you think I want him back in mine? He's a fricking psycho." She blew him a kiss. "I'm sorry, darling, but I really think I'm siding with Adam on this one. You need to be put out of your misery for all our sakes."

Vadim's face whitened. He gathered himself and came after her, his roar echoing through the valley as the sun finally set behind the trees. She didn't move, just watched the guards hold him down and contain him within some kind of magical net.

Adam smirked triumphantly and patted Ella on the shoulder.

"Don't worry, Soul Sucker. I'll make sure he never comes near you again."

"No!" Vadim roared. He fought against his captors, his claws raking at the net, and almost found a way free.

"Stop it, Morosov." She was standing right over him, her expression bored. "You'll hurt someone and just prove what an animal you really are."

He bared his fangs at her and hissed an obscenity in Fae.

She nudged his torso with her booted toe. "You're

way too scary. How could you expect anyone to live with that? I'm sorry, dude, but I have to protect myself."

Adam ordered Vadim's removal and turned back to her.

"Are you coming, Soul Sucker?"

She smiled. "I wouldn't miss this for the world."

FOURTEEN

ELLA SHADED HER eyes and looked around the vast hall, which was the length of a football field. They were back in the sect's palace, waiting for the Fae court to arrive so the "battle," whatever that meant, could start. At least Drew Spencer had gone back to Washington to prance around in his other role as head of the SBLE. She would hate to see his smirk at this point. She still wasn't convinced that his so-called judgment had been fair and unbiased. But that was a fight for another day—if she and Vadim survived this one.

It was a strange place for a fight. The walls were mirrored, and the floor-to-ceiling windows were hung with gold and silver banners. In contrast, the floor was like a stark black-and-white checkerboard that gave her a headache. Since her little alliance-forming experiment with Adam, apart from one Fae guard, she hadn't been constrained at all. She loved being underestimated. From the look of it, she was going to have a grandstand view of the battle.

Adam stood just below the balcony, talking to three other men she assumed were his sect sidekicks. They all carried swords and wore tacky gold-and-cream clothing that matched the drapes. It reminded her all too vividly of a medieval show she'd once seen in Vegas. The major differences between the men were that one was bald, one fair and one a redhead, which at least made it relatively easy to keep them straight. She already recognized their magic from their encounter in the hospital over Ms. Phelps's bed. Together their power had been formidable and definitely a match for Vadim's. But they were in Otherworld now, not San Francisco, and his powers were growing stronger every hour. He also had a secret weapon.

Her.

Keeping her shields high, she attempted to penetrate the mind of the nearest sect member. The older, balding man was already frowning at something Adam had said. Her empath senses told her he was the weakest of the four, but taking down any of the men would be difficult. From what Vadim had revealed earlier, these particular Fae were thousands of years old and extremely difficult to control or destroy, even for him.

She concentrated for a moment on learning the way the man's thoughts flowed and ebbed, identifying his signature, and then moved on to the redhead standing next to him. He was more dangerous, his mind sharper, and he was far less likely to compromise and more strategic in his thinking. The blond was the hardest to read. Something about his handsome features reminded her of Rossa and Vadim. She probed a little harder and then quickly withdrew as his barriers came up.

He glanced briefly in her direction, but she didn't meet his gaze. Definitely Fae royalty, and the one most likely to disobey Adam's orders and attempt to win glory for himself. Was he connected to the Fae king? Was he the male who had made sure the sect came after Vadim and his new mate? It seemed horribly likely, but there was nothing she could do about it now.

"Soul Sucker."

Speaking of the king... She looked up into his treacherous smiling face. He'd changed into a loose white shirt, black leather pants and a golden cloak that matched his eyes. If you were looking for a little girl's definition of the ideal prince, he'd do perfectly. Until you realized what a fucking psycho he was...

"Hey, what's up?"

He regarded her closely. "I hear you repudiated your mate."

"Re—what?" She fluttered her eyelashes at him. "What does that big word mean?"

His eyes narrowed. "Don't be insolent. I know you are far smarter than you let on."

"Really? Don't tell Morosov. He likes his women blond and dumb."

"Did you mean it?" the king said abruptly.

"That Morosov likes them dumb, or that he's a liability? Sure, I meant it."

He chuckled. "Drew Spencer said that *you* are the one who is a liability."

She hardened her voice. "I spent more than half my life in school and college being forcibly trained to become a tool for my government to use against Otherworld. That's why Spencer doesn't like me. I *hate* being told what to do."

And come to think of it, that was basically why Vadim didn't like his father too, but she wasn't going to bring up that subject right now. It was surprising sometimes how much she and her mate did have in common.

"What does your petty resentment of authority have to do with Death Bringer?"

"Isn't it obvious? He's too powerful. He wants to control me, and it's *infuriating*. Ask anyone at the

SBLE. Even when he's in his human form, we fight like cats and dogs."

"Spencer did mention that." The king contemplated her expression. "But he is also your mate."

She faced him. "As you pointed out, I had no idea *what* he was when that happened. I'm glad he saved my sanity, but I still hate being lied to, and I don't want to be held in his magical thrall for the rest of my existence."

He studied her for a long time. "I'm not sure I believe you, Soul Sucker. You certainly seemed quite taken with him when I came upon you in the glade."

"Did you watch? You're Fae. You of all people know that sex doesn't make a relationship."

He smiled, and his mind brushed against hers, seeking her true emotions. She let him see what he wanted. "You are so refreshingly direct. I almost admire you sometimes."

"Thanks, I think."

"So will you reconsider my offer?"

"To take Morosov back to San Francisco? I thought you wanted him dead." She gestured at the hall behind them. "He's pretty likely to die right here."

"What if he doesn't?"

"Then you'd better start saying your prayers."

"I have a better suggestion. I'll make sure you receive your face back, if you make sure he's dead."

"I'm already getting my face back, even if he does lose."

"You believe Adam will honor his word? He's hardly been reliable in the past."

"That's true. Damn." Ella took a long slow breath

and then let it out. "How can I help you? I don't have the weapon you gave me anymore."

He held up her battered backpack. "Yes, you do."

She made herself look deep into his cold eyes. "And if I agree to this, you swear on your own blood to let me leave here alive and return home?"

"You are more Fae than I realized, Soul Sucker. You bargain like my queen."

"To be brutally honest, I just don't want to deal with any of you ever again."

"You are an empath. Your work will bring you to Otherworld."

She swallowed hard. "I'll endeavor not to come near any Fae of your Royal bloodline. I never have in the past. How does that sound?"

He held out his hand, and she shook it.

"Good luck, Soul Sucker."

"Thanks." She took her backpack from his out-stretched hand. He damn well knew that if Vadim died so early in their relationship, she was unlikely to survive. He was quite happy to let her walk away and die. Her resolve to bring him down hardened. She gave him her best smile. "But I don't think I'll need it."

The king walked to the opposite end of the row of chairs, where the Dark Lord's emissary sat, and engaged him in conversation. Ella stared down at her backpack and struggled to control her emotions. She'd never understand the Fae and their cavalier attitude to life. If it made you that ruthless, maybe being immortal wasn't all it was cracked up to be.

"Good day, Ms. Walsh."

She looked up to see Vadim's diminutive mother taking the seat beside hers. She, at least, hadn't changed her clothes, but her leaf-green silk gown was worthy of any occasion. Despite everything, Ella took a moment to covet it.

"It's vintage Dior."

"Not magical elves? Damn. Don't tell me you can read my thoughts, as well?"

"I didn't need to. Your face gave you away." The queen smiled and smoothed the silk. "As you are mated to my son, I *can* access your thoughts, but it isn't easy. Your shields are excellent and most unlike the average human's."

"That's empaths for you. We're tricky." Ella returned her gaze to the scene below them. "How exactly will this battle work?"

"Usually, it is a series of magical tests combined with physical strength."

"And is it usual to have one man against four?"

The queen sighed. "No, but my son is very powerful. I believe he will overcome his opponents."

"You do?" Ella looked hard at the queen, but her beautiful face gave nothing away. "You're the only person who thinks so."

"Even you doubt him, Ms. Walsh?"

"I have no idea what to think."

"But you intend to aid him."

It was a statement rather than a question, and one she felt confident not answering.

"How do they stop other people adding their magic to the fight?"

"They put up a barrier, but it doesn't always work. I suspect anyone who wished to influence the outcome of the contest could get involved, if she or he had the means." The queen lowered her voice. "Like a bonded mate linked with one of the combatants, for example."

Ella glanced at her sideways. Wow, she was being remarkably helpful for someone who was supposed to be alienated from her son. She'd basically given Ella the go-ahead to help Vadim any way she could.

Below them, a trumpet sounded, and three males bearing silken banners advanced from the rear of the hall, reminding her strikingly of Vegas again, although even she didn't think she could stand having to eat a medieval banquet right now. After the men came three leashed black dragons, their fanged tongues flicking out over strong white teeth, their red eyes gleaming. The four sect dudes came next. She glanced around the hall. Apart from her, the Dark Lord's emissary, a dozen guards and the Royal family, there didn't appear to be any other spectators, which suited her fine.

Vadim walked out and she almost forgot to breathe. He was also armed with a sword, but had no other armor. He towered over the other Fae, his expression chillingly remote and focused, his black-feathered wings folded tight against his spine. For a second, his gaze appeared to alight on Ella and the queen, but he offered no sign of acknowledgment. She gripped her backpack hard and concentrated on simultaneously keeping her shields high and searching for a way through to Vadim's mind.

Ah, there he was. She breathed a little easier, only to almost squawk in annoyance as some kind of shield came up around the arena, weakening her link to a trickle. Would it be enough to maintain their connection? If she increased her power, someone might detect it. Hopefully, once the battle began and interest turned to that, she could increase the voltage.

"Is Morosov supposed to fight them all at the same time? It seems a bit one-sided."

"I assume there is more to it than that." The queen's pale beringed fingers were twisted tightly together in her lap.

The trumpets sounded again. Adam the asshole stepped forward, his voice carrying down the entire length of the hall.

"The contest between Death Bringer and the sect is to the death."

"Hopefully, your death," Ella muttered.

"Let us begin." He clapped his hands and the four sect members dispersed to God knows where, leaving Vadim alone at the far end of the hall. Ella focused her awareness of her mate and began to pray.

VADIM CAUGHT SIGHT of Ella in her pink jeans, sitting next to his mother at the far end of the hall. A more incongruous pair he could hardly imagine, but they appeared to be talking to each other. Ella's mind brushed his like a butterfly's wings. He almost smiled, and just remembered to turn it into a glare instead. He felt the hum of magical power as a shield enclosed the hall and the wavering of his mate's presence in his head. Before he could panic, she was back, a little weaker but definitely there.

Adam started shouting something about the battle being on, and then the four members of the sect promptly disappeared, leaving Vadim standing by himself in the center of the floor. Wasn't anyone going to tell him the rules? Perhaps there were none. His smile was savage and his fangs elongated, scraping past his lip. Not that he needed any rules. He was quite prepared to kill and maim as necessary to win his and Ella's freedom.

And when Ella *was* free, they'd be having a conversation she would never forget…

The tiled floor beneath his feet started to shake as if they were having an earthquake. When the dust settled, a strange array of rocks and ruined buildings covered the floor space, reminding him of the ruins of a classical city, or an overturned chessboard. Some of the buildings were high and some quite low. Presumably they were meant to provide cover for the sect as they took turns to try and fuck him up.

A flicker of movement on his right held his attention, and he turned as another massive bolder with the icy sheen of an iceberg shot up through the floor, cracking the tile. On top of it was one of the sect, his dagger poised to throw.

Vadim ducked to the side and held his hand palm up to deflect the passage of the blade. At the last moment, he realized the dagger was magically primed to find his heart, and had to increase his own power to repel it. The tip of the blade grazed his outstretched thumb and pain shot through him. With a roar, he sent the weapon spinning like a boomerang right back at the red-haired man who'd thrown it. The metal gleamed in the sunlight as it sliced through the male's silk shirt, drawing a corresponding line of stark red and a shout of rage.

The smell of his own blood and that of his opponent mingled in the air, making Vadim lick his lips in anticipation.

"Watch out behind you!"

He spun around as Adam appeared to his right, backed against an ancient-looking Roman arch, an arrow notched and ready to fly from his small Fae bow. Where the hell had that come from? Hadn't they agreed no weapons but daggers beforehand?

"That's not allowed!" Vadim shouted.

"Says who?" Adam loosed the arrow.

"Me." Vadim flicked his finger and set the arrow alight, scattering the charcoal ashes and then blowing them back in his opponent's face. Adam disappeared, coughing in a cloud of black ash. Vadim turned back to the rock face only to see it vanish again into the floor. The bald sect member sent a blast of magic across the divide, and Vadim retaliated.

Could he create his own obstacles for the sect? He tried a quick spell, but nothing happened. Things were definitely weighted against him. Dammit, he hated being so out in the open. He ran for cover. Another blast followed the first, and he dodged that one too.

"He's not as confident as the other three, Morosov. He fears you. Get in his face."

Ella was obviously intent on giving him an in-depth analysis of his enemy's thoughts. Not that he was complaining. From her position at the other end of the hall, sometimes she could see his opponents even more clearly than he could. And he was man enough to realize that in this situation, he needed all the help he could get. Instead of backing off, he ran straight toward the male, leaping the crater where the rock had stood and blasting magic from both hands. The bald one started to retreat, his terrified gaze on Vadim, his thoughts shouting out to his comrades for help.

He'd forgotten he had Ella's empath talents. They

might come in handy for tracking when his opponents intended to attack. Vadim kept going, then brought the man down beneath him. He kicked out wildly, screaming like a stuck pig. Vadim forced his head back, baring his throat.

"Tell me how to get my mate's face back."

"No!"

"Tell me."

"Morosov, Red's almost on you."

Vadim sent a surge of power through his captive and the man went limp. He wasn't dead yet, but he was definitely out of the fight for a while. He dropped the body to the ground and went to stand, only to be sent crashing to his knees again by the force of a magical blow. His left shoulder hurt like fuck, and his feathers were smoldering, never a good smell at the best of times.

And now he was pissed.

He gathered himself and ran for the next-largest obstacle, a three-foot-high wall, and threw himself over the top of it. Unfortunately, Adam wasn't on the other side, which would've made things nice and easy. Vadim took a second to check out the condition of his shoulder, where a tunnel of flesh had been gouged out. There was very little bleeding. For some reason, his thumb was far worse. He sucked it into his mouth and healed it. Because of his opponent's power, his shoulder would have to wait for some more serious magical healing. It was a nuisance, but any major wounds he inflicted on the sect would have the same longevity.

"Dude, where are you?"

Behind the laconic question, Ella's voice was tinged with a hint of anxiety.

"I'm fine. The bald one is out cold." He hesitated. *"Why do you care?"*

"Of course I care!"

"After that performance yesterday?"

"Oh, for God's sake, Morosov, lighten up! I'm trying to save your ass here!"

"And why is that?"

The silence seemed to go on forever.

"Because after that comment, I want to be the one to kill you myself?"

"I'm up for that."

"Awesome. By the way, Red's devious, Blondie is worse, and impatient with it, and you already know Adam will do anything to win. I don't think they're strong enough to take you individually, although I'm not sure what will happen if they work in pairs."

"Thanks."

She sounded pissed but remarkably professional. At this point, he'd take it. He took a peep around the edge of the wall. There was no sign of anyone among the ruins, only the acrid scent of burning. Where had the bald guy's body gone? He should've tried to secure it in some way.

"You should've killed him outright." Her voice was hard. *"None of them will give you a break, remember that."*

"You said he was the weakest. I thought to keep him alive and make him talk."

"If you insist on having a confession, it'll have to come from Adam. No one else will be believed."

"At this point, I'll take whatever I can get."

He opened all his senses and caught a hint of movement and heat to his right. A flame flicked out from

among the rubble, followed by an unearthly growl. As
the elongated form of a black dragon slithered around
the corner, Vadim's hand closed around a large chunk
of fallen stone. Glistening red eyes fastened on his,
and the dragon took off, heading straight for his face.
Bringing back his arm, Vadim launched his missile,
imbuing it with deathly magic that made it glow like
burning sulphur.

With a horrific screech the dragon fell backward, his
wing and chest caved in by the force of the blow. Vadim
didn't stop to watch the creature come to ground. It
was still capable of damaging him with its sharp teeth.
He doubted anyone was going to bind up his hurts as
they'd done for Ella. He sized up a half-fallen tower
about forty feet away and ran toward that, aware of
Ella in his mind, sharing his ordeal and lending her aid.

As magic crackled around him, setting the air on
fire, he leaped the last few feet into the tower and hurriedly climbed the stairs to the top. It didn't give him
much advantage, but at least he'd have a wider view
of the field.

"Why do they keep saving me?"

Ella's voice was in his head. He leaned against the
curved wall, breathing hard, and surveyed his sur-
roundings. Down below, the dragon lay unmoving, a
blackened shape draped over a low marble base.

"Does it really matter right now?"

"If I'm dead, you'd stop fighting."

"Like hell I would." He registered the glint of a
sword tip behind the pillar directly in front of the tower.
"Can we talk about this afterward? I'm rather busy."

"But I have a feeling it's important."

"Well, let me know how that goes for you. Can you see anyone near the half-ruined leaning tower?"

"Only you at the top. Wait. Red's opposite you at ground level."

"Where's everyone else?"

"Baldy's still out cold, and Blondie is advancing toward the opposite side of the tower."

Vadim shifted his stance and looked backward. There was no sign of the blond male, but he didn't doubt Ella's words. *"And Adam?"*

"Just hanging back, waiting to see if the others can kill you, I guess."

"Reassuring as ever."

"Hey, I'm doing my best!"

He didn't reply, as Red had broken cover and was moving steadily in a zigzag pattern toward the bottom of the tower. Vadim waited for as long as he dared and then sent off a bolt of magic, bringing a teetering column down, hopefully on the male's head. Unfortunately, when the dust cleared, Red was still advancing. A flash of blond hair behind him made Vadim aim a similar strike at his other opponent, who was also creeping closer.

"Be careful, Morosov, they're psychically linked."

"I got that."

"That means they can join their magical power together, right?"

"Right."

Vadim drew his sword. Should he descend or stay put? He'd be in a far better position if they came up individually, but he didn't believe they were going to make it that easy for him. Malevolent magic enfolded the tower from either side and closed over his head, the two powers merging and pressing down on him like an enormous weight.

With a roar, he channeled his powers into resisting the invaders, aware even as he fought them off that the stones beneath his feet were growing warmer by the second.

"They've set the tower on fire!"

He didn't bother to reply as he sheathed his sword, raised both hands over his head and punched his way through the shield like a diver launching himself from the high board. Inside his head, the two men screamed as if he'd physically assaulted them while they tried to gather the shreds of their powers and re-form the trap. But it was too late. Vadim opened his wings and flew low over the burning tower, spied Red and sent another lash of power into the man's body.

Behind him, the tower disappeared below the surface of the checkerboard; the flames extinguished. Only a cloud of smoke was left marring the perfection of the painted ceiling. He alighted on a large rock and looked back at where the tower had been. There was movement in the rubble. Neither of the males was dead yet, but he had significantly reduced their powers.

"Dammit, Baldy's awake again. That's what Adam was doing."

Vadim rubbed a hand over his smoke-rimmed eyes and spotted the gleam of a domed head running toward the spot where he'd located the other two males.

"If two didn't work, he's going to want to try three."

"Agreed."

There was a pause. *"Do you think you can handle it?"*

"Yes."

"You don't need me?"

"Not yet."

"I wonder if that's why they kept me alive, because they know I can't do anything to affect the outcome and can only distract you."

"You're not distracting me."

"Sure I am."

"You're helping me, Soul Sucker." He took the opportunity to breathe deeply before the next assault came. *"Your ability to read their minds and predict their movements is invaluable. And I might still need your magical power."*

"Don't they suspect I can help you?"

"I doubt they ever imagined that their Death Bringer would be mated to an empath. Who the hell knows what will happen?"

An arrow sizzled past his ear, and he ducked just in time, crouching low on the exposed surface of the rock. This wasn't a good place to defend himself. His gaze fastened on a series of ruins farther up the hall, and he took off, his wings opening to help him glide across the vast space. Ella would have a clearer view of him now, which would also be useful. He had a sense that he was being driven toward the end of the arena where the spectators were sitting. It would be just like Adam to want a big finale in front of those who hated and loved Death Bringer the most. His overconfidence astounded Vadim. What weapon did Adam think he had that could match his and Ella's combined power? Whatever it was, he would soon find out.

ELLA STARED AS Vadim swooped low over the arena, alighted near a ruined templelike structure and

promptly disappeared. Considering Adam had de-
signed a series of structures that were all of pale stone
or rock, Vadim was doing an amazing job of not standing out. The golds and silvers of his opponents blended
in far better.

"*Duh,*" Ella muttered to herself.

"What, my dear?"

The queen mother, who was seated on Ella's left,
looked up.

"It's okay, I was just marveling at Adam's ability to
manipulate the odds in his favor."

"He has good reason."

"Because he's afraid that if he doesn't, Morosov will
beat him in a heartbeat."

"You care for my grandson, don't you?"

"He's okay." Ella kept her gaze on the arena, where
the three sect members were slowly advancing toward
Vadim's hiding place. "He's my SBLE partner. We take
care of our own."

"He's also your mate."

"I know. That was your fault, wasn't it?" She turned
slowly to look at the old queen's composed face. "Did
you know all this would happen?"

"I had some inkling."

"Do you think I can save him?"

"I have no idea, Soul Sucker. That is entirely up
to you."

"Great. Thanks for your input." She strained to catch
a glimpse of Vadim. "If I'm so important to him, why
aren't I already dead?"

"Because they need you. Don't you know that?"

Ella thought about the unpleasant little dagger buried deep in her backpack. Should she get it out and

put it in her pocket just in case? Would Vadim prefer to die at her hand or to be captured and killed slowly? She really should've asked him before all this began. It wasn't the easiest topic to bring up. A flicker of movement below startled her. Another attack was building, and this time Vadim would be at the mercy of three of the sect members. She focused her empath powers on the minds of the attackers and started to relay her opinions to her mate.

THERE WERE THREE of them now. They were testing him. Did they sense he was reluctant to kill any of them—that for the first time in his long existence, he craved answers rather than destruction? Maybe Ella was right. She had changed him. Did he have the stomach for slaughter anymore? In the seats at the end of the arena, his father's familiar laughter rang out. Yes, he would kill. That's what he'd been trained to do. The reason he was in this precarious position today was because he'd executed his father's favorite son.

He had a far better reason to kill now.

For his mate, and for himself.

The sound of beating wings had Vadim looking up as the blond Fae dived down at him, sword at the ready, and attempted to detach his head from his shoulders. He parried the killing blow, ignoring the shock of magic that shuddered up his arm, and sent power of his own back through the metal to attack his opponent. An arrow lodged itself in his already-injured shoulder, impeding his movements, allowing the blond Fae to land and continue the fight.

He snapped off most of the arrow shaft with his teeth and carried on fighting, one eye on the movements of the unseen redhead Ella was also relaying to him in his mind. A blur of motion and Red was beside his attacker, his sword also drawn. Concentrating on pulling down his magical powers, he almost missed the arrival of the bald man. Only Ella's screech gave him that vital second to step back as the three sect members now advanced toward him.

Magic beat at him from all sides as he was slowly backed against a wall. The blond male in the center was smiling as he progressed, his blade jabbing at Vadim's chest, while the other two sought to hack and disable his wings.

"You've got this."

Damn, Ella sounded rather more confident than he felt. He risked a glance around the terrain and smiled. Baldy was wavering, Red was focused and Blondie was too angry with the other two to be effective.

She was right. He did have it.

Without disengaging his sword, he focused his magic on the wall behind the three males and blew it sky high. Rocks and chunks of mortar shot up in the air and rained down on his hapless attackers, leaving him unharmed and protected by a shield while they all staggered and fell to their knees.

"ADAM'S RIGHT BELOW the chairs."

Even as Ella shrieked the message to Vadim, her elbow was grabbed in a punishing hold and the Fae king glared down at her.

"What are you doing, Soul Sucker? You have no right to interfere in this matter."

She tried to pull out of his grasp. "Like you're not? I can sense your power blending with the sect's!"

"Be silent." His grip tightened and she almost blacked out.

"Let her be, Fergal." The Fae queen stood up, then put her hand on the king's arm, her expression furious.

"You support this attempt to suborn us? This traitor in our midst?"

"He's my son. I should never have let you take him and use him as a weapon."

"It's too late for regrets now. I created a killing machine! Your guilt can't change that. He needs to die, and his mate needs to stop meddling."

"Stop being so melodramatic!"

Ella felt like a bone between two ravenous dogs as her mind was bombarded with the intensity of the king and queen's power. The moment the king's grip slackened, she slid down to the floor, leaving the Royal couple nose to nose, and crawled back toward the view of the arena. Had the queen intervened deliberately to free her, or had she been spoiling for a fight over her son for centuries? She tried to repair her link with Vadim, but nothing happened. Either the Fae king had alerted Adam to her interference and strengthened the force field, or she was too debilitated from the Royal psychic screaming match to help.

She fought a sudden wave of panic. Had the king done that deliberately? Held her fast so that she couldn't escape his thoughts? Whatever had happened, she needed to reestablish the link pronto. Vadim might think he didn't need her, but she still wasn't sure what new tricks Adam had up his sleeve. He looked far too confident for her liking, and she needed to be alert.

While everyone else, including her guards, watched the king and queen fight, she kept creeping forward through the ranks of empty chairs toward the fighting. She peered over the balustrade. Dammit, they were about to surround Vadim! If she remained blocked from his mind, she could only hope he really did have the strength to fight off all four members of the sect by himself, because God help her, she wasn't sure if she'd reach him in time.

FIFTEEN

MATERIALIZING RIGHT UNDER the male's nose, Vadim went for Adam and knocked the bow out of his hand. He placed the tip of his blade under his enemy's chin.

"I thought you wanted to fight, but it seems all you can do is cower behind your fellow sect members."

Adam smiled. "I'm not hiding now, Death Bringer, and you are exactly where I wanted you to be."

He held up his hand, and dark power roared through Vadim, making him rock on his feet and take an involuntary step back. The malign force of the other sect members coalesced behind him. It was like being enmeshed in a suffocating circle of iron and darkness. He gathered his powers and pushed back at the boundaries that were attempting to crush him on all sides.

Nothing shifted, and he redoubled his efforts.

"Ella? Now would be a good time.

"Ella?"

Nothing. He glanced up toward the balcony and couldn't see his mate at all. Fear beat at him, and he staggered forward into Adam and felt a blade pierce the skin right between his ribs. With one stroke of his dagger, Adam could sever his keel bone, and he'd be unable to fly away. A flash of pink caught his eye, and he finally saw Ella struggling to stand up by the edge of the upper circle. Two of the guards were right behind her and closing in.

Fuck that.

No one was touching her again.

He forced himself to concentrate and fought back with everything he had. With an almighty roar, he sent the three junior sect members flying backward. They landed in a heap like broken puppets, their magic dying with them, releasing Vadim to face Adam again. This time it was his opponent who backed away, his blood-ied dagger held high in his hand.

Vadim bared his fangs in a deafening growl.

"Stay back, Death Bringer, or I will kill your mate."

"No, he won't!"

This time he heard Ella shouting out loud. She'd done something to get rid of her guards and was pre-paring to climb over the remaining barrier and jump down onto the checkerboard floor. Power flowed to-ward him from her, power he recognized as his, but with a very definite twist of Ella. He switched his gaze back to Adam.

"Stay there, Soul Sucker."

She kept moving. "I think I know why they need me to be alive."

He shot her a quick glare. "Will you just let me ex-ecute Adam before we get into that?"

"Don't kill him before I get my face back. Ouch!" She suddenly stopped and grabbed her shoulder.

Adam smirked. "That's what I was trying to tell you, Death Bringer. If you come any closer, your fa-ther will use the power of his mark to kill your mate."

Vadim didn't lower his sword or his mental shields. "Why would he do that for you?"

"Because he wants you dead."

The other members of the Royal family were advancing down the steps toward them. One of the guards reached Ella and was helping her stand. Her face was white, and her pain beat within him like a drum. He felt the shield around the arena come down.

"Don't let any of them use me against you, Morosov. Seriously, I'd rather die."

Her voice was clear and steady. At that moment, he loved her more than he'd ever thought possible.

"I don't intend for anyone apart from Adam to die, Soul Sucker." Vadim locked eyes with his father. "Why are you attacking my mate for this male? You agreed that winning this contest cancelled out all debts." He gestured at Adam. "The only reason I can't execute him right now is because of you."

"And that's a terrible mistake, Fergal." Ella limped forward until she stood opposite the Fae king. "Don't you get that you're being used? Adam wants to rule Otherworld. He *wants* you all to destroy yourselves, can't you see that?"

"Nonsense."

"*Listen* to me. Why do you think he forced Morosov back here? Why do you think he stole my face? He *wanted* him to annihilate all of you! He's still hoping you're going to carry on being a dickhead right now and annoy your son so much that he'll carry out his threats!"

"Be silent."

The king's hand shot out, and she gasped and fell to her knees, her whole body shuddering.

A low totally inhuman growl erupted from Vadim's throat. "Hurt her again and I shall willingly rip you to pieces."

"You see?" Ella gasped, her head lowered, her hand

covering her shoulder. "He'll do it, if you don't listen to me."

"The only way I will release you from your mark, Soul Sucker, is if you keep your word to me."

Vadim tensed as Ella met his father's cold gaze.

"You mean it?"

His smile was chilling. "Not quite. I no longer trust you to carry out your intended purpose. I believe I'll do it myself." The king held out his hand. "Give me the weapon you carry so secretively in your backpack."

"What weapon?" Vadim asked, but no one answered him.

"I tried to warn you all that she was weak and untrustworthy. Why do you think she was so desperate to keep her possessions shielded from your gaze, Death Bringer?"

"It's not like how he's making it sound." With some effort, Ella took off her backpack and placed it on the ground in front of her. "He was the one who gave me the stupid thing."

"And you were the one who intended to use it."

"To do what?" Vadim asked again.

She retrieved something from her bag and slowly stood up.

"Take off the mark."

The king held out his hand. "Give me the weapon first."

"*What?*" Vadim stepped in front of his mate and stared into her eyes, willing her to talk to him, to tell him what the fuck was going on.

"Give it to me *now*, Soul Sucker."

She shook her head. "No, I think I'd rather stick to our original plan." She launched herself at Vadim, a small, lethal dagger in her hand. Even as he fought her to the ground, he heard her screeching orders inside his head.

"Take it, kill him."

"Which one?"

"God, I don't know. Can't you get them both?"

He expertly rolled her onto her front, bent her arm up against her spine, and disarmed her.

"Ow! That hurt!"

She kicked out, catching him on the shin. He bit back a groan and increased the pressure of his hold. *"Stop fighting me, then!"*

"No, it has to look realistic."

A burst of mangled magic shot past his ear, making him wince and the spectators closing in on them scatter.

"Fuck it, Ella, you nearly took off my head with my own power!"

"Good!"

He moved off her and dragged her to her feet, the dagger now concealed within his massive hand. *"If I kill Adam, you won't be getting your face back."*

"I don't care about that." She hesitated. *"Do you?"*

"It's a matter of principle."

"Oh, for fuck's sake. Give it to *me* then!" She tried to head-butt him. He jerked his chin back just in time and held her out in front of him like a shield. "What the hell did you give her, Father?"

"I gave her nothing. I *assume* she obtained the dagger from the Dark Lord and his minions. When I met her for the first time, she already had a plan in place. She asked whether I would have any objection if she killed you. I told her to go ahead, and in return I would help her get her face back. In truth, you might say that this entire mess is her fault."

"That's *bullshit!* Don't you get it?" Ella kicked out and tried to get free again, but Vadim restrained her. "Adam wants Morosov to kill you all. He probably hoped that if I saw *that* massacre, I'd turn on my mate and use the dagger on him, leaving Adam king of the world."

"You are a liar, Soul Sucker. Can't you see it, my son?"

"She can't lie to me. Remember, she is my mate."

Ella wiggled around until she could see into his face, and put her hand on his chest. "*That's* why I'm still here. Your father hoped I'd kill for him, and so did Adam. They *both* had a vested interest in letting me live."

She turned to look at his mother and grandmother. "Hell, I'm the only one that *can* kill Morosov, aren't I? That's what you were trying to tell me."

"Is that true, Father?"

"She said she wanted you dead! She told Adam the same thing! You heard her!"

Vadim smiled slowly down at his mate. "She is entitled to kill me. I am hers for all eternity. But she is not going to do it at your bidding. If we combine our powers, Soul Sucker, do you think we could find the truth in Adam's mind?"

Terror flashed across his adversary's face and he tried to run past the encircling guards. Vadim stopped him dead with an entrapment spell.

"What do you think, Father? Shall I ask my unworthy opponent for his opinion?"

For the first time, unease flickered behind the Fae

king's eyes. "Why bother? What can he tell us that we don't already know?"

The queen mother stepped forward. "I would like to hear Adam's thoughts on this matter, too. If I find out that he truly wishes to annihilate our family, I want him to suffer for it." She glanced at her daughter-in-law and then at the visitor from the dark court. "Are we all in agreement?"

Vadim smiled at his father. "It seems as if you have been overruled." He released his mate and reached for her hand. "Come, Soul Sucker. Let's see what thoughts Adam really harbors in his mind."

ELLA LET VADIM lead her toward the immobile Adam. Beyond him lay the rubble of the arena and a neatly stacked pile of dead bodies. She'd heard the explosion of Vadim's power and felt it within her, but missed the visual as she was crawling on the floor. Looking at the remains of the explosion, she was glad she'd skipped it. She was totally happy that the sect members were dead, though.

Adam radiated a strange mixture of power and anxiety that drew her empath senses like a strong cup of black coffee.

"*Do you feel it too?*"

She wasn't sure whether she wanted to reply to her mate at this moment. He was being far too arrogant and possessive for her liking. On the other hand, he had just killed three males for her and threatened to wipe out a whole bunch of his superpowerful family... She couldn't buy devotion like that for all the money in the world. Such immense power was curiously addictive, which explained a lot about the lure of elderly politicians for younger women.

"Will the net hold?"

Vadim ran an experienced eye over it. "I think so. We can't make it too strong, or we won't be able to penetrate it."

"Makes sense." Ella reached out her hand and gently probed between the strands until she touched Adam's arm. He hissed a curse and tried to shift away from her, but his bonds wouldn't allow it.

"Wow. There's a lot going on in there."

"I noticed that too." Vadim came up behind her and put his hand on her shoulder, strengthening their bond with his physical presence. "He's full of shit."

She wanted to grin at his cool tone. *"Where's everyone else?"*

He glanced over his shoulder. *"Right behind us, why?"*

"We should put a guard on your father, and a couple on the other side of Adam in case he manages to break free of us."

"I had the same thought." She felt the quick rush of him communicating with someone else. *"My mother will watch my father and will command the guards to move into place."*

Ella nodded, her senses already engaged with the delicate task of feeling her way into another sentient being's mind. With a male as old as Adam, it wasn't easy. He was fighting her at every turn. But if she took a more direct route, she might inadvertently damage his memories and destroy the very information she wanted.

"Even if I find something, how am I going to make this work?"

"Remember, we all have a familial link. You relay the information to me, and I'll amplify it and send it onward. They can't accuse us of lying, then."

"True. Where do you want to start?"

"Home in on his guilt and his fear."

She probed deeper and felt Vadim's power and physical presence steadying and supporting her. Being inside Adam's head was like splashing around in a sewer. His delusions of grandeur, arrogance and his obsession with magical power made him a fearsome enemy and one who, despite his current position, still hadn't conceded defeat.

She'd dealt with enough monsters to know to seek the most heavily protected areas of his mind, to pick and probe until the walls crumbled and the intent behind the thought was revealed. Ah, there it was...

"Here you go."

Like a skilled weaver extracting a single, delicate thread, she removed the memories and thoughts and spun them into Vadim's mind. Images of his three darkhaired victims were followed by those of Brad Dailey, Ms. Phelps and herself. Each memory was as clear as a diamond and saturated with satisfaction. Adam thrived on their terror and loved pushing them to take that final step and kill themselves. Shielded behind his enjoyment of his trophies' pain, she discovered his pure loathing for the Fae family who currently surrounded him.

ADAM MADE A gurgling sound, but Ella and Vadim's magical hold on him was too powerful to allow him to speak.

"Keep going, Ella."

She plunged deeper and relayed Adam's agreement to aid the Fae king in his vendetta against his son, his satisfaction at the ending of the trial and his conviction that he and his fellow sect members would finally be strong enough to overthrow not only Death Bringer, but also his entire family.

"Ah, the Soul Sucker finds the truth." The older queen's voice sounded far away. "Adam *is* guilty. He truly wished to destroy us all."

A flash of bright, bitter anger seared Ella's senses, and she flinched as she saw the moment Adam had stolen her face. He hadn't reckoned on her coming after Vadim or expected the depth of power a bond between a dark Fae prince and a human empath would deliver. His hatred of her was a clear, shining blade.

"That's enough, Soul Sucker."

She was shivering. She turned her face into the comfort of Vadim's shoulder.

"You don't need to exhaust yourself. He is already doomed for his treasonable thoughts." He stroked her hair. "My parents are arguing again. My mother believes my father should be executed alongside Adam."

"No!" She gripped his arm. "That's—" She turned back to Adam, who was now smiling at her. "That's what he wants!"

"Why?" She addressed Adam directly. "Why do you want the king in particular to die?"

Beside her, Vadim had gone still. "What is it, Ella?"

She reached through the net again and sought Adam's skin. Something wasn't right. He was puzzling her, his walls ever shifting, his true personality hidden behind...

She opened her eyes.

"Who is he, Morosov?"

The row behind them was growing louder as the Fae took sides.

"What do you mean?"

"Think." She felt him open his mind to hers while she kept the link to Adam wide. "Adam's not his real name, is it?"

AN ABYSS YAWNED at Vadim's feet, and he pulled Ella roughly away from Adam.

"Tell me something before you die."

A superior smile lightened his opponent's all-too-familiar features. "Why would I tell you anything? Can't you use your human pet to force the information out of me?"

"I could." His hands clenched into fists. "But this is between us. It always has been. Why is that?"

Adam shrugged. "You're supposed to be the most powerful being in Otherworld. You work it out."

"You always hated that, didn't you? That I had all the power, that I was the chosen one. Is that why you took over the sect?"

"The sect welcomed me. They appreciated my powers."

"I'm sure they did. If you die, will my mate get her face back?"

"How would I know? I've been alive for almost as long as you have. I'm supposed to be immortal. Why would I bother to find out about the effect my death has on others?"

"Then free her from the spell."

He fake-sighed. "I can't do that when I'm trapped. My powers aren't working."

Ella touched his arm. "I don't care about my face, Morosov. Don't let him go free."

"How noble," Adam sneered. "But it isn't really about you either, is it, Soul Sucker?"

Her fingers sank into Vadim's flesh. "He wants you, right?"

He nodded, his gaze not leaving the other male's as he sorted through a myriad of memories and impressions and tried to blend them with Adam's pilfered thoughts.

Behind him, he was aware of his father moving toward him. He intentionally raised his voice.

"You wear my brother Ciaran's face."

"So?"

"When I first saw you in San Francisco, I said that you were a fraud, because my brother was already dead."

"Because you'd killed him, and things Death Bringer kills never survive."

"That's what I believed." Vadim drew in a slow breath. "It appears I was wrong."

"What?" His father's jarring voice bellowed in his ear. "Are you suggesting this is really Ciaran? How ridiculous is that? Good God! Death Bringer, will you do *anything* to bring this family down?"

Vadim kept his gaze on the prisoner. "Is that why he helped you?"

Adam blinked very slowly. "That's for me to know and for you to find out."

"I can do that for you, Morosov," Ella said softly. "All I have to do is touch him again." She looked up at him. "This is what he was hiding. He didn't really want my face, he wanted you back."

"For revenge."

"Even though you obviously didn't kill him after all. Was he always jealous of you?"

"Of course. My father professed to love him the most yet spent most of his time training me—his personal weapon."

"That isn't true." Adam practically spat out the words. "I always knew I was loved, while you were hated and feared."

"But you were willing to do anything to get power like mine, weren't you?"

"I did what anyone faced with an impossible situation would do."

"Forced a confrontation between us? Used your twin sister as bait?" Vadim fought to control his voice.

"She loved me. She was willing to help me in any way she could."

"That's not love," Ella said. "That's stupid."

"I regret having to lend you my sister's face, Soul Sucker. You are not worthy to wear it."

"Strange, it doesn't bother me in the least."

Adam sighed elaborately. "It amuses me to know that my brother will have to live with it for the rest of his unnatural life."

Vadim drew Adam's attention away from his mate, who looked ready to do him harm. "Did you kill her?"

"Who, Nia? No, she was weak. She couldn't live with the idea that she'd betrayed you by pretending I'd died in your attack. She was more than willing to listen to my suggestion and take her own life."

"Is that what gave you the idea for your little game, then?" Ella asked. "To take her face as a trophy?"

"Yes, Soul Sucker, how astute of you to notice."

He snarled. "I obviously underestimated your intelligence."

"Most of us do." Vadim recovered his veneer of calm. "So if we assume that you follow the sect's usual rule of three, and that you wanted my face next, whom did you choose to complete the pattern?" Adam's gaze flicked momentarily to Vadim's right. "Ah, you wanted *Father's* face, because once you had his, no one would remember you as Ciaran, and you could move on with your plan to control the whole of Otherworld."

"*What?*"

In his desire to get up close and personal with the captive, the Fae king tried to push past Vadim, who put out an arm to hold him back.

"He intended to kill you. Didn't you get that?"

"That's impossible! I—" The king suddenly broke off as if aware that his estranged spouse and mother-in-law were regarding him suspiciously. "It's not true."

"Why would I lie?" Adam said. "I'm not expecting to come out of this encounter alive, are you?"

Blustering, the Fae king turned to survey his audience. "The man is mad. He obviously wants to implicate as many of us in his crimes as possible. Perhaps Death Bringer was right in the first instance, and Adam was trying to annihilate our whole family. Isn't that rather more important?"

"Nice try, Fergal." Ella pretended to clap. "And, by the way, that was my idea, not Morosov's."

Vadim reached out and took her hand. He half turned to face his family. "For once I'll agree with my father that the state of the realm is rather more important than the state of his conscience. What do you want me to do about 'Adam'?"

He couldn't call that monster by his brother's name. From what he'd sensed in the other's mind, all vestiges of humanity had been leached from his soul over the intervening years. Adam cared for no one and thrived on power, hatred and vengeance.

His grandmother raised her chin. "What do *you* wish to do with him, Death Bringer?"

Vadim went still. Beside him, Ella squeezed his hand hard.

"It's okay about my face, it really is. I don't care if you execute him. He's done enough harm in his lifetime even for an immortal Fae."

Vadim stared at his brother for a long quiet moment and then raised his hand.

ELLA WANTED TO close her eyes, but she owed it to her mate to watch to the end. She couldn't let him destroy himself again. Didn't his family understand the terrible burden he'd carried with him for *centuries?*

"Morosov…"

"No!"

A bolt of the Fae king's magic shot between her and Vadim, releasing Adam from his bonds. With an exultant cry, he rose above the ground and grabbed for Ella.

"Get off me, you idiot!"

Vadim rose too, his huge wings unfolding, claws out, fangs extended.

"Let her go!"

Twenty feet up in the air, Adam held her out in front of him, and her legs dangled like a doll's. "Father, kill her!"

She looked down at the Fae king's face. The wound on her shoulder started to throb like fire.

"Don't be stupid!" she shouted. "If you kill me, Morosov will kill you and Adam will have won *everything!*"

"She's right." Despite his aggressive stance, Vadim's voice was eerily calm. "Now release her, Adam. This is between us. It always has been."

She glared at Vadim. "Don't you dare fight him! That's what he wants! Why are all you Fae so *dumb* sometimes?"

She tried to turn to see Adam's face, and he was smiling. The door to the hall crashed open. Beyond it was the long corridor leading to the trophy room. Was he intending to gather his trophies on the way out, or did he intend to destroy everything?

His trophies...

She looked from him back to Vadim and then at the Fae king.

Sets of three. The blonds, the brunettes and the final set of Fae royalty that would never be completed....

"Give me the dagger and give me your power."

"Don't be stupid."

"Don't argue with me! I think I know how to fix this!"

"Ella..."

"Please. Trust me."

A second later, the blade was in her palm. Below her, the Fae king held up his hand, and the pain in her shoulder began to spread throughout her entire body. Without allowing herself to think any longer, she used Vadim's immense strength to free her right hand and, turning, plunged the lethal blade into Adam's throat. As he screamed, they started to fall. By the time they hit the floor, she was beyond feeling anything at all.

SIXTEEN

THE MOMENT ELLA turned to strike Adam, Vadim lurched across the space and just managed to knock some of the power out of his father's spell. Adam started screaming, blood gushing from his mouth, and fell, bringing Ella with him. Alighting beside them, Vadim picked his father up by the throat and shook him like a rat.

"What the fuck were you doing? If you've killed her, I'll—"

A cool hand touched his arm. "I'll see to her, my son."

Vadim didn't release his grip. "He still dies."

"I wasn't aiming at her, you fool! I had a clear shot at Adam!"

Vadim didn't even deign to answer that; his attention all on his mate, who lay sprawled over Adam's bloodied corpse. Blood oozed through her jacket from her left shoulder. His mother knelt in front of her and took her hand.

"She's still alive."

Vadim exhaled and loosened his death grip around his father's neck a tiny fraction. "You are very lucky. Now she will be able to watch me kill you in person."

"I didn't intend to harm her. If I had, all I needed was to call in my mark. I was aiming at Adam!"

He bared his fangs an inch from his father's face. "Release her from your mark *right now*."

Sweat glistened on the king's unlined forehead. "It is done. I swear it."

Vadim dropped his father and went over to where Ella had fallen. His mother had disentangled her from Adam, and she lay on her back, her eyes closed, her battered backpack supporting her head.

"Will she be all right?"

"With your father's influence now removed, I believe she will." The queen hesitated. "She is a fine mate for you, my son."

He sank down onto his haunches beside them and reached out a shaking hand to touch her unnaturally dark hair. His mother had already used magic to clean her obvious wounds and remove Adam's blood. "I know. Even though I didn't appreciate it at the time, you and grandmother picked well for me."

"We knew our disapproval of the match would make you want it more fiercely." She smiled and briefly patted his arm. "You must both come and visit us, often."

"If that is your wish, and if Ella agrees." He hesitated. "You no longer require my presence here in Otherworld?"

"I think you deserve a better life, don't you?"

Ella muttered something, and Vadim's gaze shot back to her. "Mother, *look*."

As he watched, her face started to dissolve, the black hair and pale skin receding to reveal her usual fair hair and disgruntled features.

"How the hell did that happen?"

"Adam is dead. Perhaps his powers died with him."

"I bloody hope so, after all that effort," Ella mumbled.

"Soul Sucker." Vadim took her in his arms and sat her in his lap. She leaned against his chest as if she belonged there. "You are alive."

"Of course I am. I told you that you needed me, didn't I?"

He drew her even closer against him. "You shouldn't have done that."

"What, killed that monster?"

"You didn't even know if he could die."

"I was pretty sure that if the knife would work on you, it would work on anyone."

"But it was my responsibility, not yours."

"You aren't just Death Bringer anymore, remember?" She put her hand on his cheek. "Don't you think you've suffered enough?"

He swallowed hard as she held his gaze. Had anyone ever done that for him before? Taken on his burden? Killed for him? He didn't think so.

He slowly exhaled. "I do not have the words to thank you."

"That's okay. I have that problem a lot." She kissed his mouth. "How about we call it even?"

He wrapped his arms around her, buried his face in her neck and breathed in the strangely reassuring scents of Pop-Tarts and bubblegum.

"What's going to happen now?"

She was already wriggling to get free and move on. With a sigh he released her.

"My mother is still insisting that my father hang for his part in this matter. So far, she hasn't asked me to administer the final blow, but I'm sure it's coming."

"Can we leave?"

"Soon, hopefully. There are a few things I need to take care of here." He hesitated. "Although obviously, you can leave whenever you want."

She rubbed her left shoulder and looked away from him. "I'm okay to tag along with you for a while. This is still an open SBLE investigation, you know."

He let her scramble out of his lap and went to stand himself.

"Hey, what about your arm? You're bleeding."

In his concern for her he'd totally forgotten about the wounds he'd suffered during the fight. "I'm fine. I should be able to fix it myself, now all the sect members are dead."

"I could do it for you."

"It's okay, I think I can handle it."

"You're just worried I'll blow your arm off."

"Having seen the way you use my power, it had crossed my mind." He let his palm hover over the wound and said the necessary words. Once the head of the arrow came free, the pain quickly eased. He wished it were that easy to control the pain in his heart.

"Your magic is extremely hard to manage. I completely blew up a troll the first time I used it."

"That was probably quite messy." He glanced over to where the arena had been and saw that someone had already tidied everything away. The room looked perfect and far removed from the violence that had erupted earlier and taken four lives...

"What's wrong?"

"I was wondering where they'd put the bodies."

"Let's go and find out."

She headed for the huge doors, and he followed her as meekly as a lamb.

ELLA TRIED NOT to look up as Vadim walked alongside her, but he was being rather too quiet for her liking. Had she really offended him by stepping up and slaying Adam instead of letting him do it?

"Are you still mad at me for killing Adam?"

"No."

He kept walking. It bugged her that she had to take the occasional skip to keep up.

"That's it?"

"You did what was necessary, and for that you have my gratitude."

"Oh. That's okay, then."

Maybe her emotional attachment to him had misled her into thinking he was more vulnerable than he truly was. He might only want to see the bodies to make sure his brother really was dead this time. She paused at the door to the trophy room, which stood open, the guards dismissed. Hopefully there were no black dragons lurking around either.

"Can we go and look in here?"

"Of course."

He waited for her to walk past him into the vast room.

"I thought most of this stuff would've disappeared with the death of the sect."

Vadim turned in a slow circle, taking it all in. "I suspect there are still other members. We just don't know about them yet."

"Good point." She carried on through the room, heading for the back wall.

"What are you looking for?"

"My face." She sighed. "I'm going to kind of miss it, and then there's all that hassle of getting a new driver's license, passport…"

"Ella—"

"Hey!" She spotted Brad Dailey's face. "It worked!" She looked over her shoulder at Vadim. "Was Ciaran a blond version of you?"

"Yes."

"I hoped so." She whistled. "It was a bit of a risk, but I'm so glad I went for it."

"For what?"

There was a hint of impatience back in his voice, which made her feel much happier. She moved out of the way so that he could see the three faces on the gold plinths.

"Adam's replaced you," Vadim said slowly. "Did you expect that to happen?"

"Well, I thought it might work. The only thing is, what happened to my face? I hope I didn't end up on your brother. We definitely do need to check out those bodies."

He caught her hand. "You chose to kill him because you *hoped* you'd exchange faces?"

"Yeah, I guessed there needed to be a group of three to spring the spell, and as the Fae Royal thing wasn't going to happen and Brad and Ms. Phelps were already dead, I reckoned Adam needed one more victim. I still didn't get my face back, but it did stop him adding me to his list of trophies." She shrugged. "I bet he didn't think he'd be the one doing the dying this time."

"Why didn't you share this theory with me?"

He was towering over her now, his beautiful blue eyes narrowed.

"I wasn't quite sure which configuration was going to work. Originally I thought he wanted you, Nia and your father, but when that all changed, I substituted my own plan."

"And didn't tell me."

Each word was spaced out and radiated fury. She gazed up at him and tried a smile. "You were rather stressed at the time. I didn't want to worry you."

"Stressed… And when, *exactly* did you come up with this idea that Adam was attempting to complete a hat trick of Fae royalty?"

"Dude, I told you that ages ago. When we were in that protected glen. When Adam had me up in the air back there, my theories kind of coalesced."

"You mentioned only that you believed Adam wished to rule Otherworld."

"Well, how was he going to achieve *that* unless he got rid of you and your father, who are both more powerful than he was?" She rolled her eyes. "Men are so dumb sometimes."

His hand shot out and he pinned her to the wall. "So you were not trying to save me from having to kill Adam. You were merely carrying out your half-baked *theory* to get your *face back?*"

His tone was withering. She smiled into his storm-filled eyes. "Oh, no, I was trying to save you all right. The theory part was just a bonus."

She held her breath, but instead of kissing her, he dropped his hand and turned away from her. She frowned at his broad back. Why wouldn't he kiss her?

"We should go and check out the bodies."

She pushed away from the wall. "Sure."

He didn't say a word as they walked down the endless hallways; his mind was closed to her as well, which was starting to tick her off. In the main hall, she spied Rossa in conversation with one of the gatekeepers.

"Hey!" She waved at him and he strolled over.

"You're both alive! You look great now, Ella." He grinned at the unsmiling Vadim. "It's awesome that you beat all those guys. I knew you could do it."

"What are you doing here?" Vadim's question was distinctly uninviting.

"Your mother called me in to keep an eye on the place while everything's up in the air."

"She called you?"

"I have skills." Rossa raised his eyebrows. "I also happened to be right here, so she didn't have much choice. Were you looking for her?"

"No, we were wondering where they'd put all the bodies."

"Oh, right. They're in the place of worship, which is down this hall and then to the left."

"Thanks." Ella smiled at him. "And thanks for everything."

Rossa preened. "It was nothing, babe. Anytime, for you."

As they moved on, Vadim said something under his breath in Fae, but she chose to ignore it. After a moment he cleared his throat.

"He didn't exactly do much, Ella."

"He was very helpful to me when I first got here."

"Because he'd been ordered to keep you safe."

"I know that." She kept her gaze on the hallway.

"But he was *terribly* sweet about it, and he did help me get into this place."

He resumed muttering in Fae.

It seemed to take forever to get to the chapel, or whatever it was called. The doors were gold and marked with a myriad of religious symbols from both the human realm and Otherworld. Inside, portraits of members of the sect lined the wood-paneled walls, the most prominent being one of Adam that hung over the ceremonial table at the front. About two hundred candles had been lit, and the waves of heat coming off them were extreme.

"Oh my, the cult of Adam. All bow down."

He was blond in the picture and looked far too benevolent for her liking. To the side of the main altar was a row of four open coffins. Vadim had already moved toward them and stood looking down into the last one, his expression unreadable.

"Is that Adam?"

He nodded but didn't take his gaze away. Ella went to join him.

"Well, that's definitely not my face." She angled her head to one side. "He would've looked odd with it anyway, and I don't think I could've brought myself to try and take it off a corpse." She shuddered.

Vadim turned away and checked out the other coffins, where Red, Baldy and Blondie had been laid out, all magically restored to their full beauty.

"What will happen to them now?"

"I believe there's a vault beneath this space where sect members can choose to be buried. Unless there are new instructions from their families, I suspect the four of them will end up there."

"And then maybe we can pull the whole place down around their ears?"

"Would you like that?"

"It would certainly make me feel safer about coming back here."

"But it might enrage the remaining members of the sect, who are already going to be in disarray due to the demise of all four members of their council."

"You're no fun anymore. What's wrong with a bit of vengeance?"

Even as she said it, she knew she'd erred. He turned away from her.

"I'm sorry. That was a stupid thing to say. You've probably had enough of death and vengeance to last you a lifetime, a Fae one at that."

"Shall we go and find my parents?"

"If we must. Your father is really starting to get on my nerves."

"Starting to? He has that effect on a lot of people."

"And he's up to his neck in this plot."

He held the door open for her. "You'll never prove it. My mother might get angry with him, but she doesn't have the ability to take his power away."

"Who does?"

He smiled then, but it was bleak. "I do."

"But you won't."

"As you said, I'm no longer prepared to be Death Bringer." He hesitated. "The ironic thing is, if Ciaran had asked me for my powers, I would've willingly handed them over to him."

"But you couldn't." She poked him in the chest. "Why do you think they chose you rather than him in the first place?"

"I've never thought about that."

"Well, it's obvious to me. You have integrity and balance and...*goodness* inside you. If Ciaran had your powers, Otherworld would be a very different place and none of your family would still be alive."

He stared down at her. "Why does everything seem so simple to you, my mate?"

"It just does."

His smile this time was much better. "I will try and accept your counsel in this."

"Cool. Now let's go and find your adorable family and get the hell out of here."

THEY WERE GATHERED in the entrance hall, and it was obvious to anyone who'd ever been in a relationship that the king and queen still weren't speaking to each other. Ella glanced at the queen mother, who smiled graciously at her and drew her to one side.

"Soul Sucker, as a representative of the SBLE, are you satisfied that this case is now over?"

"I will be as soon as I write up my final report. Would you like a copy?"

"It depends on how detailed you wish to make it."

Ella paused. "What are you hoping I'll leave out?"

"The parts about your family."

"*My* family?"

The queen opened her blue eyes wide. "You are part of this family, my dear, whether you want to embrace it or not."

"If I leave your family's antics out, that doesn't leave me a lot to put in my report."

"Exactly, granddaughter." She patted Ella's arm. "Perhaps I might make a suggestion. If you simply state that you tracked down Adam to the sect's palace and disposed of him. You were the one who killed him, my dear, so what else is there to say?"

"What about the family vendetta and Death Bringer?"

"Surely they are of no interest to anyone at the SBLE?"

"What about the king?"

"I'll take care of him. He will not be allowed to conspire against your mate any longer."

"What about Ciaran being Adam?"

"The history books tell us that Ciaran died a very long time ago. Why resurrect him only to kill him again? Why not let him *be* Adam? You will only cause your mate pain."

Ella contemplated the ageless face of the queen for a long moment. "And if I do this, what's in it for me?"

A smile lightened the other woman's features. "You are more Fae than you realize, Soul Sucker. You certainly haggle like one. If you omit my family from your report, I will no longer seek Death Bringer's permanent return to Otherworld."

Ella glanced over at Vadim, who was talking to his mother. "Suppose he wants to return?"

"He doesn't, my dear. He wants to be with you."

"Are you sure about that?"

"Why do you doubt him? He will not leave you for all eternity."

"That's the bit that scares me." She stared at the back of his head and then nodded. "If he doesn't want to stay here as Death Bringer, then I agree to your terms."

"Excellent, my dear. Now I suggest you take him

home before he comes to blows with his father again. Those two will never share a universe amicably."

She escorted Ella back to Vadim's side.

"Are you ready to go, Morosov?"

He looked down at her. "If that is your wish."

"I think I've got enough information to close the case, how about you?"

"There certainly isn't anything else worth staying for. My mother insists she can deal with my father and that I shouldn't worry about her."

"She's a strong woman." She linked her arm through his and led him toward the exit. "She'll be okay. Did she tell you she invited me back for dinner?"

"She invited you?"

"Well, she asked both of us."

He looked down at her. "Is that something that would appeal to you?"

"Dude, she promised to show me her closet. I bet she has some amazing clothes in there that she is just dying to give away to her favorite new relative."

One of the guards opened the door, and they were outside in the bright sunshine, totally alone. A gust of wind blew her hair into her face, and she pushed the blond strands behind her ear.

Blond…

Ella kept moving toward the wood and Vadim caught her hand.

"We don't need a portal, if that's what you're looking for."

"That wasn't what I wanted. I just don't want anyone at the palace spying on us."

"While we do what?"

She looked over her shoulder at him. "While I kill you."

The moment the shadows swallowed them up, she turned on him. "When were you going to mention that I had my face back, *asshole?*"

He raised an eyebrow. "When I felt like it."

"What the hell is that supposed to mean? Don't you think it was rather important?"

"To you, obviously."

"You're still sulking about me killing Adam for my face, and not just to save you."

He leaned back against one of the trees, his massive arms folded over his chest. "I might be. Or maybe I thought you might like to see how it feels to be left out of the loop."

"When did it come back?"

"Just after Adam breathed his last."

"It makes sense. How come no one else mentioned my face? Your whole family just stood there and said nothing."

"What I find fascinating about you, Ella, is how you get all bent out of shape about the little things and yet can deal so calmly with death and disaster."

"Because those things are easy."

"Not to everyone. And while we're on the subject of things you find uncomfortable, do you want me to return to San Francisco with you or not?"

She realized she was scowling at him. "It's up to you."

"That's a typically evasive Ella Walsh answer."

"It's not evasive. I'm not going to tell you how and where to live your life."

"Do you think I want to stay here?"

"I can see why you might." She gestured at his awesome body. "Here you can be in your true form, have all your magic around you and be the most powerful being in Otherworld."

"But I'd already given that up before I even met you."

"Only because you felt so guilty about your siblings." He went to speak, but she pressed on. "But at least that's over. You know you didn't execute your own brother, so if you wanted to come back here, you could."

He contemplated the grass in front of his feet for so long that Ella wanted to scream.

"Sometimes I am tempted." He held out his hand and flexed his fingers. "To feel such power running through me again is addictive. But I also fear that power. If I came back, I would eventually be corrupted just like my brother."

"Not necessarily."

He half smiled. "I appreciate your faith in me. In this instance, I know I would become too powerful or succumb to the lure of the dark king's court and destroy my own. It has already been foretold."

"By whom?"

"By many seers, including my grandmother."

"That's definitely a kicker."

"And what do you want, Ella?"

She tried to laugh. "I've never been a long-term planner, you know that."

"And I know why. You didn't think you'd have a life to plan, did you?"

She shook her head.

"Is it still all too much for you?" He spoke very

gently, his words barely reaching her on the breeze, as if he was afraid of startling her.

"What do you mean?"

"Me, the mating bond, the prospect of us being together…"

"About that. You're immortal, right?"

"Technically, yes. But you could kill me, or I could choose to die for you."

She grimaced. "Neither of those options appeal to me at the moment. Why would you even *want* to come back to the SBLE, where you have to pretend to be something you're not, and hide your powers and true self?"

"Feehan knows what I am now. I won't need to hide anymore."

She pointed at him. "You can't walk down the street looking like that!"

"Other shape-shifters manage to live in your world. I'm sure I'll find a way to stretch my wings occasionally. Why are you offering me so many reasons not to come with you?"

"I'm not, I'm just trying—"

"What if I asked you to live in Otherworld with me?"

"I…"

He smiled as she stuttered into silence. "It's all right, I'm not that stupid. Forcing you to make such a choice at this moment would only result in you storming back to San Francisco alone." He studied her. "Perhaps that is what you'd prefer—an ultimatum, a reason to walk away."

"That's not fair. I haven't insisted you come back with me, have I? I've tried to give you a choice."

His eyes flashed fire. "You won't force a decision on me, because you're afraid I'll take you up on it. You're afraid I'll walk and leave you, like everyone else has done."

That hurt. She drew in an unsteady breath. "I'm scared, Morosov."

"Of me?"

"No. Of myself."

"I can't fix that, can I?" He sighed and walked toward her and she tensed. He held out his hand.

"We still have a job to do. The rest can wait until later. Let's go back to the SBLE and close this case once and for all."

SEVENTEEN

THEY MATERIALIZED IN her office. Ella blinked up at Vadim, who had already resumed his human form. She touched his starched white shirt.

"I actually miss the feathers. How weird is that?"

He stretched and rolled his shoulders. "It feels strange to be back in this form. I miss my wings."

"What about your immense powers?"

He smiled. "Oh, I still have those."

"Not all of them, right?"

"Why, are you worried? I don't intend to use them unless I'm provoked."

"Seeing as I'm the person who provokes you the most, that isn't very reassuring."

She went around the desk to turn on her laptop. "Time is weird in Otherworld. How long have we been away? Five days?" She looked back at him. "Does that feel about right? It seems like a long time to me."

"I have no idea."

"And it's about two in the afternoon, so we missed lunch. Dang it."

"I'm sure you'll survive. Let's see the boss first, and then you can eat."

She headed toward Feehan's office, Vadim at her side. It was strange not having him towering over her. It was also strange the way he'd resumed his chilly personality so fast. The door was open, so she gave a perfunctory knock and kept on going.

"Hey, Mr. Feehan."

"Come in—Ella! Vadim! Good Lord! How good to see you! Sit down!" Feehan jumped out of his chair as he waved them into the uncomfortable seats in front of his desk.

"I must confess, I didn't think you were going to make it out alive."

"Neither did we," Ella said. "But here we are, like two bad pennies."

He resumed his seat and beamed at them. "I'm delighted to hear that." His expression faltered. "Unless... well, I suppose, of course, you'll both be wanting to resign, being as you're Fae royalty."

"Not really." Ella didn't dare look at Vadim in case she cracked up. "Unless you want us to resign?"

Feehan glanced covertly at Vadim and then away. "Not at all!"

"It's all right, you know. He won't hurt you."

"I never thought he would. Although—" Feehan studied Vadim more closely "—I never realized what you concealed beneath that perfect human exterior. You were quite impressive. What exactly do you shape-shift into?"

"I can shift into virtually anything. The being you saw in Otherworld is actually my true form."

"True form." Feehan swallowed and straightened his tie. "Okay. Well, that's a new one on me."

"I don't expect to revert to it in this world, unless it is absolutely necessary."

"Good to know, because *that* would cause a major panic."

"By the way, we solved the case," Ella said brightly.

"I did wonder about that, since you have your face back." He stood up. "Shall we gather the rest of the team in the conference room?"

They followed him out into the bigger room across the hall and waited as Rich and Andrew filed in and high-fived Ella. Liz was next.

"Oh, you're back! We thought you were dead!"

She hugged Vadim and then Ella, who grimaced at her partner. "I love the confidence everyone has in our abilities, don't you? Of *course* we're back!"

"My Fae-Web said differently." Liz took a chair right next to Ella. "In fact, there were a couple of times when one or other of you was almost dead." She shivered. "I hate that."

"It was close at some points, but we made it."

Feehan stood at the door, gesticulating to someone. "Come on, Sam! We haven't got all day!"

Sam appeared, carrying a greasy paper bag that smelled suspiciously like fast food.

"Dudes!"

"Do you have fries in there?" Ella reached over and poked the bag. "Can I have some? You can't get a decent meal in Otherworld to save your life."

Sam tossed her the bag. "You can have them all. It's so cool that you're okay!" He turned to Vadim. "And I hear that you're, like, some awesome winged black devil, man. *Sweet!*"

Between mouthfuls of fries, Ella managed to mutter, "Trust me, he's more chicken than devil."

Feehan shut the door and sat down, his expectant gaze turned toward her.

"So tell us what's been happening."

Vadim opened his mouth, but Ella hastily swallowed down her fries and started talking.

"We killed Adam and I got my face back. That's it, really."

"I'm sure there's more to it than that, Ella," Feehan said encouragingly. "Can you elaborate?"

"Adam was the leader of an ancient Fae sect that liked to collect things. One of the things he wanted was three humans with blond hair, so that he could steal their faces."

"Which is why he targeted Brad, Ms. Phelps and you."

"Exactly." Ella nodded. "Morosov went ahead of me to Otherworld to liaise with his family members about Adam's whereabouts. With our combined information, we tracked Adam down to a palace where the sect had its headquarters."

"So how did Vadim end up on trial?"

Her partner sat forward. "Well—"

Ella cut across him again. "It was Adam's doing. He convinced the Fae council that Morosov was responsible for a murder."

Sam chuckled. "Like Vad would hurt a fly."

"That's when Mr. Feehan and I were called as character witnesses." Liz frowned. "How the hell did you get out of that? With Spencer moderating, I thought you were both goners."

"Morosov managed to convince the jury to commute the murder charges into combat to the death. Adam agreed."

"*You're making all this up and leaving a hell of a lot out. Why?*"

Ella ignored Vadim's sharp question. "He was totally nuts. I think he really wanted to kill Morosov with his bare hands for messing up his trophy hunt. He also blamed me for coming after him. I wasn't supposed to do that, and I'd spoiled his fun."

"So what happened then?" Feehan asked.

Ella tried to look convincing. Even if Vadim wasn't buying it, everyone else was.

"We were taken to the sect's stronghold, and the four leaders, including Adam, went after Morosov in a weird game of deadly hide-and-seek."

"Four against one?" Sam shook his head. "That's, like, so not cool, man."

Ella smiled at everyone. "You'd be surprised. Morosov easily destroyed the first three, and when Adam tried to use me to get away, I helped kill him." She sat back. "As soon as Adam died, my face changed back to normal."

"Wow." Sam whistled.

Liz stared at Vadim. "You're Death Bringer."

He inclined his head a wary inch. "What about it?"

"The most powerful being in Otherworld."

"I was."

"Why would you give that up?"

"Because I no longer wished to be anyone's trained assassin. I will kill if I have to, but never again at another's bidding." His mouth curled in disgust. "A weapon in the wrong hands is always dangerous."

"But you could destroy the human world."

"If I wanted to, I suppose I could." He glanced over at Ella. "But while my mate lives in this realm, I promise you will all be safe."

Ella cleared her throat. "Does anyone have any more questions?" Everyone looked at her. "About the case, I mean. I don't think we'll be able to get Brad's and Ms. Phelps's faces back, seeing as they're dead, but we can certainly try... What?"

"Don't you realize that you hold the fate of humankind in your hand, Ella?" Liz grinned. "You'd better stop pissing Vadim off immediately."

"I don't think that's possible." She managed a fake sigh. "Perhaps he'll have to learn to be nicer to me first."

"Very funny, Ms. Walsh." Vadim wasn't smiling. "Mr. Feehan, is the nurse Delia still at the hospital, or has she recovered?"

"She's still there. We have her under SBLE guard. There's been no change in her condition."

Vadim rose smoothly to his feet. "Then I think that if everyone is satisfied with Ms. Walsh's version of events, we can consider this case closed. Despite these latest revelations about my reputation, I assume you still wish to employ me, Mr. Feehan?"

"Sure I do." Feehan smiled up at Vadim. "I consider you an asset to our team."

"Then I'll be off to the hospital to see what I can do for Delia. I'll see you all later."

"Do you want me to come with you?" Ella asked.

He turned to look at her. "No, thanks."

With a cool smile, he left, and she slumped down into her chair. So, he was annoyed with her. What was new? Didn't he understand that she'd just been trying to protect his ass?

"He's not very happy with you, is he?" Liz murmured.

"Men."

"What did you do?"

"Killed someone he wanted to dispose of himself."

"Adam?" Liz lowered her voice even more. "By the way, you left out a load of stuff from your story."

"How do you know?"

"Because I'm a Fae-Web specialist, dork. I see the truth, I can't avoid it." She hesitated. "He really is incredibly dangerous, Ella. Don't you think you should've left him in Otherworld, where he belongs?"

"To be ordered to kill on command like a hunting dog? He hated that existence, Liz. It destroyed his soul."

"Then who will keep order in Otherworld, now?"

"I don't care, as long as it isn't Morosov. He deserves a break."

Liz started laughing. "Trust you to end up with Death Bringer."

"I know, it's sort of like mutually assured destruction, isn't it? I'm the person who makes him the maddest in the whole world, and he can't kill me because I'm his mate." She patted her heart. "It was obviously meant to be."

"Don't even joke about that, honey. The Fae live forever, remember, and often plan for things hundreds of years in advance. They've probably been waiting for you to turn up to neutralize Death Bringer for centuries."

"I suppose so." Uneasily aware of the Fae queens and their meddling, she got to her feet. "And now I need to go and type out that report."

Liz winked at her. "Before you forget what you said."

"Something like that." She hesitated. "Are you free

for a quick drink after work? I think I need some alcohol before I have to face Morosov again."

VADIM GOT A taxi to the hospital, which gave him plenty of time to brood about the incredible story Ella had cooked up for their team. What was worse, apart from Liz, everyone seemed to have lapped it up and not questioned a thing. He still wasn't sure why she'd gone to so much trouble to truncate the truth. Did she not want his coworkers to know how dangerous he was? Or was it simply a matter of getting away with the shortest report in SBLE history? He shifted on the patched leather seat. Being in his human body still felt strange and constricting. The sense of not being *himself* surprised him. Was it possible that Ella was right and he should've stayed in Otherworld?

He was pulled out of his thoughts by the arrival of the taxi at the hospital. He paid off the driver and headed to the administrator's office on the fifteenth floor. At the staff desk, he recognized Jose and headed straight for him.

"Hey, Morosov, isn't it? How's my favorite girl?"

"She's fine. Unfortunately she had to type up a report at the office, so she couldn't accompany me."

"Damn. What can I do for you, man?"

"I wanted to see Delia. Is she still on this floor?"

"She is. Let me show you to her room. She's stable, but that's not saying much. We're just hoping her body will come out of this by itself at some point."

Vadim followed Jose down the hallway right to the end, where a tall SBLE security guard sat outside the door on duty.

"Thanks, Jose."

"You're welcome. Let me know if you need anything."

Vadim exchanged pleasantries and credentials with the guard and was allowed into Delia's room. Apart from the regular *drip, drip* of something going into her arm, the tick of machines and her faint breathing, the room was quiet. He sat on the side of her bed, took her limp hand in his and studied her face. She opened her eyes and looked right through him.

He could still sense Adam's magic clinging to her and set about cleansing it. Having Ella's empath abilities made the task much quicker and easier than he had anticipated. He gladly took the dark magic into himself. One of the benefits of having been blessed and cursed by both Fae courts was that almost no magic could harm or hold him for long.

As he worked, Delia's color returned and she began to breathe more deeply and evenly. Her eyes closed in a more natural sleep, and Vadim sat back. Within a few minutes she became restless, her head turning on the pillow. The monitors around her bed started to flash and bleep with activity.

She opened her eyes, and he got to experience how a prince in a fairy tale must feel as she stared at him. But she didn't smile. She just looked terribly confused.

"Is this a dream?"

"Not anymore." He let go of her hand, then stood. "You'll be fine now, I swear it."

He could hear the sounds of activity approaching down the hallway and stepped swiftly out of the room. The security guard was on his feet, his weapon already out.

"Sir?"

"It's fine. She's waking up." He nodded at the approaching cavalry. "They'll make sure she's going to be okay."

To avoid any embarrassing questions about exactly what he'd been doing, he chose to leave in the opposite direction and walked unhurriedly to the stairs. The elevator doors opened, reminding him of Ella and how he'd gotten her over her claustrophobia with the magical power of mated sex. He got on and descended to the main entrance. It was raining a little, and after a quick look around to see if anyone was watching, he magicked himself a raincoat over his favorite Armani suit.

When it rained, the city wilted as if it needed sunshine to thrive, like a struggling plant. Out toward the sea, the sky was the same gray, making everything blur into a miserable mess. He turned up his collar and decided to walk back to Market. It would take a while, but he needed time to think, and he wasn't anxious to see Ella until he had time to put his thoughts in order.

A flash of diamonds brought his attention sharply to an alleyway on his right, and he stopped walking.

"*Mother?*"

She smiled at him from within the gloom of the dirty passageway.

"There's something I wanted to ask you."

"Which couldn't wait?"

She bit her lip. "I couldn't speak of it in front of your father." She hesitated. "If you want to return to Otherworld for good, I think I may have the answer."

ELLA SIPPED HER chocolate martini and stared at her newly restored reflection in the mirrored bar of the hotel. It was definitely cool to be blond again, although she missed her aristocratic nose. The whole team, except Feehan, who had rushed off to take his wife shopping, had decided to come and have a drink, celebrating her safe return. They'd also told her that since Vadim was immortal and she was his mate, he was probably loaded and that the drinks were on her. She only hoped her bank account could stand it.

"Come on, Ella, cheer up." Liz clinked her glass against hers. "You're twenty-seven, you're mated to the hottest guy in the universe and you still have your crummy job!"

"Lucky me."

"Hey, birthday girl!"

Rich interrupted to kiss her a sloppy goodbye, then weaved his way unsteadily from the bar toward the street. Sam and Andrew had already gone to get tacos. She wondered where Vadim was. Had he left the hospital? She'd left a message for him on her desk to say where they were, but he'd be able to find her anyway.

"Ella, what's up?"

She put her glass down carefully on the bar. The possibility of anyone overhearing her in the roar of conversation was slight, but she still leaned in close to Liz.

"If you were Morosov and had all that power, wouldn't you want to stay in Otherworld?"

"I thought you said he didn't want the power."

"He *says* he doesn't, but I'm not sure if I believe him."

Liz finished her drink and ordered two more. "Do you want me to be honest or supportive?"

"There's a choice?"

"Everything I've seen in the Fae-Web about Vadim tells me that his number-one priority is you."

"Jeez, don't say that."

Liz stuck her finger in Ella's face. "Which means that *you* are the problem."

"Gawd." She made a face.

"Why can't you believe that he wants you and wants to be with you? Dammit, the male is a hero. He *killed* for you."

"*Because...*"

"Listen to me, when I first met Doug, I really didn't see myself settling down with a hairy shape-shifter." She smoothed down her immaculate white skirt. "It just so wasn't...*me*, you know. But the more I got to know him, the more I realized I couldn't live without him, and when we first had sex—*shut up, Ella*—we bonded, and I knew I'd never be the same without him. The question you need to ask yourself is whether you'd be happy if Vadim wasn't around anymore."

"I can't think about that."

"Because it scares you too much, right?" Liz picked up her glass again. "The thing is, you two have done this thing half-assed and backward. You're bonded, so you need the sex, but you haven't had time to get to know each other yet. How could you, when you've been expecting to go nuts this week?"

Ella scraped a piece of chocolate off the side of her glass with her fingernail. "That's what he said."

"And he's right. Why don't you give him a chance?"

She'd told him that too, because she was scared. "I suppose you're right."

"I usually am. Look how many scummy boyfriends I've steered you away from over the years." Liz's cell phone rang and she checked the screen. "It's Doug. He's on his way to pick me up. Do you need a ride to the ferry?"

"No, I'll be fine. I'm supposed to be meeting Morosov here. I'll walk with you to the door, though."

She hadn't heard a thing from Vadim since they returned to the city. The silence was starting to unnerve her. What would it be like if he wasn't with her at all? It wasn't just that she'd miss the sex. She'd miss him. How had she come to depend on him so fast? It was totally against everything she believed in. But what was worse—not allowing him to be with her or being with him and wondering when he'd leave?

Outside the rain has stopped and the unpleasant stench of trash bins and wet tarmac drying in the sun surrounded her.

"There's Doug!" Liz waved enthusiastically at a blue minivan.

"Nice wheels."

"Shut up." Liz grinned at her. "He's coaching a shape-shifter soccer team, so we have to go and pick some of the kids up."

"God help your opponents. If a decision goes against one of your team, does someone get eaten?"

"That's why we need to practice." Liz kissed Ella's cheek. "I'm really glad you survived, hon. See you tomorrow."

Ella was busy making faces at Doug over her friend's shoulder. "Thanks for everything."

She waited until Liz was safely in the van and then retreated into the hotel lobby. She saw a shape-shifter litter in her buddy's immediate future. Where now? Should she send Vadim a text?

"*Ella.*"

"*Hey.*" That was cool and calm enough, wasn't it?

"*Can you meet me in Golden Gate Park by the Japanese Tea Garden?*"

"*When?*"

"*I'm already here, so whenever you're ready.*"

She deliberated ordering a cup of coffee from the bar to clear her head, but the alcohol in her system might help her relax more and say what needed to be said. She went to the bathroom, and after checking everyone else had gone, she closed her eyes and sent herself to where Vadim was.

It didn't take a second until she was sitting on a bench looking out over the beautiful gardens. Here the rain had stirred the scents of nature rather than the city, and a heavy, flowery perfume hung in the air.

"Ella."

She looked up to see Vadim in front of her. His black hair was damp from the rain and slicked back away from his amazing face. He'd somehow acquired a raincoat to protect his designer suit.

Of course he had.

"You really are quite beautiful in both your forms, Morosov."

"Thank you." He indicated the bench. "May I sit with you?"

"Sure." She patted the seat. "It's a bit damp, but nothing that'll kill you. Not that anything can kill you anyway."

"Only you."

"I knew I should've kept that dagger your father gave me."

She kept talking like a flipping idiot. Why was she

so nervous? Why couldn't she stop being so glib and just shut up?

He looked down at his clasped hands. "There's something I wished to discuss with you."

"Then go ahead. How's Delia by the way?"

"She'll be fine. I managed to detach the remnants of the spell from her mind."

"Cool."

She waited as he took another deep breath and then realized she could hardly breathe at all.

"My mother came to see me."

"When?"

"Just after I left the hospital. She said that if I wished to return to Otherworld, I would be offered the leadership of the sect."

"Oh." She forced a smile. "That's...great."

"You think I should take it?"

"Well you're the perfect man for it, aren't you? With your power, you could keep that bunch of idiots in order and provide a counterbalance to your father's evil schemes."

"That's what my mother said."

"I told you she was smart."

Silence fell between them, broken only by the odd drip of rain from the trees.

"If I took the job, would you come with me?"

She swallowed hard. "And live there full-time?"

"As my mate, you would be treated with great respect and bear the title of princess."

"Me?"

"Yes."

Indignation thrust through her hurt and made sitting still impossible. She shot to her feet. "And what about our jobs here?"

"Feehan would understand if we left."

"And what would I do in Otherworld, apart from traipse around, being a princess?"

He looked up at her. "Most females would think that being mated to the most powerful male in Otherworld and being treated like royalty were gifts in themselves."

"But then most females don't realize what a dork you are, do they?"

He blinked at her. "What's wrong?"

"What's *wrong?* I spent my whole day writing a lovely fictitious report to keep you and your family out of trouble with the SBLE, and this is the thanks I get."

"What does the report have to do with anything?"

She glared at him, her hands on her hips. "I made a deal with your grandmother!"

"You did what?" He rose too, his expression darkening.

"Your grandmother asked me to keep your family out of our report, and in return I—I made her promise something. Not that a promise means anything in Otherworld, apparently. What was your mother *thinking?* Doesn't anyone talk to each other over there?"

She was babbling again...

"What did she promise you?" He was close enough now that she had to look up at him. He put his hands on her shoulders. "Tell me."

"That she wouldn't ever ask you to return to Otherworld."

"And why would you ask her for such a thing?"

Magic sparked from his skin and made all the hairs on her head stand upright. She raised her chin.

"Because I don't want you to go back there. I want you to stay here with me."

He didn't react in any way or move an inch.

"Did you hear me? I don't want you to go."

His smile was slow but quite beautiful, like the sun emerging from behind a cloud.

"And why is that, Soul Sucker?"

She almost stamped her foot. "You're going to make me say it?"

"Of course I am. I've killed for you and threatened to annihilate my whole world just to keep you safe. What are a few little words in return?"

"They're a big deal to me!"

"I know." He briefly rested his forehead against hers. "Would it help if I said them first?"

"No one's ever said it to me and meant it."

"I mean it. I love you, Ella. I always will."

She swallowed hard. "Okay. Me too."

He straightened up. "Ella…"

"All right! But you have to promise not to do what your mother wants, and go back to Otherworld."

He placed his hand over his heart. "I promise."

"You should go and tell her that right now!"

He smiled. "And let you out of my sight at this crucial moment?"

She faced him. "You've already told her no, haven't you? This is all a setup." She jabbed herself in the chest. "I've killed for you. I even sat and typed that stupid report to keep you safe! Isn't that enough? Why do I have to say the stupid words?"

His smile faded. "Maybe because no one has ever said them to me and meant it either, Soul Sucker."

"Oh, God." She whispered, "Vadim, I—"

But he had already disappeared.

DAMMIT! WHAT THE hell was wrong with him? Where had that pathetic, needy statement sprung from? He knew she loved him, knew it in his soul. Why was he so determined to make her say it?

He picked up the nearest pillow and sent it spinning, smashed his fist against the wall. It wasn't enough. He needed to get out. His glance slid over the rest of his destroyed hotel room and he quickly made things right again. There was no reason to burden the staff with extra work because of his petty tantrum.

God, he needed to be free.

In a second, he magicked himself north to the immense sequoia forests and changed form. Here at least he could fly undetected and act like the animal he was. He flew for a while and then perched at the top of one of the massive trees and watched the sun go down. The scent of pine and eucalyptus filled his lungs, and he breathed deep.

"Morosov, is that you up there?"

He squinted down and saw Ella's upturned face at the bottom of the massive trunk. She'd never let him get away with disappearing on her. She'd even followed him to Otherworld to save him, without caring for her own safety. Without answering, he swooped down, picked her up and flew her up to the top of the tree.

She opened her mouth and he put his finger against her lips.

"Don't say it."

"I'm not going to say anything, I'm going to

scream!" She gave a convulsive shudder. "I'm terrified of heights."

"You are?"

She nodded, her fingers digging into his flesh.

"It's all right. If you say it now, I won't believe you. I was wrong to try and force the issue."

She nipped his finger and he snatched it away.

"Listen, you big dope. I never thought about it from your side before. I only thought about my issues. You haven't exactly had it easy in the parenting department either, have you?"

"No."

"We're both a bit gun-shy."

"Yes."

She kissed him softly on the mouth. "If you won't let me say it, can I show you instead?"

"Be my guest."

She looked down and instantly clutched hold of him even tighter. "Here?"

"I won't let you fall. I'll never let you fall."

"I suppose I'll have to trust you, then."

"Yes, you will."

She kissed him again, and unaccustomed warmth unfolded in his chest. She might not be a conventional female by the standards of her own world, but in his, she was a true warrior.

He respected that.

With a wave of his hand, he had her naked and straddling him, her hot, wet core pressed against his hard cock, her nipples tightening against his chest. He lifted her over him and let her slide down slowly over his willing flesh. When he was deep inside her, she started to move on him, and he planted his feet firmly against the tree trunk to hold them both steady.

He slid his hand into her blond hair and wrapped it around his fist until she tilted her head for his kiss. Such a beautiful female, and his for all eternity—if he played his cards right.

Her inner muscles squeezed his cock, and he lost his train of thought.

Her feelings flooded his mind, of her first meeting him at the SBLE offices and admiring his ass, of their being stuck in the elevator shaft and the shock of their unexpectedly erotic mating.

"Ella…"

More images. This time of her hurt and betrayal, and of her need. She'd never let him see such things before, never let him in so completely. She was giving him the gift of herself, reminding him that love comes in many different forms and showing him her most vulnerable self. He doubted anyone else even knew such an Ella existed.

"I'll never leave you, I swear it on my blood."

He wrapped his thoughts and love around her and held her there, in his mind, in his arms and in his heart.

"VADIM, CONCENTRATE. CAN'T you tell I want to come?"

"Come, then."

He buried his face in the curve between her neck and shoulder. She climaxed around his shaft, and he gave himself up to her until he couldn't give anymore, then followed her into bliss.

After a long while, when it was completely dark and even he was starting to feel cold, she touched his cheek. "Can we just go home?"

"I'd like that."

"So would I." She glanced up at the sky. "Can you fly me there?"

"Like this?" He scooped her even closer and anchored his arm around her hips. He pushed off the branch and they were airborne.

She clutched at his shoulders. "Wait! My clothes!"

He kept flying. In a while she might remember that she could do magic and fix the problem herself. But he sure wasn't going to mention it…

Revenge was sometimes rather unexpected and remarkably sweet.

* * * * *